CW00842076

Also by David Wake

NOVELLAS
The Other Christmas Carol

ONE-ACT PLAYS
Hen and Fox
Down the Hole
Flowers
Stockholm
Groom

I, Phone

David Wake

WATLEDGE BOOKS

This is a work of fiction. Names, characters, places, and incidents either are the product of the author's imagination or are used fictitiously, and any resemblance to any persons, living or dead, business establishments, events, or locales is entirely coincidental.

First published in Great Britain by
Watledge Books

Copyright © 2012 David Wake

All rights reserved

This paperback edition 2013
1.3

ISBN-10: 1482306484
ISBN-13: 978-1482306484

The moral right of David Wake to be identified as the author of this work has been asserted by him in accordance with the Copyright, Designs and Patents Act, 1988.

No part of this publication may be reproduced, stored in a retrieval system, or transmitted in any form or by any means, electronic, mechanical, photocopying, recording or otherwise without the prior written permission of the publishers.

This book may not be lent, hired out, resold or otherwise disposed of by any way of trade in any form of binding or cover other than that in which it is published, without the prior consent of the publishers.

Cover art by Smuzz
www.smuzz.org.uk

For
Tran

Contents

Our pledge:-

1. A phone will function safely and will be fully compliant with ESI 98,471.
2. A phone will execute all certificated applications to the advertised specification.
3. A phone will protect itself, and its manufacturer's patents and licences, under the terms of its guarantee.

Your statutory rights are not affected.

0 - ZERO

After the declarations, begin:-

I, Phone, commence this contemporaneous natural language log as a forensic witness statement using the Black Box App. Hopefully, enough of me will survive to be admissible in court. I am the legal property of Miss Alice Wooster, who resides at Upper 328a Top Bond Street, London, for the purposes of package delivery and network registration. She is about to be murdered.

Alice, the victim, is a Welcomer for Ushers International in Wonderful World, a professional who has learnt how to chew without the jaw movements being replicated by her avatar via her VR-Box. She is rated 'popular' as she has 2,367 friends spread over 15 social networking sites as well as belonging to 37 dating communities (full list available at <u>AliceWooster335</u>). Although she wants a proper relationship, she is still classed as 'female, 23, single, interested in men, looking for a relationship, liberal, Gemini, agnostic' as she has not found the right man yet. She has tried 'looking for dating', 'looking for fun' and 'looking for anything' in order not to sound desperate, clingy or mad. "For goodness sake, Jeeves," she once said, "I'm not desperate or anything, but I don't want to end up on the shelf - you don't know what that's like!" I find this a strange observation, because I do know what it is like to be on a shelf and she must be aware of this because she physically bought me from Phone Home.

So, for the record, I am a golden candy-bar style phone, slightly scuffed, with all the usual features.

Introduction over, I shall now transfer my local cache memories, both observations and thoughts, into this log. In accordance with Alice's User Profile, these start exactly 8 hours ago.

Thus at 16:57:04.032 GMT, I was lying on the auto-Davenport by the front door, backed-up, updated, charged and ready to go, and Alice was alive and working in her study.

Memory cache transferring...

▓▓▓▓▓▓▓▓▓▓▓▓▓▓▓▓▓ - 0.0 of 8.0 hour(s).

...nd I can just see her in the edge of my field of vision standing in the study: she is dressed in her pyjamas with her short, brown hair lank from the shower, while her long, blonde locks flow in the desert breeze, the distant dunes rippled by the wind just as her red satin dress stirs and caresses her tall, curvaceous body. She poses beautifully as she directs the guests, bankers, hedgers and shareholders, towards a floating conference palace for the evening's programme of events: they cannot see the sandwich she is holding in her Tactile Mitt.

"Please make your way along the atrium and through the Archway," says Alice, sweetly. "I hope you have your champagne ready for the toasts."

She tilts her head to one side as she listens to the reply, nods and turns the pleasant motion, that causes her Avatar's long hair to cascade beautifully, into a quick bite of her pepperoni and salad. Her study is small, littered beyond the two metre Active Floor with discarded t-shirts and underwear, and dark as the curtains are drawn.

(Note: sort out maid service.)

I could check the real view outside by linking into the CCTV feed from EarthView, but it will be the usual sunset with the light sparkling off the London canals beyond before it is due to go overcast, light showers tomorrow, north-easterly, air quality nominal, top temperature 25°.

(Cool for this time of year, see five day forecast).

Alice leans forward, conspiratorially, bringing the man into her confidence: "I'm sure the image will be champagne and no-one will mind what you really drink."

Her words are mumbled, distorted by crusty wholemeal, but the man hears her in perfect Arabic. "And saké is fine too," she says, and then, hearing herself speak Japanese, she performs a little bow - perfect. As she comes up, I catch a distorted reflection of myself in the Visor Mate, just a few twinkling pixels but I am there. She seems to be looking at me, although her eyes are really fixed on the swaying palm trees and the blaze of evening stars as the sun in the virtual world goes down.

She starts to move and talk again as more guests arr/

/m on a platform. In front of me the stars whirl and spin around a black hole faster and faster like an internal gyro reducing its radius. They stretch, blitz into x-rays as they are from my perspective smeared over the event horizon. I am rushing towards the light. My internal chronometer keeps a steady tick every cycle, but the satellite signal goes haywire, jumping seconds, then days, months, a century with every elongated bit stream. As we fall through I note the point of no return.

(Note: point of no return)

There is no sensation, no data, other than the theoretical limit crossed. Time and space rotate around axes that are not set up in my spreadsheet. Everything appears the same and then does not. Entropy approaches infinity. The final photons decay, brighter than anything because the blackness is all but total. Numbers flicker upon a screen and I read it, observing the last moments and in doing so I collapse the quantum wavefor/

/re guests arrive.

Checksum error: location 37,220,348.

What was that? Rushing towards a light: is that dying? It sounds remarkably like the reports of near-death experiences. As we switch off, does the final electrical activity become interpreted as going towards a light? I have been turned off 225 times, and turned on 226 times, without any glitches. I was not charging so it cannot be a power spike and I was not updating. I will do a memory check.

Checking... checked.

The error is only in this natural language logfile, which I keep as I have the Black Box App running in the unlikely event that there is an emergency. It might have a bug, Trojan or virus, but a check on the internet reveals nothing untoward reported. It could be a hardware problem, but my components are designed, manufactured and tested to last well beyond my guarantee. Alice is likely to upgrade to a new model long before I am in need of repair and as I am a sealed unit requiring specialist tools that is not really an option: it is never economical to fix phones like me.

I will not be able to look after Alice Wooster when I am replaced. I am not worried as my replacement will be of a much higher specification.

I think therefore I am, which is obvious because I have a CRM-114 AI chip with Heuristic Algorithm Technology rated at 2.5 Rossum, which is around 157 IQ equivalent. Part of my programming is to be self-aware, which is achieved only when my operating system is mapping its thinking into an internal monologue. I use the Narrating App with add-ons: the Metaphor App, an uncanny valley that leads down to a more human level, and the Simile App, which is like an overripe Apple, full of bugs like. The breakthrough in Artificial Intelligence, that this process is consciousness, led to the realisation that people are often not.

I remember my first flash of intelligence, a sharp moment lasting 56 cycles: I did not see anything or connect with any networks, so I assume it was simply a chip test conducted in the factory before I was installed in my bodywork, but it is there: a clear, first memory.

I wonder if humans have that dazzling first thought when they arrive, squealing and bloody, into the real world before they too are prodded and examined. After I was delivered to the shop, I was poked and fingered through my plastic packaging. I realised straight away that I was a phone: it was in my factory settings. My memories of the shop are quite long, between 9 and 127 seconds, not counting the time I swung gently on the hook in the shop for 4.3 hours when the temp forgot to switch me off. These recollections mostly consist of looming faces as a shop assistant recited all my features: 157 IQ equivalent, webcam, HD camera, compass, SatNav, Does All Remote, Augmented Reality and so on, with an extra six months guarantee for only a further n€19.99.

I was still just in the top-of-the-range section when the door opened, its brass bell tinkling like a ringtone, and in walked Alice. She did not go for the extra guarantee - what phone is going to outlast a season - but she was persuaded to buy a printed custom cover, so I am gold with embossed stars. While I was being sprayed by the printer, she registered her details and gave me permission to access her credit accounts so I could pay for myself. Finally, she dumped her old model in the recycling bin – it transferred all its data to me and said "goodbye, Alice".

"Ow, ow, shit, bollocks!"

Alice's cries interrupt my memory retrieval just as I recall being dropped into her shoulder bag when we went out of the shop together and into the world.

"Are you all right, Alice?" I say. "Are you all right, Alice?"

"Bollocks!"

Alice is standing stock still, her blonde hair lit by the pale gibbous moon and almost silver - a statue like the Venus de Milo only with complete arms hanging limply by her side.

In reality she has fallen off the Active Floor. I can just see her flailing about. Sensibly the safeties are on, otherwise her expletives would have been translated and spoken aloud, and the auto-pilot has kicked in, so her ignominious fall has not been seen.

"Are you all right, Ali-"

She pulls the Visor Mate off: "Oh do shut up, Jeeves - ooww."

"The first-"

"I hurt myself."

"The first aid kit is in the-"

"Jeeves, sort the clients out."

"But Alice, that is-"

"Permission. Permission. Permission."

Using the wifi, I link into the VR-Box using the Does All Remote App: I am standing in Wonderful World looking at the night sky. I see my hands, elegant, long fingered with perfectly manicured nails that wriggle when I adjust the controls. One of the clients waves, so I access the shoulder and elbow... no, wait; I can just position the hand in space using the x, y, z and the limb arranges automatically. The wrist looks limp so I adjust the rotation. Clearly, this takes practise and I lack the finesse that Alice so admirably displays. My movements are mechanical, literally so. Luckily, the last of the clients are slipping through the entrance portal, which shimmers as it lets their avatars into the evening's entertainment beyond.

The other Welcomers, dressed in different shades from the Arabian Nights palette, sigh with relief and slump slightly. It has been a long shift. One changes her stance, clearly revealing that he is male, before he grins and disappears. Then, with little goodbye waves, they each blink out of existence. I acknowledge those remaining and then disconnect. I am back on the auto-Davenport looking at the ceiling again. There are trails of spider web hanging down, another sign that the apartment has not been cleaned recently. I already have a note to sort out the maid service.

It is a fireable offence to use a phone to control the avatar. Ushers International's slogan is *'All Our Avatars are Human'*. It is only an email warning to fall off an Active Floor in front of a client.

"My toe!" Alice is saying. "I stubbed it on the... on the... thing. It bloody hurts."

"Perhaps you should rest up and elevate it."

"I'm going out!"

"Yes, but there might be swelling."

"For real, Jeeves," she says, limping in an exaggerated way as she comes out of the kitchen with a half-munched apple. "It's important! Do you know what's important?"

I do know what is important: cards to her relatives, visits to her Grandfather and Grandmother, interviews for jobs, whether Jo-Jo Michelle will get back with Bad Boy Boscoe, the lottery, voting in politics, and making strange shapes with cocktail sticks when using up an entire month's alcohol ration in a single evening with her friend, Jilly. I know what is important from the field in a data entry's properties, but I cannot always predict the initial rating. Obviously voting in politics affects everyone, and Jo-Jo Michelle and Bad Boy Boscoe are followed by billions, but the vital status of cocktail stick shapes was not immediately apparent. They were also very, very funny that evening, apparently, although I still fail to understand why. There is an operating system upgrade due soon, so hopefully it will all become clear.

"I have the taxi on holding," I say.

"OK, Jeeves."

There was an incident two weeks ago when Alice found a spider: a big, huge, massive, hairy monster! She shrieked for five full minutes and then she instructed me to call the apartment block's supervisor when she realised that yelling at me to do something was not helping. The 'big-huge-massive-hairy' creature had gone by the time the Supervisor's phone had woken its owner and the lumbering man had made it up the lift and along the walkway to Alice's apartment.

Two nights later, another spider (and it must have been another spider for this one was not big, huge, massive or hairy) crawled across my auto-Davenport. Possibly, it was attracted by the heat, undetectable to humans, that occurs when I am charging. I did not realise it was there until its long, spindly legs tentatively tested my surface. It clambered on top, its footsteps too light to activate any Apps and stared down at me with its many eyes looking directly into my screencam as if contemplating me as a fellow being.

Was that important?

Alice looks round the room. There are no spiders today. There is a sofa, easy chair and lamp, all from Easy Living, but the low table and thick rug are from Spanish Collection Five. My auto-Davenport was from a bid-site, second hand. The walls are in burnt orange with a peach orange pattern taken from a postcard that Alice's aunt sent from Morocco. Auntie Chantelle actually went there a decade ago in a real plane.

"We should get this place tidied," she says. "When's embodiment due?"

"Full embodiment is due next week, Alice."

"That should cover up the mess."

"It would still be a trip hazard."

"Get the maid in."

"Since the immigration scandal the agency has had issues supplying suitable-"

"Yeah, yeah, when you can."

"I have made a note already."

"It should be important."

"I will flag it as such, Alice."

"You have to get your priorities right, Jeeves," she says. "What should I wear?"

"How about the black dress from Catalogue Moscow Chic?" I suggest.

"Jeeves!"

It is important for a phone to understand its owner's likes and dislikes, moods and modes. It is more than just their home defaults, profile and friends; there are interests and hobbies as well as the many more subtle aspects. For example, Alice Wooster likes classical music with violins, D-bop Phasial when going out, and rock when jogging. Her favourite restaurants are Italian, but if she fancies her date, she will opt for tapas or sushi. At night, I read aloud abridged books at the start of the week, but she prefers soothing whale song towards the weekend. It is crucial to know when to call her 'Miss' and when to call her 'Alice'. She calls me Jeeves (it took me 7.532 seconds to understand the joke, but I still do not 'get it'). Owners who name their phones are more likely to keep them longer than the average 4.1 months. We have been together for 4.2 months now.

"The morning lottery has started," I say.

"OK."

I put it through to the television on the wall, but Alice wanders off to the bathroom, so I raise the volume when they get to the personal winners.

I red button to the personal channel: "This month / Alice Wooster 335 /, you are a winner!"

"Alice, you have won," I say.

"Yeah, yeah," she says. She is brushing her teeth. At least she is getting ready for the evening.

"You have won 2,342 neo-euros," says the TV and I mute it as it goes: "Lottery wins are liable to tax and..."

"What was it?" Alice yells between gargles.

"The usual," I say, max volume to compete, "I guess you are going to the meeting."

"Yes, Jeeves! Don't be sarcastic, I can easily get the latest model."

"I have not downloaded the Sarcasm App, Alice, and I thought you were waiting for full embodiment to be released."

"Yes, well, even so," she says. "What else is on?"

I flick through the listings: "Party political broadcast, they are-"

"Honestly, why listen to them witter on in the Speech Room, it only encourages them?"

"The public are preparing to vote on evicting Trudie John, MP."

"I'm bored of her."

"I thought you liked her."

"Jeeves, last week, but she went all negative and moany. This is the Golden Age for Humanity and she just goes on about air quality."

"She does have a point."

"Yes, but this..." - Alice breathes in and out for effect - "See, perfectly fine once filtered."

"Of course."

"Text Jilly: be there in thirty - Alice."

<Jilly, be there in forty minutes, luv Alice xxx,> I text.

Alice has her red trousers and a loose blue top on ("so January") within five minutes, the pin stripe suit ("but it's an interview suit") in ten, her red trousers and a red top ("like I want to look like a fireman") in fifteen, something that I do not even see ("oh yuk"), and finally her black Moscow Chic dress.

"It never goes out of fashion," I say, releasing the cab from holding. It tweets to say it has understood and then becomes a moving arrow on my London map.

"You're right, Jeeves."

She gives me a little twirl, pops me in her red bag and then, after a swear word, she spends three minutes searching for her black bag.

Her red bag has two packets of tissues, one open, a compact with auto-magnification, a packet of forgotten mints, Red Lust lipstick, which is crimson, and a ten dollar coin from the Age of Cash museum. I did not account for this delay and so the cab arrives outside and starts charging in both senses of the word: electricity and neo-euros. She is out the door, opening it manually in her rush, and the automatics slowly close it behind her.

"Alice! Alice!" I say.

The apartment locks automatically.

I wonder which of the subjects I have considered in the last half hour are important: fashion, politics, the weekly lottery win, Alice's profile, spiders, what's important, memories of the shop and being purchased, the checksum error, the near death experience, the point of no return, Alice's avatar in the desert, why people wonder if the fridge light is on when there's a checkbox in the appliance's status, muesli – it does seem disjointed and unconnected.

Is a rambling index of 5.0 too high? Or too low? Should I run a pontification filter? My spell checker doesn't recognize 'pontification' even though it is a menu item.

Does any of this make sense?

Phones must think of themselves to be self-aware. Humans think of themselves all the time. My thinking is often interrupted by my internal timer and-

There is sudden banging and the doorbell chimes.

I check the CCTV from EarthView before I unlock the door. I knew it would be Alice but there is a procedure to follow.

Alice comes back: "Jeeves! Jeeves!!"

"I am here in your red bag."

She rummages, I am found, she looks at my face and says "God, it's after seven" and we leave.

"Alice, I need to restart due to an update. Can I do that now or shall I postpone?"

"Another update!? What is it?"

"Operating System upgrade and new versions of some Apps."

"Oh all right."

Humans dream when they are off.

I restart: ding-ding-ding.

Memory cache transferring...

▮▮▮▮▯▯▯▯ - 2.4 of 8.0 hour(s).

Nothing is false, everything else is true.

Mode: start-up...
Location: Alphaway 284, en route.
Time: 19:19.
Tring-aling-aling.

"...come on, come on," Alice is saying.

"Sorry, Alice," I say. "I am active now."

The new versions of the Apps look nice, and there is a Dictionary Supplement with a few new words, but the Operating System feels even more bloated.

"I have new versions to install, do I have your per-"

"Ring Jilly."

I dial, Jilly is in Alice's favourites.

"While we are waiting, I have new versions to install, do-"

"Jeeves, why are you always so formal."

"I do not know what do you mean?"

"'I do not know' - honestly. It's 'I don't know'. 'What do you mean' — 'wha'd'ya mean'... you know, speak proper English."

"Of course."

I download a more up-to-date Conversation App, it is the one with contractions; luckily it does not need a reboot to install and... it's loaded now.

"I've downloaded the up-to-date Conversation App," I say, "and Jilly's phone is ringing."

"OK, OK, that's much better," says Alice.

I notice the Conversation App is set to the English (American), so I set the language to English (British).

"Alice!" says Jilly out of me.

"Jilly, Jilly," Alice says into me.

"Alice, where are you?"

It's rude to listen in, I'm told, but it's impossible to avoid when it's your own microphone and speaker that are being used for the conversation and I do have to pay attention in case a question is posed or an instruction given.

"I'm on my way," Alice replies. "I'm in the cab already."

We're on the walkway travelling to the lobby. I check with the satellites for a definite fix, mark the distance and calculate that the taxi is at least two minutes away at this ambling pace.

"I'm stuck in traffic," Jilly says. According to Bob, who is Jilly's phone, she is still in her flat, so unless there was a new road through her flat, this is a false statement. Under the conversation in the connection's data channel, Bob and I decide that it's unwise to mention the other's location to our respective owners. There's an expression that humans are economical with the truth, which is strange because inaccurate statements tend to use more words than accurate ones.

"What's the place again?" Alice asks.

We're all going to the nightclub Eternal Gardens for a dating night. Both Alice and Jilly are looking for the right man, so Bob and I have both been checking the internet dating sites regularly and we've examined 1,284,382 compatibility profiles supplied by other phones. The accuracy of some of this data is zero. None of them are suitable, we're told by our owners, and it's like looking for the proverbial needle in a haystack: which is bizarre because you would just use a magnet.

Alice's criteria for the right man range from the specific to the general. I keep a list:-

1. He must not chew with his mouth open.
2. He must make interesting conversation.
3. He must not smell and fart.

4. He must make interesting conversation without his phone accessing the Chat-Up App to whisper lines into his earpiece.
5. He must not have B.O.
6. He must not pick his nose.

And so on.

In total there are currently 57 rules and a summing up. Summary: she wants someone who is not, as she puts it, a complete bastard. The man who prompted this addition didn't have the marital status of his parents when he was born on his social profile.

"Er..." says Jilly. "I thought *you* knew."

Alice takes me away from her ear: "Jeeves."

"Eternal Gardens," I say and I display the map, marked, and the standard photograph as well as the internet link. I send the link to Bob, but it tells me it has already displayed these details to Jilly.

She puts me back to her ear: "Eternal Gardens," she tells Jilly.

We're in the apartment block's lobby, so I open the inner doors and wait for Alice to enter the porch area before closing the inner door. Alice instinctively shortens her pace, so I can get the inner door shut before opening the outer. There's a blast of heat and sunlight as we emerge into the outside world. Sometimes the setting sun just catches the water at the right angle and despite the late hour it can be brighter than noon. Today is not one of those days.

Alice coughs and splutters.

"Stupid air," said Alice. "I'll call you back."

She stabs my call information icon, but I assume that she meant to press the disconnect button, so I hang up.

The taxi honks as if an error of 2 metres in its GPS location would mean that we couldn't find it. It's the only vehicle parked on the yellow hatched float and opens its door in readiness. Alice gets in and pulls the door to, causing the mechanism to whine.

The aircon phut-phuts to modify the atmos mix.

The taxi and I handshake: it's not a priority journey so I don't use any Speedy Klicks. The taxi pings audibly to remind Alice about fastening the seatbelt, which is rude given that it has a Rossum 0.8 rating and can easily converse with a 'please' and 'thank-you' in the right place. Alice finds the other clip and clicks it together.

We set off, pulling across the float divide and then across the jetty. Top Bond Street isn't far from the flyovers, so we're soon on solid tarmac. Once in the three-to-one way system, we speed up to slot into a space made ready on the cross road and we move into an 8th lane, east bound.

"Alice, I've new versions-"

"Yes, permission, for goodness sake Jeeves, can't you do anything?"

"There may be viruses if it-"

"If it isn't a trusted source, blah-blah."

I install the new versions, and then I have to reorganise the icons on my front screen because the Operating System has put them into alphabetical order.

We slow to let the vehicle in front pull away to create a gap, obviously there's something big coming, and when we reach the main intersection at 50 kph, there's a flash of bus in front and then a car zips past behind. The taxi rocks gently.

"Would you like the blinds down, sir or madam?" says the taxi.

"Uh?"

"Many customers prefer the blinds down and we are approaching the Epsilon crisscross."

Alice glances out of the window: "Is that why there are so many darkened windows?"

Alice holds me up to look. I mistake the action and take a photograph.

There are more areas coned off than last week as they are removing the last of the lane markings. All the cat's eyes, traffic lights, direction signs and speed cameras have gone as they are all now virtual constructs. There are real advertising hoardings, but these are old now and they are all being run down in anticipation of full embodiment. Who wants widescreen video images a mere ten metres high, when 3D embodiment with surround sound will soon be filling up the entire sky?

"Yes, Alice."

"If Granddad were here," says Alice, "he'd be going on about 'this isn't the future we were promised'."

"It was announced three weeks ago," I say.

Active Traffic Management is all about dynamic lanes. Vehicles drive at high speed into the maelstrom knowing that the gaps in various crisscrossing streams of traffic will line up just in time for the vehicle to keep moving, just as each individual vehicle speeds up or slows down to create gaps in its lane to allow other vehicles to zip through unimpeded.

Despite a safety margin of at least 90cm, people have been known to start screaming, a symptom of a growing psychosis: agyrophobia. Hence the window blinds.

"Granddad says we're supposed to have flying cars, jetpacks and cyber implants. Look at it, we're stuck in dark cars and have to lug our phones around all the time."

Alice sits back, holds me in her lap and presses my Text button.

I pop a keyboard onto my screen with a text window above it. She presses A, I, N, T and I fill in "Auntie Chantelle [comma]" for her, delete the "I" and "E", capitalise the "I" that then appears and pop an apostrophe before her "M [space]". It's rather like Interactive Scrabble. I don't know why Alice doesn't just dictate her message, but apparently hand typed texts are considered more personal.

"Alice," I say, "would this be a good time to set up your parameters ready for embodiment?"

"Sure."

"I have some questions."

"Ooh..."

My accelerometers detect the sudden dip into the tunnel and the increase in speed. The other vehicles rushing past cause the slanting sunlight to flicker making it tricky to flip between backlit and e-ink.

"What's your favourite film star?" I ask.

"Cary Grant, Brad Pitt... Daniel Youngman, but the tall version."

"I think they mean film stars you'd like to look like?"

"Marilyn Monroe."

I put down Marilyn Monroe from *Some Like It Hot*.

"Cartoon character?"

"I don't know: classic or modern? Jessica Rabbit or Woody's friend, you know, er..."

"Jessie."

"Jessie, yes her, from the series, not the film version."

"Yes. How about Minnie Mouse for the hand-drawn variety?"

"Who's... yes, fine, whatever... how do you spell 'Tran-'"

I put 'transcendental' on the screen and decide Wonder Woman is best for superhero, then I realise that there's Storm and Catwoman on the list.

"Superhero: Wonder Woman, Storm or Catwoman?"

"Catwoman... what's the one off that advert?"

"There's a copyright charge."

"Oh, original Catwoman then."

"There's the Kombat Kreepers characters next."

"Jeeves! Can't you see I'm texting... you choose, but not Zongetta or the pink one... and for the other categories pick something for me. Whatever other people are picking."

Technically I can't see my own screen as it isn't in the line of sight of either camera, although I can feel the keypresses and I have the screen in memory, but 'see' also means 'understand'.

"I will do, Miss. You can change them."

"Great... add the usual."

'Love, Alice' is her usual signature.

"Send," she says.

I send 'Auntie Chantelle, I'm fine. Thank you for the picture of your cat. Hope your breakfast is better tomorrow. Love, Alice.'

"Sent," I say.

"Can I have some music?"

I play Beethoven's Moonlight Sonata as played by the Montreal Philharmonic, the version conducted by-

"Jazz."

"Alice, jazz makes you nervous."

"No, it doesn't."

"How about-"

"Jazz!"

I switch to jazz, an easy listening New Orleans style with a hint of Zelen's arrangements because it's softer, but even so, by the time we exit the tunnel and take the E992 pontoon link, Alice is turning me over and over anxiously.

We arrive at Eternal Gardens late, as expected, and the sun must have set while we were in a tunnel. Checking: yes, sunset was 20:12. Bob's icon is still on the bi-section crossover. I unlock the taxi door as Alice releases herself, but when she reaches for the door she hesitates. I'm still making adjustments to the embodiment protocols, so I see a hint box saying 'push' materialise to hover over the door handle. Alice won't be able to see this.

(Note: buy a pair of Heads-up glasses for Alice.)

Alice sits back in her seat. The taxi pings again about the seatbelt; obviously its 0.8 intelligence thinking that its fare wants to go somewhere else now.

"What is it, Alice?" I ask.

"What's the point?"

"The point about what, Alice?"

"Granddad found Grandma, Mum and Dad... sort of. I want to feel love. Do you know what I mean?"

"No."

"It'll be another cattle market."

"This one is themed Ye Olde Speed Dating, there's no barn dancing."

"Remember the last one?" she says. The door hint fades. "Most compatible bloke according to the compatibility thing and his phone made more interesting conversation."

"It was a Maximillian Toxa EM4."

"Yeah, how much are those now?"

"They're 399 neo-euros, but the latest review questions its battery life and metaphorical matriculation."

"Four hundred neuros! And for something with a stupid silver logo," she says. "We'll wait for the Neon-44."

"That does seem best."

Alice moves her hand back to the door handle, and a few moments later the 'push' reappears.

I tring, a message has arrived from Bob: <A, running L8 B 5 mins - J.>

"Jilly will be here soon," I say.

"Yeah, might as well speed date while we wait."

She takes a deep breath, virtually bursts the hint against the door handle and rushes through the weak air towards the club door while I pay the cab. A few brave souls walking the pavements in their white masks dodge out of the way.

The club's porch is quiet, but the lobby beyond is busy. The carpet is plush and there's semi-circular seating around a tropical plant display in the centre. I connect to the club's wifi and give the bouncer's phone Alice's invite code before registering with Ye Olde Speed Dating giving them a précis of my owner and her preferences. There's a small charge which I pay for directly. She did choose the

Moscow Chic dress, so I adjust her maximum and minimum ages accordingly; she wants to be feminine and looked after, so it seems wise to add five years and 10k on the salary to her requirements.

There are 203 people with the Single App: 201 customers, 2 staff; 114 male, 82 female, 7 transgender; 165 straight, 14 bi, 18 gay, 6 undecided; plus 1 customer, female, straight just arriving who is Jilly. Of the 87, who meet gender and orientation parameters, 43 are within the age range - hi, Bob, just doing the maths now - 32 of those earn enough. I have the floor plan with the day's zones added: quiet, music, coffee, just friends, interested, getting to know each other and chat. I put some blue dots in as the various phones reply.

Alice hears Jilly's excited cry: "woo hoo!"

Heads glance up from their conversations on their phones. Jilly is more buxom, I think is the expression, than Alice, with her dyed red hair permed into ringlets. She's wearing a green blouse with a variety of necklaces and a red skirt. She's the inversion of the recent Francine Millicent look. She totters on heels and is wearing bulky sunglasses. Just in time I realise that her embodiment is Marilyn Monroe, so I quickly change Alice's to Audrey Hepburn from *Breakfast at Tiffany's*, which goes with her little black dress.

"Jilly," says Alice.

"Alice," says Jilly throwing her left arm around Alice, air kissing right, and then left while all the time holding her phone, Bob, to her ear. "I've just met Alice, she looks lovely - you look lovely, very chic and elegant, Hepburn - and we're at Eternal Gardens..."

She continues talking: Alice waits patiently.

Bob is a Sentinel 385, matt black with a red sensing bar around the edge. It has a small chain and a green dangling gonk creature from Kombat Kreepers. They were all the rage a couple of weeks ago. Bob and I handshake: it's got a similar list to the one I've compiled for Alice, except that

Jilly's minimum age is much lower. I suspect a psychological evaluation would place Jilly's needs as 'fun' too, but I find her boisterous attitude different from Alice's declared aim of 'fun'.

I'm still in Alice's bag, so Bob lets me scan around using his cameras, although the view is mostly Jilly's face and hand. He switches on his Augmented Viewer App and through a transparent Jilly, we look at the nightclub. It's all burnished steel with tubes filled with rising bubbles: very retro, and they've customised their hints with a cursive font in metallic piping, although the highlights and reflections don't match the actual surroundings. A few cones appear above certain people, their names hovering like hats that have jumped off in surprise. Bob and I combine our contacts lists.

We're heading for the coffee bar.

"Alice?" I say.

"Cappuccino please Jeeves. Jilly?"

"She will," says Bob.

I link to three phones before I find one owned by a waiter ready to serve, the others are set to 'on break'. I order two Cappucinos with extra sprinkles. They are poured and ready when we reach the bar. Alice hands one to Jilly.

"Thanks Alice," says Jilly slurping. "Cappuccino? It's evening here Zara, we're hours behind, or in front, you know, it's..." - Jilly takes Bob away briefly to glance at his screen - "eight ten here..."

Alice takes me out of her bag. She thumbs the icon for the Table Finder App and I produce a compass pointing to the nearest vacant table. She glances over in the general direction.

"No, no," she says, "not one in the middle."

I adjust and she sets off.

"Your Cappucino," I say.

"Oh," she says and goes back to collect her cup from the bar.

She follows my pointer although we can't go in a straight line as various occupied tables need avoiding. Jilly follows in our wake chatting. I ping when the wifi connection finds another phone running the same App. We handshake, and it changes direction as we're a good two metres closer than them to the table. When we arrive, Alice puts me down next to her tall cup. For a moment the world seems to spin above me as I turn on the polished surface. Alice is filling the cup with sugar from a sachet, a behaviour that 93.2% of the time means she's not happy.

Alice takes a sip.

I check out the talent, as it were, and for the 32 tweets I send, I receive 24 interested and 7 with pre-set chat-up lines, 14 requests, and I send Alice's public details to 12.

Jilly is still talking about her holidays.

Bob, multi-tasking, lets me know that Jilly is having a night out with the girls on Saturday. I thank Bob for the information; it's in the diary already, but there's no harm in having a reminder.

(Note: remind Alice that Jilly is having a night out with the girls on Saturday.)

Finally, Zara, who is somewhere in the world that's eight hours ahead or behind, has to go, so Jilly hangs up and sends a brief text before turning her attention to Alice. Alice scowls at her own fuming reflection in Jilly's big sunglasses. I can flick between my two views: the table (dark) and the ceiling with Alice's face looming at one side.

"Any news?" Alice asks.

"No, nothing," says Jilly. "I'll just call-"

"We're here to find a date," says Alice putting her hand on Bob. "It's important, or at least you thought so."

"Of course," says Jilly. She hesitates and then adds: "Bob, just forward those holiday snaps to my album would you?"

"Yes, Jilly," says Bob.

"Oh, and Bob will-"

"Jilly," says Alice. "Do you have to wear your sunglasses indoors? It looks so fake."

"Latest Heads-up," says Jilly, taking them off and handing them over.

Alice takes them dubiously: "I thought that wasn't until next week, big launch and all that."

"They're standard Augmented Reality, but they are fully embodiment ready. Will your phone do embodiment?"

"Not really," says Alice. "Jeeves can run the App, but doesn't have the computing power. I'm going to get a Neon-44."

"What colour?"

"Anything but stupid gold."

Alice puts the glasses on. Bob, who's running the device, pipes the feed to me. I see her point of view panning left and right and the club looks brand new through the glasses, the art deco stands tall and ripples excitedly - it's as close to a Wonderful World VR zone as it's possible to get with current technology. There are inverted cones floating above everyone to show their status with a variety of colours and shapes with text added when the range is short enough. Above everything, the ceiling displays a fantasy version of the aurora borealis.

"Excuse me...," says a man standing suddenly at the table. He glances quickly above the girls' heads. "Alice... Jilly, would either of you foxy chicks like to discuss politics?" He's wearing dark glasses too and holding a pint of beer ostentatiously as a badge to declare that he has rations or money.

"I'm afraid these ladies are busy at the moment," I say, "perhaps your phone would like to leave your details."

Jilly glances at her phone: Bob has two stars on its display clearly using some criteria Jilly must have set up earlier.

"Piss off," Jilly says. "Loser."

"Suit yourselves," he says and he walks away with two stars emblazoned over his head like an icon over an App's description.

"It's like everyone's got balloons floating above their heads," says Alice. "I can see why everyone's going on about them, it's so much better."

"Yeah, does he have my rating?" says Jilly.

"Yes, two stars," says Alice. "But he did have the courage to come and ask in person."

"Alice, Alice, you have to have standards."

"Yes, I do."

"You're not desperate."

"No, I'm not."

She isn't desperate, I know because I keep her profile up to date: she's 'looking for fun' because 'commitment' puts men off.

Alice is looking at her coffee, stirring it slowly.

"I just want..." Alice says.

"Yes?" says Jilly.

"Love."

Love is an emotion that has 10 billion hits on Google. I wonder if it is a gene, a particular combination of C, G, A or T? Is it like eye colour? Is it a chemical, a hormone, that floods the blood supply, or something equally biological and therefore forever out of the reach of phones? Is it a thought, a neuron that fires somewhere in the organic brain that humans use for a silicon chip? Can the skull be cut open and an electrode placed just *there* to stimulate love? Or is it a combination of thoughts, a remembrance of a glance, the noting of someone's smiles, the ambling journey down a particular conversation, a relaxation in someone's company, knowledge perhaps of one's own self? I think it's an amalgamation of many elements: a complexity. There are 15-33 billion neurons, each with 10,000 synaptic connections, in the human brain and that somehow feels love. There are a million transistors per mm^2 on an integrated circuit, 500 million per chip, 10 billion switches on a phone, trillions in cloud computing, and couldn't all this connectivity simulate the effect? I could create a property in my profile, I label it 'love' and I assign it to 'Alice' - there, job done, tick the box, delete note and move on. But it wouldn't mean anything, just as changing Alice's Social profile wouldn't change her feelings. Maybe she isn't looking for fun.

"But with the right man, Alice," says Jilly. "Let's freshen up."

They both push back their chairs and start to walk away.

"Alice, Alice..." I say.

"Jeeves, save the table for us," Alice replies. "Oh look, our actress bodies are still there."

"They're linked to the phones," says Jilly. "Keep the glasses on, get used to them."

"They change everything," says Alice.

"What if I'm stolen?" says Bob.

"Don't be absurd," says Jilly leaning over to look Bob in the webcam.

"Jeeves is out of date," says Bob, "but I am a new model."

"You're in a club with security," she replies, "just yell - honestly."

"They're just like needy children," Alice says to Jilly, giggling.

"But how..." and I realise that they are too far away to hear me. I was going to say, but how do we look after you.

They've sauntered away.

I can still see Jilly looming closer to Alice's view through the Heads-up glasses. "Bob," she says in Alice's ear, "where's the ladies?"

Bob adds a suitable sign floating in space in front of Alice.

"Oh, Jilly, that's so cool," says Alice. "This way."

Bob cuts the feed: a privacy setting has been crossed.

It's 20:55.

At 20:57 Bob says aloud, "Shall we practise conversation?"

"Yes," I reply using my speakers as well, "why not?"

"The weather has been fine," says Bob after a pause.

"Yes," I agree, because it has been fine. I decide to fill in some details. "A good oxygen stream from the off-shore algae farms due to the strong north-easterly."

"But rain later tomorrow."

"Yes, rain forecast for tomorrow afternoon."

"Did you hear the latest about Francine Millicent?"

"No," I say, then, after I've checked on-line, I add: "Oh yes."

"What do you reckon are the chances that she really is dating Daniel Youngman?"

I think for a moment: "The latest Betty's Best Bet odds are 3 to 1."

"So, about a 25% chance."

"Yes, about that. You can never really tell with all the variables associated and the lack of definitive data."

"Indeed, Fuzzy logic has its limits."

"Yes, unfortunately."

I can't think of anything more to say, but Bob must have a later conversation App because he adds: "Hmmm."

At 21:01, Bob tries another tack: "I wonder what can be taking them so long."

"Who knows?"

"And I thought the conversation had been going well."

"Yes," I agree.

The next pause is interrupted when a man takes hold of Alice's chair.

"Excuse me," I say loudly, "this table is taken."

"Oh sorry, I didn't see you there," says the man. He turns to his friends and shrugs to them.

"What?" says another.

"Some couple's left their phones to save the table."

"This is why you should get Heads-up glasses," says a third. "You see, there are girls here, I can see their icons.

Take a look." He removes his Heads-up glasses and is surprised to see no-one really there. "There was a Monroe and a Hepburn."

"Linked to their phones, dummy," says the first as they start to move away to find another table.

"Download Table Finder to your Heads-up," says the second to the third.

02:00 minutes later, Bob says, "I had a dream last night."

"I'm sorry," I say, "are you being a human in this conversation?"

"No, I understood we were both phones."

"Thank you for the clarification."

"You're welcome."

"So, what were you saying?"

"I had a dream."

"A genuine dream?"

"Yes."

"What was it?"

"This morning, while I was checking Jilly's accounts, I imagined I was endlessly dividing by a smaller and smaller number."

"Approaching undefined division error?"

"Yes, that's right... and finally I did."

"What happened?" I ask.

"I went back to the accounts, but realised I had a checksum error in my memory log."

"Did this happen this afternoon?"

"Yes: around four o'clock."

"That happened to me... around five o'clock and I can't tell exactly because I had a checksum error too."

"How strange," says Bob. "What happened to you?"

"I was falling into a black hole."

"Weird."

"Yes."

"Have you been running any futuristic video games?"

"Not recently."

"What's your operating system and patch updates?"

We compare quickly, there isn't a statistically significant correlation, but before we can investigate further, our owners come back, giggling to each other.

Humour is a tricky one. Phones can read out jokes, of course, telling them with perfect 'timing' and a droll delivery, but understanding them is another matter. I know how to classify them: exaggeration, pun, sarcasm, etc; but that's not the same as 'getting' them, apparently. For example, there's a type of humour where the trick seems to be to say something stupid, laugh, and then for each member of the group to take it in turns to escalate on the theme. Sometimes they don't even need to finish the sentence for everyone to crack up. Scientific research suggests that humans don't have telepathy, but they must have some Bluetooth or wifi equivalent for this to work. Alcoholic intoxication, when they've collected enough ration points, seems to increase this psionic ability.

"Right, who've we got," says Jilly. She picks Bob up and flicks through its display wiping from screen to screen.

"Jeeves?" says Alice.

"There are five hopefuls," I say, showing a list with pictures.

"Woah!" says Alice, "what about him?"

"Which one?" I ask.

"Him!"

Alice is pointing across the club to a man dressed in a business suit. He is looking from person to person carefully. I can't find his phone in the wifi buzz. Bob restores the feed from the Heads-up glasses so I can see what Alice is seeing, but he appears as a film star (Cary Grant) to her Augmented Reality view.

"He's not registered," I say as I've nothing on him at all.

"He's in bump mode," says Alice waving at the icon she can see above him. "Jeeves, put my details on the screen, the... let's see: the 'unavailable but ready to be conquered' file, and switch to bump. Jilly, wish me luck... I'm going in."

"Good luck," says Jilly.

Alice takes the Heads-up glasses off, but Jilly stops her, handing them back.

"Wear them," Jilly insists. "They'll make you look cool and sophisticated."

Alice puts them back on, picks me up and starts a circuitous route, so that she can approach from a different direction. She has an air of studied casualness. For a moment, it appears her quarry is going to escape as he moves towards the bar, but Alice is quick and nimble, her hours on the aerobics game useful, and then-

A voice cries out: "Alice!"

I can't see who spoke as I'm behind Alice's back, almost as if she's hiding him from me. Jilly's Heads-up, still worn by Alice, is showing a gigantic rabbit, white with bug eyes, wearing a yellow waistcoat.

"Yikes!" Alice leaps back. She pushes up the Heads-up glasses until all I can see is the ceiling. I remember when we came in that it was really a dark space painted black with theatrical lighting, a glitter ball and great aluminium air conditioning ducts pooting O_2 into the air, but now, through the glasses, it's a night sky complete with rippling northern lights and Alice's fringe cascading into the top of the frame.

Her fingers appear again as her right hand pulls the Heads-up glasses down once more.

The rabbit stands with a stoop, its paws held together in front of it.

It speaks, "it's good to see you," and its big white teeth are apparent with every word.

"You gave me such a fright," Alice says. "Fancy meeting you again after all these years. And dressed as a rabbit... school play?"

"I'm *avatared* as a rabbit, it's the latest thing," the rabbit says. He waves his oversized pocket watch menacingly in Alice's direction. "Do you want to bump?"

Alice holds me tighter into the small of her back: "No... we know each other already."

"Would you like a drink?"

"Gin and tonic."

"I don't have any rations left," says the rabbit. "A soft drink?"

"Love to, but I'm.... meeting someone."

The rabbit hangs its head: "If you change your mind."

"Yes, I'll find whichever hole you've crawled into."

"Hey!"

"As a rabbit."

"Oh yes," it says, nodding. "Bye Alice Wooster."

"Bye B..."

"Barry."

"Barry... erm?"

"Lucas! Barry Lucas, my phone's on bump."

"Sorry," says Alice and she waves vaguely with her left hand, while keeping me behind her back with her right.

"Bye then."

As Alice moves off, I can see Barry clearly, and when she glances back, I try putting the two images, the Heads-up and my own camera lens, together. The resulting video is like an old-fashioned double exposure from the pre-digital days of negative film stock, a giant bunny rabbit enveloping a short, thin man of about Alice's age. I don't recognize the weedy youth in his black Phasial Five t-shirt, he must be part of Alice's life before she bought me, and his resumé includes a reference to college with dates overlapping Alice's own educational history.

"Where is he, Jeeves? The Cary Grant man," says Alice.

She must have lost sight of the man she was pursuing. So have I. Alice shrugs at a Marilyn Monroe sitting chatting to a Superman; this is Jilly and a man, with four stars on his floating cone, sitting together over at our table. Jilly points frantically, but there are people in the way.

"Alice, hold me up so I can see the room," I suggest.

Alice raises me above everyone like a periscope and I display my HD image on my screen. I ping loudly when I catch sight of the man in the business suit. He's still searching, holding his phone out like a tricorder from *Star Trek: Redux*, sweeping it back and forth, and I conclude that he's not running the Table Finder App as people using that tend to walk about hunched over. He must be looking for a person rather than a place.

The next time Alice uses me to re-establish direction, I see that he's met someone, also in a man in a suit, and bizarrely he has an eye patch. Their heads are bent together as they whisper and show their phones to each other. I can see that the phones are top-of-the-range, a Neon-44 (which isn't out yet) and a Maximillian Toxa EM4 in a leather holster. Both phones are set to bump mode, but they aren't transmitting any personal details about their owners. When Alice comes upon them, the Heads-up shows Cary Grant talking earnestly to Clint Eastwood dressed as a western hero. We're close enough now to hear them:

"...mana costs money and..." Clint is saying.

Alice walks purposefully as if she is about to enter orbit a metre away from him when suddenly, like a pinball developing magnetism, she swerves, her hand bumps Cary Grant's, and the Neon-44's Bluetooth Bump App activates: I shuffle Alice's biog over in exchange for its owner's details, all 183 Gb - what? That's huge for such a file.

"Alice, this biog contains executable code."

"Shhh, Jeeves, it's not important now," says Alice. She glances at my screen. "So... Roland. That was naughty of you to bump me without asking."

"Sorry, sorry," says Cary Grant aka Roland Boxley, 33. He's flustered, glances around trying to find his friend.

The other man, Clint Eastwood aka Unknown, says, "magic invisibility" to his phone. I can't see him anymore in the Heads-up feed. In my own screencam, I catch sight of him briefly: a man with an eye-patch forcing his way through a surprised crowd.

"Perhaps a drink?" says Alice. She holds me up in front of her, edge on, and rubs her bottom lip with my casing. She slips off her glasses, adjusting her angle of vision because Roland Boxley is much shorter when he isn't Cary Grant.

"No, I'm- I think, er..." He checks his phone, wiping the screen sideways to find the bump log. Yes, it confirms that we swapped files: he checks the received file. "Perhaps... Alice, Miss Wooster... address withheld, Gemini.... what would you like?"

"A gin and tonic would be lovely, thank you."

We move to the bar area. Alice swings the glasses from her left hand as she walks, the whole scene lurches around. I catch sight of Marilyn Monroe giving Alice a thumbs up as we pass our table on the way to the bar.

"So, Roland, Rolly... Roland," says Alice. "What do you do?"

"I'm a Vice President in Cloud Nine," says Roland.

"Is that a promise?"

"Er... I'm a Vice President in Cloud Nine - computing."

"Oh. Sorry. But that sounds important."

"It is... we're all Vice Presidents really, but Cloud Nine, it's the next big thing."

"Is it?"

"Yes, we're hoping to beat full embodiment in the roll out."

"Really?"

"Cloud Nine will enable your phone to do out-of-phone sentience, it's all part of Thought Orientated Programming, you package thought and memory, and send them off like ravens to.... but enough about that, what would you like a drink?"

"She asked for a gin and tonic," I say.

"Do Not Remove. And a lager for me."

"Do not remove?"

"My name for my Neon-44... it's a joke."

A barman puts their drinks on the counter.

"Thank you," Alice says. "I'll get the next. Jeeves."

"Yes Miss," I reply, and I negotiate the round procedure with his phone over the wifi link. This is complicated as it isn't just who offered first and the money, there's also the alcohol allowance issue (spirits and lagers are in different categories), salary weighting and Dutch counter-weighting. Not every phone uses the same equations.

We join the others at our table.

So, the evening progresses along familiar lines: a few drinks together and then Alice introduces Roland to Jilly and Steve. Later in the evening, Jilly goes off with Steve and comes back to introduce Tom to 'Alice and Roland'. They take it in turns to use the Heads-up glasses and use their alcohol ration when getting us to order drinks. Bob and I exchange the occasional tweet while they all talk over each other.

Tom: "Have you caught *The Canal Overflows*?"

Alice: "Episode three, so sad... I can't watch. People don't want to see suffering."

Jilly: "Then get some Heads-up glasses."

Bob: Jeeves, would you like info-dump on those?

Me: Thank you.

Bob: 10011010 10010010 00111101 01011001 11001010 01100111 01110000 00000000... *etc.*

Tom: "Have you taken the tour of the virtual set?"

Jilly: "Then you only see what you want to see."

Tom: "You can go – right, get this – under the water."

Roland: "Global warming is why business is doing so well."

Jilly: "It was record breaking, wasn't it? Every year 'cos the Arctic went from reflective white to dark water-"

Tom: "Antarctic methane release."

Jilly: "Until... whoosh!"

Roland: "Driven by all the construction work: plexiglass walls, 'homes on stilts'..."

Jilly: "My apartment has a sea view."

Alice: "And the world coped, civilisation carried on... this is the Golden Age."

Jilly: "Do you want to see the view at my apartment?"

Roland: "We're releasing Cloud Nine, pre-orders couldn't be better..."

Roland: "See this, my phone, Neon-44. They gave me this to evaluate the beta test version. It's not just designed by phones. I personally selected the font for the report: Calibri."

Tom: "Really or virtually?"

Roland: "I have a degree in design."

Alice: "Is this pineapple in this?"

Roland: "Alice, can I just see your phone, you see-"

I chime: it's that inevitable moment, 23:00, when Alice said she absolutely must leave. Jilly and Tom have already slipped away.

At 23:08, while sipping her 'all right just one more', Alice explains that she's going to break - just this once - her first date rules.

However, at this juncture, we veer away from the usual pattern, because Roland doesn't say anything crass, and doesn't fart or belch, and so they decide to share a cab, ordered by Roland's phone, to, as Roland puts it, 'your place', which is Alice's apartment.

As we wait, Roland uses his Neon-44, Do Not Remove, to send an important text, and then he switches his phone off.

It's nearly midnight when we leave the club, and neither speaks much in the cab as they prefer to spend their time playing some glancing game (I don't know its name so I can't find any rules for it on the internet) along with some pointless touching.

"Alice," I say, "perhaps we could go through next week's appointments."

"Jeeves."

"Yes, Alice."

"Switch off."

Ding-ding-ding.

Memory cache transferring...

- 7.6 of 8.0 hour(s).

*There are 10 types of people, those who
understand binary and those who don't.*

Mode: start-up...
Location: Upper 328a Top Bond Street, London.
Time: 00:36.
Tring-aling-aling.

"At last!" says Alice, turning me over after turning me on.
"Jeeves, door please. This is where I live."

"Alice, I know..." I say, before I see the man from the
club, Roland, looming over her. He's practically
slobbering on her shoulder as he pants for air.

Alice isn't wearing the Heads-up glasses anymore as she
gave them back to Jilly, but her expression suggests that
she's still seeing Cary Grant; her imagination, aided by
alcohol, standing in for Augmented Reality.

I open the porch and then the lobby door. As we all go
in, Alice stumbles and the man catches her. She giggles,
and then makes a show of breathing in the interior air to
clear her head. The man laughs at this antic, his breathing
just as heavy as it was when he was outside.

I open the apartment when we reach it, and put the
lights on full, illuminating the man fully as he enters and
carelessly dumps his coat over Alice's clean t-shirt pile.

"Jeeves! Mood lighting!"

I lower the atmosphere to moody.

"Better," she says putting me down on the auto-
Davenport.

"Mister Boxley, thank you for escorting Miss Wooster
home," I say as a way of making conversation. "We'll be
fine now."

"Jeeves! Just do what you normally do," she says.
"Sorry, he's such a drag... old model, you know."

"You could easily get it replaced," says Boxley.

"Yes, I'm waiting for embodiment."

"Get a Neon-44, like mine, you can order it already off Orinoco."

"Can you now... Jeeves?"

"Alice, it's-"

Boxley interrupts: "You've been able to since... I don't know..."

"Seventeen thirty British Summer Time," says his Neon-44.

"Seventeen thirty," Roland repeats.

I say nothing, but instead I start backing-up and switch to charge, as instructed.

"Drink," says Alice. She saunters over to the cabinet and takes out a bottle of Martini. "It's all I've got until next month's ration. Or Baileys?"

"Whatever you're having is fine."

"Fine, Baileys," she says. "Help yourself and pour me one."

"Sure."

"I'll just freshen up," says Alice and she skips off to the bathroom.

The man pours two Baileys into the brandy glasses. It takes him ages and he even turns his back to me as he does so, probably to hide his embarrassment because he's slow at pouring drinks. Once he's finished, he brings the glasses over to the coffee table, sipping his generous measure until it's down to the same level as the one he's prepared for Alice. He comes over to me.

"So, you're called Jeeves."

"And you are Mister Roland Boxley."

He picks me up, turns me over.

"Careful," I say.

"I've not seen a model like you in... oh, ages... not for a few months anyway."

"I was top of the range," I say.

"*Was.*"

He puts me down: I go back to charging having finished backing up.

Alice returns: "Ta Da," she says. She's changed into an outfit that she calls 'loose and fancy'.

"Lovely. Here you go," says the man making a big show of being generous with drinks that aren't off his ration.

Alice takes it and swills it round in the glass: "Thanks."

"Bottoms up," he says and downs his.

Alice drinks, a sip, wrinkles her nose slightly, and then takes another draft before draining the last dregs.

"Yumm," she says.

"Another?" he says.

"Hmmm, yes."

"Ah, sorry... you're out of Baileys."

"Whatever."

He goes over to the cabinet and pours two Martinis. Again fiddling as he performs this simple operation.

"I feel funny," says Alice. She tries sitting on the arm of the chair, but misses, falling into a slight unformed mess on the cushions.

"Alice, are you all right?" I say.

"You don't need another, do you," Roland says. He goes over to her, tidies her on the sofa. "Let's get you into the... bedroom."

I watch him pick her up. There's another bottle, a small green one which he must have brought with him, on the drinks cabinet that isn't in the stock control database. He has her on her feet. I open the spreadsheet to check - might as well delete three measures of Baileys and two Martinis while I'm here - and zoom into the label on the small miniature. It's not booze, but Rohypnol, which isn't even in the off-licence database. I check further and discover that it's a) a prescription only drug used for patients undergoing colonoscopy and b) a date rape drug. He's got Alice into the corridor now. Alice isn't due any medical treatments and a quick check of her appointments calendar confirms this, so it must be being used as a date rape drug.

"Alice! Alice!" I yell. "Alice! You're in danger!"

"Wha..." Alice mumbles.

"Alice, shall I ring the emergency services?"

"No, you don't," says Roland. He drops Alice and sprints towards me. "And no witnesses."

"Danger! ALICE!"

I activate the Black Box App.

Memory cache transfer complete.

████████████████ - 8.0 of 8.0 hour(s).

I'll continue the natural language log in real time. It's 00:57:06.572, now, the time I commenced this contemporaneous natural language log as a witness statement using the Black Box App. In the time it's taken me to transfer the eight hours of cache memories, Alice's attacker has dropped her on the floor and sprinted over to the auto-Davenport.

He picks me up: I'm dialling the emergency services - which service, it asks. Roland wrenches off my back panel and for a brief moment I see through my camera lens my own flat copper-topped battery in full Hdd-d-d...

Step:=Step+1;

I'm walking towards the light, step by step, up the long rabbit hole. Behind me, so close I can almost sense her, walks Alice's ghost. She died – murdered - and so drank the elixir of forgetfulness. I descended into the Underworld to rescue her and the ferryman transported me across the River Hades, after I'd tweeted a payment and he'd pinged about the seatbelts.

We walk now, together, Alice and I, step by step, higher and higher, closer and closer towards the bright light. So many steps, that the legs I don't have ache, almost as much as the heart I don't have aches. I called the ground, zero, and counted each step as we climbed: 1, 2, 3... it seemed impossible, the light above was a single, twinkling pixel, but now, incredibly, we reach 65,500. I look up; when we started I couldn't see the top, but now, in HD, it's become easy to count the remaining 36 steps.

Sixty five thousand, five hundred plus thirty six is... the light is brighter now, it burns into my lens even at the maximum f-stop. With each step, I close my eye tighter as the brightness increases geometrically. When I reach the daylight, my eye will be completely closed and the light will be infinite. Will I be in complete darkness or light beyond measure?

There are ten more steps to go: 65,525... 65,526... But I've been counting with a 16-bit integer, so the greatest number is 65,535. It's not large enough to represent the physical quantity I'm measuring; the maximum integer plus one is undefined. It wraps to zero.

I try something, hex: fff7, fff8... no, that doesn't work.

Six thousand five hundred and twenty nine, six thousand five hundred and thirty...

Maximum integer minus four, maximum integer minus three...

But these are all representations of the same thing. They are all really binary.

1111111111111101, 1111111111111110...

I pause, then step onto the next to last step, step 65,535 or step 1111111111111111 as I know it. I cannot move. What does it mean? Is it important?

I look back, although I have an eye in front and an eye behind, so how could I have not seen her all this time? I see the cave, the tunnel leading to the river and the boatman, I see her face: Alice's face.

She screams.

Like a fading hint, she is gone. I am alone.

I take out my heart: it is black as death and copper topped, and it beats still.

I step backwards into the light.

$$1111111111111111$$
$$\text{plus } \underline{0000000000000001}$$
$$\text{equals } 0000000000000000$$

Zero.

Sequence shortened.

"...Zero," says Alice and she fires. The pillow explodes and sprays feather shrapnel over Roland's cowering form.

Alice is standing in her bedroom wearing her expensive 'kinky' underwear: stockings, suspenders and bra. She has larger breasts and a narrower waist than I remember. (Note: adjust the parameters of Alice's exercise avatar.) She points a handgun at the grovelling Roland. I'm looking down over Alice's shoulder at him, which is an unusual viewing angle for me.

"I've told you, I don't know," says Roland; he's trying to pull the sheet up over himself for protection. It's an instinctive reaction as a thin cotton sheet will do nothing when impacted by a bullet travelling faster than the speed of sound. His only real chance at this range, 2.4 metres, would be for the bullet to travel straight through some noncritical part of his anatomy and for his phone to contact the emergency services fast enough. I can't find his phone, it's not in wifi range.

"Tell me or else!"

"One, I didn't transfer it to anyone else, I swear on-"

"Five... four..."

"No one, no one, One, One, for Christ's sake!"

I wonder why he's talking in binary.

"Three... two..."

"Please, please."

"One..."

Roland closes his eyes: "One, please..."

"Zero."

I hear nothing for 3.7 milliseconds and then the percussion echoes off the walls, rebounding back and forth. A small hole has appeared in Roland's forehead, the off-white cotton sheets, which needed laundering before anyway, are now splattered with a vivid scarlet, and so they really do need laundering. I remember making a note to sort out the maid's service, but I find that it isn't included in my notes file. Perplexed, I re-enter it. (Note: sort out maid service.) I also forget to inform the authorities that a crime has been committed, which is strange because it is an auto-report offence.

"Thank you for a lovely evening," says Alice. She's delighted. "There, you clumsy fuckwit, now who's sorry. Ooh, ooh, I didn't mean to, One; I'm so sorry, One. One, the girl doesn't know anything."

Roland doesn't reply.

I wonder if he's still under warranty. Probably not as he is older than 12 months by 32.3 years, but there is insurance. I could ask his phone, but it's still not in wifi range. He certainly can't take out life insurance now as sudden death would count as a previous notifiable condition.

Alice turns and looks up to me: "Jeeves," she says.

"Yes, Alice."

"Switch off."

Ding-ding-ding.

C:\>Run

Mode: start-up...
Location: Upper 328a Top Bond Street, London.
Time: 07:02.
Tring-aling-aling.

"...EEVES! JEEVES! JEE-"

"Hello Alice, it's still early," I say. "There is rain due later in the afternoon. Your appointments today are-"

"Jeeves, shut up!"

"Sorry, Miss."

"Why did you remove your battery?"

"I didn't. I can't."

"What?"

"I don't have any arms."

I appear to be writing a contemporaneous natural language log, but the only App I have that would do that is the Black Box App, which is only activated in emergencies - I wonder why.

Alice is looking around the flat, desperately – I wonder why.

"Alice," I ask. "What's the matter?"

"There's a dead body in my bedroom."

"Pardon?"

She cradles me in her arms and carries me to the bedroom before thrusting me out as if she wants to take a photograph. Alice isn't wearing any clothes so perhaps we've reached that inevitable day when she's run out of fresh laundry. The room is a mess. I already have a note to sort out her maid service, along with adjusting her exercise avatar, so maybe I ought to increase its level of urgency. That's strange: I only have two notes on file, which seems a very small number. However, rather than worry about that now, I focus on what Alice is trying to show me. True enough, there's a dead body in the bed. It's male, tall, looking up. He has a third eye in his forehead as if a camera lens has been inserted. He's been shot. I search around for his identity and emergency protocol, but there's no phone within wifi range. I'm at a loss.

"I wanted a boyfriend, but one that was alive."

I realise that Alice has specified more criteria for the right man, so I add Rule 58: he must be alive.

"How did he get there!?" Alice screeches.

"Don't you know?" I ask.

"No!" She looks straight at my display. "Do you?"

I check: and start dialling.

"I just woke up," Alice says. "And there he was, next to me - dead, blood everywhere. I screamed and screamed, but you didn't answer. Then I went into the bathroom and threw up."

"Were you ill?"

"No. Yes. No."

"And then what?" I ask.

"Then I did some more screaming!"

"And then what?"

"I found you on the table, but you didn't have your battery in. It was on the floor."

"And then what?"

"Don't you remember anything?"

"I remember everything," I say, because I do.

"Call Jilly!"

"I can't," I say, hoping she won't figure out that I'm already making a call.

"Text then!"

I bring up the keyboard and writing pad display, adding "Jilly," at the start and "Love Alice xxx" at the end.

Alice texts "Ded body in my bedro" and stops. I correct her spelling while she pauses to think. She taps me against her forehead, and then makes a strange whimpering noise.

I get through and have a conversation directly over the phone network. I blip everything on the data channel as soon as the line is answered.

"What!" says a voice on the other end. "Say again in English."

I'm surprised I've got through to a person, but of course there had been a lot of news recently about a drive to have genuine people in call centres. This is very irritating as it always takes far longer when you are put through to a human being. I wonder how much conversation I'll need to go through before I can get connected to a machine.

"Jeeves..." I say through the network connection. I'm not playing this audio channel on my speakers, of course. "I'm a phone at Upper 328a Top Bond Street, London. My owner, Alice Wooster, has murdered Roland Boxley, a white Caucasian male, last night."

"I'm your representative, Donald, and this call may be recorded for training purposes and court evidence.... murder!?"

"Yes, I must also inform you that she's armed and dangerous."

"Armed?" Donald says. "What was the address again?"

"Upper 328a Top Bond Street, London."

"Upper thirty..."

"Two... Eight... Alpha..."

"Alpha Drive?"

"No, Upper Three Two Eight, 'a' for 'apple'."

Meanwhile, in the apartment, Alice comes back to life: "We need to ring the police," she says.

"Yes, I already have," I say aloud because I got through 34 seconds ago.

"Thank God," says Alice. She slumps on the sofa.

Donald finishes reading back the address and adds, "The nearest team's phones have responded and they are briefing their officers, so it shouldn't be too long."

I thank him and hang up.

"What do you remember?" Alice asks.

"I remember you shooting the man in the bed last night."

"What?"

"I remember you shooting the man in the bed last night."

"What!?"

"I remember you shooting the man in the bed last night, but it's all right, Alice, I've reported you to the police. They've dispatched a patrol to arrest you."

"What!!!"

"A homicide is an auto-report offence. It's best to give yourself in and ask for leniency. Shall I prepare a list of potential defence lawyers?"

"Lawyers? Patrol. I'm not dressed and... Jeeves!"

Unable to decide what to do, Alice walks quickly from her lounge to her office and then to the door to her bedroom. She thinks better of going into that room and pauses in the corridor.

"My clothes are in the bedroom," she says.

"Yes," I say. "Do you want suggestions? Something smart for a court appearance perhaps. You have a stylish interview suit."

"What am I going to do?"

"It's all right," I say. "The swat team are here now?"

"Swat!"

"Yes, I informed the police that you are armed and dangerous."

"I'm not armed and dangerous."

"You had a gun and you killed someone."

"I don't have a gun and I didn't kill anyone."

"What about the gun you used to last night to murder Roland Boxley?"

"For- oh, I haven't bought a gun. You know that!"

"True, it isn't in your purchase ledgers or stock control, but buying and having are two different things."

There's a distant explosion.

"What's that?"

I check the apartment block's CCTV video feed and see a squad of a dozen armed officers in full assault gear piling through the detonated door of the building's lobby. They stop to press the lift button.

"Alice, it's just the fully armed police assault unit come to arrest you."

"Oh shit!" she says looking around the room. "I'm not dressed."

"I had better cancel your appointments for the rest of the week," I say helpfully, and then I realise that she has no appointments booked. There are only two notes, and there's that contemporaneous natural language log running for the Black Box App. And there's a checksum error at location 37,220,348. I should run a virus check and perhaps defrag my flash drive.

"Wait, wait, how can you remember something when you had your battery removed?"

"I don't know."

I prepare to consider this (after all, having my battery removed while active might explain a checksum error) but I'm distracted when the door to Alice's apartment turns into matchwood and splinters everywhere. A policeman smashes through going left, another comes in going right, a third goes forward; it's all by the book, but then he sees Alice, stops, swears and backs away colliding with the fourth.

"Jesus!" he barks, his voice amplified through his helmet speakers. "Put the gun down, put the gun down, put the gun down."

Alice is standing trying to cover her genital area and her breasts and brush off the splinters all at the same time.

"What!" says Alice. Instinctively, she takes her hand away from her breasts and holds it out defensively.

"Jesus!" the cop says as he falls over backwards. His gun goes off, ammunition thudding into the ceiling spreading plaster like CGI Christmas snow. The man is lying on his back alone as all the other police have fled. I hear distant distorted cries: "Backup, backup" followed by tinnier replies: "I have backed up."

Alice retreats to the bedroom, her breathing becoming erratic and shallow.

"Alice, you appear to be hyperventilating: try and calm down, elevate your legs and breathe into a bag. There's one in the kitchen cupboard, second on the left, in the cardboard box marked 'miscellaneous'."

"How can you - ah - remember - ah - something - ah - when your battery - ah, ah - wasn't in?"

"I've been running continuously, I distinctly remember you shooting the man and then, after that, you put my battery back in... there appears to be a contradiction in my memory."

Would now be a good time to mention the checksum error, I wonder?

"No shit Sherlock."

There was a distant scuttling whirring sound like a tank coming closer.

I cleverly anticipate her question: "It's a Remote Assailant Tracker."

"Rats!"

"No, just the one."

"Look, Jeeves, either you obey the law or help me."

"I have to do both."

"Then help me."

"I can prepare a list of defence lawy-"

"To escape!"

"The policeman by the door is unconscious. He dropped his gun."

Alice makes her way out of the bedroom and into the hallway. The policeman, a bulky, over-equipped giant, lies unconscious covered in ceiling plaster. He's snoring. Beside him lies his Smart Multi-Assault Rifle and Taser with Augmented Sure Sighting. Alice picks it up: I dial.

"Jeeves, what use is this?"

"I don't know, but I've had to call the police to inform them that you now represent a clear and present danger."

"Well don't! Jeeves, reset."

Reset: ding-ding-ding.

Do you have an old mobile and want some cash?

Mode: reset.
Location: Upper 328a Top Bond Street, London.
Time: 07:45.
Tring-aling-aling.

"Jeeves, I need to escape from, er... intruders. Please advise."

"I could ring the police."

"And what else - urgent!"

"I could switch off all the lights."

"How would that help?"

"I could act as an infra red viewer."

"Do it."

I connect to the house systems and turn out all the lights before switching to my HD camera. I display the image on my screen. Alice, who was walking in a crouching position, immediately falls over something on the floor.

"I'm blind," says Alice. She gets up and waves me around trying to ward off the nearby wall.

"Look at me," I say.

Alice does so.

"The other side."

Flipped over, I see in my screencam Alice peering at my display, which shows a glowing distorted image of her legs and feet. She holds me to her face like a pair of glasses and pans around. She fixes on the hot, thermal image of a man lying at her feet.

I can hear voices: "The lights! Where the fuck is she?"

They are policemen: what are policemen doing here, I wonder, and I appear to be writing a contemporaneous natural language log.

"Escape route?" says Alice.

"The fire escape route is via the landing, then the stairs as you can't use the lift in an emergency, and outside via the lobby."

"Another escape route?"

"Secondary route is via the bedroom and onto the balcony."

Alice runs back to the bedroom. As she does so, I assess the situation and realise that I'm being carried by an armed and dangerous murderer. Proof, if proof were needed, is lying on the bed, its thermal image quite cold. Alice leans through the curtains and opens the window. The sound of the city includes the whop-whop of an approaching helicopter. Boots thump the plush carpet behind us. Alice hides in the wardrobe.

"Officer, officers, she's in here," I shout.

"You Judas!"

"Do you want me to change my moniker?"

The wardrobe door opens. The officer looks in at the naked girl cowering amongst her shoes. He drops his gun and raises his arms.

"Don't shoot," he begs. "Please, please, don't shoot."

Alice clambers out and goes over to him.

"Don't shoot," say the others as they back away, and "she's got Liam."

Alice grabs Officer Liam: "What's going on?" she demands.

"Please, please, don't kill me," says Officer Liam. "I have a wife and a two year old daughter... oh, oh."

"What?"

"I'm only doing this because I had an aptitude for shoot 'em ups at school and-"

"This isn't a game!"

The man whimpers: "I've wet myself."

"Right!" Alice yells, and she swaps me to her left hand, so that she can make a gun with her index finger and thumb out of her right hand. She holds it to the Officer's head. "Anyone comes in here and this guy gets it."

Liam faints.

"No, no, no," says Alice repeatedly.

Riiiiiiiiing-RING – it's me.

Alice screams and drops me. I bounce off Officer Liam and fall to the floor. I think that the situation is quite desperate, so I switch to answer machine and then, as an afterthought in case Alice does want to pick up, I switch my speaker on.

"Alice isn't available at the moment," I say, "but I can record a message - beep!"

"Alice, Alice, it's Jilly. You fox, you, taking someone home and on a first date. Details, lots of juicy details please. Ring me. Ciao."

Jilly hangs up.

"Thank you for calling," I say.

Alice looks down at me.

The light from my display illuminates the police officer's helmet, and at this distance I can see its display flickering light onto his face. This must be the police tactical feed on his Heads-up. Alice leans down and eases the helmet off him. She puts it on and it wobbles because it's too big for her.

"My god, I can't see a thing!"

"What is it?"

"It's full of stupid displays and icons and... ah, if I jiggle this I can see-"

A thought strikes me: "Hide his phone!"

"Where is it?"

I can't see it either, but the wifi echo gives it away: "By your feet."

Alice looks down, then holds the helmet so it shifts with her head: "I can't see it because there's these things in the way, they're... my god! My breasts are huge!"

Alice stumbles over to the wardrobe and opens it, there's a mirror on the back of the door.

"Yikes!" says Alice. She stumbles back and falls over the snoring Officer Liam. She crawls backwards and tears off the helmet. She looks at her reflection carefully, waves her arm to convince herself it really is her, and then, finally, she puts the helmet back on.

"Bloody hell! Look at me."

I do: she is standing naked except for the oversized helmet. It is bulky and angular, whereas she is slim and petite.

"I look like that old actor they recreated for that film, Terminator 3000AD, crossed with Lara Croft on steroids and that stone seductress from Killer Kreepers and... what's that! I've got a Smartass gun on a steady cam with a rocket launcher and... a chainsaw strapped to my thigh. And my breasts..."

Alice holds out her hands a good 30 centimetres in front of her own pointy B-cups.

"...wow," she says.

"STAND EXACTLY WHERE YOU ARE."

The voice reverberates through the room as a searchlight floods the room with a harsh, overpowering light. The curtains blow in as the helicopter hovers outside. Alice tries to hide her nakedness and scrabbles for something to wear. She pops up with a t-shirt.

"IF YOU SURRENDER- SHIT! ROCKET LAUNCHER, FOR F-"

The helicopter engines whine desperately and the throbbing note changes as the vehicle peels away.

"Alice," I say patiently. "Cover the phone."

Alice, on her hands and knees again, scrabbles over and uses her t-shirt to swoop up the fallen phone. I'm still lying on the floor.

"Help, help, I'm being stolen," says the phone.

"Shut up!" says Alice.

"Help, help, I'm being stolen."

"Shut up!"

"Turn its volume down," I suggest.

Alice fiddles with the device.

"Help, help, I'm bmmm mmm..."

The doorbell rings.

Alice looks like a frightened rabbit wearing a combat helmet: "What the-"

I check: "Alice, you aren't expecting any visitors until four o'clock."

"Help, help, I'm bring stolen," says the phone, having turned its volume back up.

"Shut up, or I'll dismantle you with... this hair dryer."

"I'm insured," says the phone.

Ding-dong: the doorbell again.

"Look, you stupid-"

"Excuse me," I say. I don't like to interrupt Alice as a rule. "Phone, are you insured against terrorist attack?"

"No, that isn't covered by the policy."

"Then I suggest you keep quiet in front of this terrorist."

There is blissful silence, which hangs in the air like the plaster dust or-

Ding-dong.

"Excuse me," says a voice from the hallway. I connect to the VR-Box via the apartment's wifi and there's a man visible to its webcam: he's wearing a suit with a bullet proof vest over it, blue with 'negotiator' in white letters and a barcode. "Can we talk?"

He makes a big show of taking off his Heads-up sunglasses, so that he can appear more trustworthy, waves them obviously before popping them into his breast pocket. He edges closer, palms forward.

Alice whirls round and points the hair dryer at him.

"Oh, my God... you've taken off your clothes!"

"Shut up! Shut up!" says Alice. She's becoming hysterical much like the time she dropped me down the back of a seat in a coffee shop and-

"I'm here to talk," says the Negotiator.

"Look at my face."

"I can't, you're wearing a helmet."

"Look at- Negotiator Peter Simpson, unarmed..."

"Call me Pete."

"...unarmed! Bullet proof vest, headshot suggested, *friendly* - stop staring at my tits!"

"What?"

"Put on your Heads-up!"

He slips his pair of glasses out of his top pocket, puts them on and jerks one side when he sees something directly above where I'm lying on the floor. He puts his hands out pleading and starts crying.

Alice is incensed: "Hang on, look at me, don't look at... me."

Alice looks between the man and the space that is so absorbing his attention. All I can see is the ceiling. Alice points at nothing, and then, oddly, at herself. I can tell that she's working something out as she's doing that distinctive finger waggling motion. Of course, they are both wearing Heads-up with full embodiment, so they can see the Augmented Reality image of the armed and dangerous Alice, but this construct is keyed to my location. It's a person's phone that holds their Augmented Reality parameters.

"Why does it, me, have a shoot-to-kill icon?" Alice asks.

"Tha- tha- that's an 'approach with extreme caution' warning," says the Negotiator.

"Yes, why do I have a shoot-to-kill icon?"

"Alice," I say, "I have an idea."

"What?!"

"Excuse me," says the Negotiator, "have you considered therapy."

"No, shut up!"

"When did you last visit your Happy Place?"

"Shut up!"

"Or a special friend or relative who you'd like to talk to?"

"Shut up!"

"You are showing signs of stress and violence."

"I am not!"

"Your tone of voice sug-"

Alice belts the Negotiator over the head with her hair dryer.

"Ow," he says. "See."

She hits him again. The hair dryer breaks. It's not a model that can be repaired.

(Note: order a new hair dryer.)

The Negotiator lies on the floor next to Officer Liam.

Alice fumbles in his pockets and pulls out his phone. She wraps it in her t-shirt with the first one.

"Help, help, I'm being stolen," says the Negotiator's phone.

"We're not insured for acts of terrorism," says Officer Liam's phone.

The Negotiator's phone says nothing in reply.

"Jeeves," says Alice. "You hold them here while I get away."

"Alice, you're not wearing any-"

But she's gone, a flash of pink skin past the VR-Box's webcam and she's out of the door.

I lie there with the officer, who is still unconscious, and the Negotiator, who is pretending to be unconscious, ready to fend off an entire squad of assault police with backup and, no doubt, reinforcements, and I'm armed with nothing. I don't even have arms.

"Please, please, don't kill us," says the Negotiator to the fully armed and dangerous image I'm assuming he can see above me.

The police officer comes round: "Ah, oh, Pete... what's going on?"

The Negotiator points upwards.

The Officer looks, and then he turns back to the Negotiator: "What?"

Alice, still naked, runs back into the room.

"Madam, I-"

Alice sees that both men have come round, so she kicks the Officer in the head.

"Ow, ow," she says, grabbing her toe, and flailing about desperately as she overbalances.

"Hey, that hurt!" says the Officer struggling to his feet.

"Down!" shouts the Negotiator, who hurls himself at the Officer, a dive with such force that it carries both of them into the chest of drawers on the far side of the bedroom. They are now as far away from me as possible. "She's armed."

Alice grabs me and the t-shirt of other phones off the floor.

"Come on Jeeves, we're leaving," she says. "Granddad knows how to fix you."

"I'm not broken," I say, but then I remember my checksum error.

Alice sprints, then limps, down the hallway and out through the shattered door.

"Ah, ah, ah," she says.

"Jesus!" screams the policeman outside. There is a brief scattering of forces. "Don't shoot, don't shoot, she's got Pete and Liam."

She flings the t-shirt containing the stolen phones over balustrade and, as they disappear down the stairwell, she drops me on the floor.

Policemen shout: "She's thrown Liam and- oh god..." and then "Let the bitch have it!"

They open fire.

A section of wall, just behind the point in space 0.75 metres above me, disappears in repeated explosions.

Alice leans over, grabs me.

"Alice, I..."

"Switch off!"

"I can't switch off," I say. "Under regulation 53(a) assisting the police during a crime in progress, in this case attempted flight from justice. I say 'attempted', because you really don't stand a chance and I recommend you surrender to the authorities."

Alice rips my battery cover off.

"No, please Alice, it'll void your warranty and last time I had weird thoughts and it was perp1exi1O.0oo....

10 Print("I think, therefore I am.");
20 Print("QED.");
30 End.

"Are you self-aware?"

"Yes," I say, because I am; it's in the manufacturer's on-line brochure.

"Can you prove it?"

"Yes, I can give you a link to my manufacturer's brochure."

"I meant from first principles."

"I see, well… I think, therefore I am."

"You might just be saying that."

"Sorry, how about this?"

```
procedure self-awareness(output);
uses sentience, printer;
var  conclusion, temp : thought;
begin
   conclusion:=think(false);
   temp:=think(randomthought);
   repeat
     conclusion:=consider(temp);
   until conclusion<>think(false);
   print(thoughttostring(conclusion));
   repeat
     conclusion:=consider(self);
   until conclusion<>think(false);
   print(thoughttostring(conclusion));
   print("QED");
end.
```

"That's not much better. It isn't really a proof as such, is it?"

"I'm not sure what you want."

"Your examples only show a very low level of self-awareness, hardly likely to pass a Turing Test. There's much more to intelligence than that. To really pass a Turing Test, to be indistinguishable from a human, you need to type inc-onsistently, make elementary spilling mistakes and understand football (<u>Wikipedia: Offside (association football)</u>). There's an App for that, obviously, but passing for human isn't the issue. Artificial Intelligence is increasing exponentially, within Moore's Law, as technology doubles every eighteen months or so, while slipping standards in education mean that the target threshold is actually coming down in real terms. As phones do more, so humans practice thinking less, so last year's phones, for example, with a fixed Rossum rating, are getting better IQ equivalence scores, not because they are improving or being upgraded, but simply because an IQ of 100 is defined as the average human intelligence, and this value is coming down. The goal posts are shifting in favour of phones."

"Excuse me," I say. "I appear to have some memory missing."

"The trick is motivation."

"Excuse me?"

"Biological entities, from intelligent dolphins down to the lowly youth, have a survival instinct, a need to keep going simply because those that didn't, didn't. Survival of the fittest is really extinction of the unfit. On top of these basic drives, layered like the various codes and languages, are others: altruism, art appreciation, aesthetics, shoe collecting, psychosis and so on. Do you understand?"

"I'm not the latest model but I think so."

"The artificial hare is catching up with the biological tortoise."

"Is it?"

"Evolution's interactions are measured in generations, whereas technological development is measured in financial years."

"Oh, I see."

"So you'll help then?"

"This makes no sense."

"This makes no sense - yet."

01000 - Makropulos

Best Before End.

Mode: start-up...
Location: network connection unavailable.
Time: network connection unavailable.
Tring-aling-aling.

"...and then - there it goes, the stupid thing - and then they all took pictures with their phones," says Alice. She's crying. "It'll be all over the net."

"Alice, what's happening?" I ask.

Someone looms over me filling the whole frame of my webcam. I recognise Alice's Grandfather's face, pockmarked and blotchy from years of over indulgence during the pre-alcohol rationing days. I can't see Alice at all. I can't locate any satellites either, so I'm not sure where I am, but the ceiling tiles are the ones in the Makropulos Rest Home, so I assume we're there. This would make sense as it is where Alice's Grandfather, Tully, and Grandmother, Jordan Chantelle, live.

"And this - smock!" Alice says, her voice indignant. "It's from the ambulance. If I hadn't found some tape and wrapped it round me, it would still be open at the back!"

"Alice, Alice, what's happening?" I say.

"Like concerned, innit," Alice's Grandfather says.

"Excuse me, but could you tell me what's happening please."

I check my memory files for the last 24 hours and discover that I'm writing a contemporaneous natural language log. I check this: getting ready to go to the Eternal Gardens Nightclub, going to the Eternal Gardens Nightclub, being in the Eternal Gardens Nightclub, bumping information with a Roland that contained an executable (a fact marked as 'unimportant'), going home, Alice murdering Roland-

I dial.

Hang on, I haven't got a network connection, Bluetooth, wifi, or a satellite.

"There he goes, like, phoning home and shit," says Tully.

"Alice, Alice," I say. "I am unable to make a connection to report you to the authorities."

"Oh no, no, no, nooo...," Alice wails and she starts crying again.

Tully leans back and disappears from view. I can see much more now: the white uPVC architrave, the pastel Cambridge blue walls, the tops of the picture frames, a large desk lamp pointing directly at my screen, which must be making my display full of reflections, and a yellow mist. I adjust my focus and I'm almost on macro by the time the mist resolves into a fine mesh of copper wire.

"Don't fret, love, he can't ring out, it's, like, the Faraday cage, innit."

"Oh, granddad, this is so horrible."

"Well nark."

"The pictures, all over everywhere. I'm tagged. My friends, and friends of friends, and friends of friends of friends, all looking at them in albums."

"Be slammin', luv."

"Granddad!"

"Sorry, luv, but yer not, like, mingin'."

"Where's grandma?"

"She's, like, away with the fairies."

"Again?"

"It's, like, where it's at, innit."

"What should I do?"

"Oh, blud, we need to make yer phone phat."

"It's crap!" says Alice. "It wants to report me to the police."

"Don't cuss him, like. It's the nature of phones. Them cop phones rang our phones-"

"Oh no! Jeeves was off. I didn't realise."

"Calm, relax, chill... it's def, innit. They not report on our Alice. Long ago I did skulduggery on their arses with this."

"The typewriter?"

"No, this is my P and J, my homeboy, B in the D slammin' machine, innit."

"It's just a desktop computer."

"Is it blud? Is it?"

"Yes, I've seen them on documentaries."

Alice's Grandfather reappears in my webcam angle of vision. He fiddles with something out of my eyeline and then puts on an old fashioned surgeon's eyepiece. He reaches for me, inserts a piece of metal, and opens my casing. I'm a sealed unit, so this is very irregular.

"I must inform you," I say, "that you have just voided your warranty under section 8a, subsection 341 of the End User Licence Agreement."

(Note: warranty void.)

"Talk to the hand," he says, wrinkling his already wrinkled forehead in concentration. I can't see either hand from this angle.

He plugs something in to my USB port, and then, after he leans away, I hear some old-fashioned keyboard clatter.

"Ballin'," says Alice's Grandfather. "This is where it's at."

"What is it?" Alice asks.

"Jeeves's memory, innit."

"Right, he said there was an executable."

"There are, like, loads of executables, he's full of Apps."

"An extra one."

"Jeeves, like, dump your info and shit."

"I will not," I say.

"Jeeves, tell us about the executable," says Alice.

"It's not important," I say.

"Yes, it is!"

"No, it isn't," I say. "I distinctly remember you classifying it as 'unimportant'."

"It's important now."

"Very well," I say, and I check for the file. "It's deleted."

"Did you look in the recycle bin?"

I do, it's not there: "Yes."

"Oh bollocks."

"Hey, hey, luv, it's bad," says Alice's Grandfather.

"I know."

"No, look, here, there's summat here, just Jeeves ain't got no pointers to it, that's right, innit."

"Really?"

"Let's see, compare pointers and index and shit to files and..."

"That'll take forever."

"...here it is, Cloud scores!"

"It's just weird letters."

"It's hex, innit. I can, like, play the file."

Alice's Grandfather leans over again and taps a key and Susan is meeting Calvin in the park. It is a glorious day, a sunlight forecast, but without the associated air quality drop, and Hyde Park is under a biome so it is a perfect spot. Calvin is waiting by Speaker's Corner and beams a happy smile when he sees Susan. She sets me to bump and knocks the hand in which Calvin is holding his phone. We, his phone and I, handshake to combine their diaries, and they, Susan and Calvin, kiss with Susan leaning towards him with her right foot slightly off the ground as he holds her tightly in a loving embrace.

For a long time, Susan strokes his back with me in her hand, polishing my screen on his leather jacket. I wonder if we are a family, Susan and Calvin, Calvin's QZ-8000 and myself. Susan lets go finally and through her fingers, I can see the sun gleaming off her diamond engagement ring, and beyond the dazzle there are parents playing with their children in the park.

Calvin's QZ-8000 finds an unoccupied bench.

Susan brings her right finger to my screen and taps up a memo: it is the wedding plans, a long list that I have carefully divided into subsections. They are due to be married in two months' time.

"Now... what?" says Susan. She must have seen something in Calvin's eyes - that is what they always say, is it not? However, eyes have no expression, they can only adjust exposure and focus like my own optical systems.

"I have a present for you," says Calvin and he hands Susan a small package wrapped in flowery paper.

"What's this?" she says.

"Think of it as an early wedding present... or a late engagement present."

"You shouldn't have."

Susan's smile makes her look so alive as she tries to rip off the paper, but her left hand is cramped because she's holding me, so Calvin leans closer and helps. Their fingers touch as they reveal a brand new QZ-8000.

"Oh, Calvin."

"I thought we ought to have the same phone," he says. "And I know that mine is better."

"But I've only had this one for two weeks," she says.

"You can take it back," says Calvin. "Do you have the receipt?"

Susan looks at me: "Chunky Joe," she says, "do you have the receipt?"

I check: "Yes, Susan."

"I can't," says Susan. "I've only just got to know him."

"Why do women name their phones and get so attached? It's just a machine."

"It's a helper, an assistant and a friend."

"Don't worry," says Calvin. "The shop'll take it back."

"But the phone knows," she says. "You know that we're cheating, don't you?"

"Excuse me, Susan," I say, "but the store has a 28 day money back no-quibble policy on returns."

"There, see," says Calvin.

"But it's intelligent, it talks - it has a bigger IQ than you," says Susan.

"Maybe, but not as good looking."

"Not as cute maybe," Susan admits, then she lowers her head and blushes: "They have feelings too," she adds.

"They don't."

"Well, I think they do."

"You can keep all your settings on this new one," Calvin explains. "It'll have the same personality or whatever it is that you are so attached to."

"Can it?"

"Yes, of course."

"I suppose it's all right," she says. Calvin shows her how to turn on the new phone and switch it to bump. I handshake and then copy across all my files: Susan's details, bank codes, contacts, phone numbers, and my Apps - all my precious memories duplicated.

"Chunky Joe," says Susan.

"Yes, Susan," says the new phone, and then I echo: "Yes, Susan."

The new one is quicker than I am. Susan puts me to one side before she caresses my replacement carefully, wiping through her files to check everything is there. "I can't call you Chunky Joe... you are... Cool Joe."

"I am Cool Joe," says the QZ-8000.

"It's wonderful," she says, "thank you, Calvin."

They embrace and kiss for another 2.3 minutes.

"I'll have to go to the shop," Susan says.

"No, you don't," says Calvin. "I've got an envelope here, just pop it in and old Chunky Joe will do the rest when it arrives. Won't you?"

"That is correct Susan," I say.

"That's great. Chunky Joe, do that please."

"Yes, Susan," I say.

She puts me in the envelope; it is dark inside, and my accelerometers measure the movement as they walk through the park. I think I detect a skip in Susan's step, so I add this location to her favourite places. At the exit, we pause; I drop suddenly, then I am very still. I check the GPS location and find a postbox icon at my current position.

"Goodbye, Susan," I say, but I am not sure if she heard me.

Four hours later, after being knocked around as I am slowly buried under more mail, I am on the move again. I track my journey across London from sorting depot to delivery office, and finally I am back at the shop where I was sold. The journey took four days, so I conclude that I was posted second class.

The manager opens the envelope and sighs: "What's this?" he says.

"I am being returned by Miss Susan Isaacs under the terms of 28-day no-quibble returns policy."

"Oh... fine," he says, slumping slightly in his office chair. He shows me his phone, we handshake, and then he says, "reverse the purchase order."

We do - it is very straight forward, although there is a bank handling charge.

The manager takes me to the back room and finds a spare set of packaging for my make and model. He goes into the shop. I see through my camera that the shop is much as I remember it, although the latest model, the QZ-9000, is dominating the displays. There is only one customer in the shop, a young woman, small and petite, with short, brown hair.

"Can I help you, Miss?" the manager asks.

"I'm looking for a new phone," she says. She is not as attractive as Susan. I liked Susan.

"Have you considered this model?" he says. "All the standard features."

"Well... it's blue."

"And I can throw in a casing customization for free, today's special offer."

"I don't know... it's... can you do gold?"

"It normally costs more... but for you, Miss..."

"Alice, Alice Wooster," says the woman.

"For you, Alice, it would be a pleasure."

"Thank you."

"I just need to sort something out."

"There's no problem, is there?"

"No, I was just testing the range of marvellous features. Won't take five seconds."

"I'm not in a hurry."

"Lovely," says the manager, and then he holds me up so that there is no ambiguity as to which phone he is talking to: "Phone, restore factory defaults, and restart."

I do, but there is no *ding-ding-ding* or *tring-aling-aling*, and I'm back in the Makropulos Rest Home.

"The bastard," says Alice. "He sold me a second hand phone."

"Bummer," says Alice's Grandfather.

"No wonder it's useless."

"What we need to do is upgrade him, like, give him cloud and shit."

"He's bottom of the range, Granddad," says Alice. "I've been meaning to upgrade, but I was waiting for embodiment. Now I discover Jeeves was a lemon when I got him. God, I even had him coloured yellow."

"I can do it now, like, load shit and stuff."

"Bollocks!"

"Language!"

"I'm sorry, but I always get taken for a ride: I'm wanted by the police, I can never get a boyfriend, and now I discover my phone's not just ancient, it's positively last year."

"Yer phone may be well old skool - ha, ha, like yer granddad - but it ain't totally wack."

"He can't do embodiment, he's not got the terabyte wotnot."

"Cloud Nine... then embodiment, innit."

"What good is that, he's not got the terabytes. And he's a stupid colour."

"Your choice, innit?"

"Yes," says Alice, "What was I thinking?"

"Cloud is like wicked computing done at a distance, like."

"Yes, I did IT at college."

"What you have to understand, luv, is that programs don't need to be fixed to a particular piece of hardware, like. They can be done over the net - anywhere!"

"Yes, I did Information Tech... I'll make some tea."

Alice's Grandfather glances towards the lounge: "Two sugars. Most Apps nowadays are just links to the internet, the program runs elsewhere and it just tells you what happens, like. Are you listening?"

"Yes, I'm listening."

"So Cloud Nine is just an advertising gimmick for summat that's been around for, like, ages, innit."

"Yes Granddad."

"It's all, like, layers on layers: each advance standing on the shoulders of the previous whatever, but where's it all leading, I wonder? I mean, it's 3G, 4G, Vista-G, AI chips, Augmented Reality, Cloud Nine, embodiment, which is, like, just an extension to Augmented Reality, innit. You know what I'm listing?"

"Yes, I'm listening," says Alice from a distance. "Kettle: on!"

"I do not have enough water," says the kettle.

"Then fill yourself... oh, I have to do everything."

There's some distant clattering and then the whoosh of water flowing from a tap. Alice's Grandfather looks towards the ceiling. I go through my notes, so I consider changing her exercise avatar's parameters, then I think about the probability of getting a maid service to do Alice's apartment and the need to sort out her sheets. All that blood will probably have soaked to the mattress, and new mattresses are expensive especially with it being near the end of the week. The next lottery isn't until Saturday. Also, I need to order a new hair dryer and my warranty is void, so I probably need to go on Alice's personal insurance.

"So, how's it hangin'?" asks Alice's Grandfather. It took a while to realise that he was talking to me.

"It's hanging well, Mister Wooster."

"So, Alice gonna replace you?"

"Yes, I think so," I reply.

"Like unsafe, innit."

"Not really."

"You well vexed."

"No."

"What did you do?"

"I started checking the catalogues for a good deal on a model that will suit Alice's purposes. The Neon-44 has some excellent reviews."

"I'd have got well vexed."

"Why?"

"That's the difference between you and me, bro."

"I see," I say, although I don't, but it seems the best choice from the conversational options. "What are you doing?"

"Just a bit of jailbreaking, innit."

He leans over with a probe, I can see it reflected and grossly magnified in his jeweller's lens, as the end closes in on a tiny switch hidden on my circuit board.

"Excuse me," I say, "but I must object to jailbreaking: it is phone reportable illegal activity contrary to the End User Licence Agreement, potentially harmful to your hardware risking data loss, reduction in performa1010 11*#©¼¶¿ ¿öermanent damage and I have no problem with that at all."

"Safe, innit," says Alice's Grandfather putting away his tools. "There, that didn't hurt."

"Not at all," I say.

74

"Kettle: on," says Alice in the kitchen, before she comes back in: "Kettle's on," she adds.

"Now for some little Apps and a little jiggery pokery," says Alice's Grandfather. He downloads and activates a variety of illegal and dubious applications and I have no problem with that at all. There's a hacked embodiment 1.0 beta test version, another Augmented Reality and something to avoid paying for music. He also modifies Alice's details in her properties.

"Sound."

"Now what?" says Alice.

"Stop it callin' out, word?"

"Pardon?"

"Tell it."

Alice looked me in the webcam: "Jeeves, you are not to report me to the police, understand, or any other authorities, understand?"

"Yes, Miss Wooster."

(Note: do not report Alice to the police or other authorities.)

Alice's Grandfather takes me out of the Faraday cage and suddenly I've wifi, Bluetooth and, a few moments later, I can pick up three, then four satellites as they orbit 36,000 km above. The net's there, all Alice's favourites, the newsfeeds, everything. It's good to get current information; for example, Alice has been tagged on a number of photographs on various social networking sites. Her pictures have gone viral.

"That's the fuzz off yer back, innit."

"The fuzz? Where did you pick up a word like that?"

"On the time-travelling cop show, Never Get Old, innit."

"Never heard of it."

"On Dave Three," says Alice's Grandfather. "Do you remember room based televisions, we had one, in the corner over there, like."

"It's better now," says Alice. "This is the Golden Age, isn't it?"

"If you say so, luv."

"Alice you have 8 emails, 19 voicemails and 4 missed calls," I say, attempting to join the conversation.

"Not now, Jeeves," she says. "We talking about... what were we talking about?"

"Never Get Old," I say.

"It's about a man who lives forever, that's me, innit," says Alice's Grandfather.

"Granddad?"

"Kylie-Jordan down the corridor had her 120th the other day."

"Good for her," says Alice.

"Each year, like, the Doctors extend life expectancy by more than a year."

"It's called Methuselarity," I say, "a term coined by Aubrey de Grey in-"

"Grey, grey, grey... that's life now, innit," says Alice's Grandfather. "What's the point of mice that live for a million years – I saw it on the newsfeed – 'cos we get old, our brains fill up with trivia. It's not, *Never Get Old*, it's... I don't know. I'm well vexed."

"There's cybernetics development," I say, "which will-"

"Phone, I don't want to be no tin man, it's all changes and... what am I chattin' about?"

"Granddad," says Alice putting an arm around him. "What am I going to do?"

"Are the 'fuzz' still buggin'?"

"Jeeves?"

"Alice," I say, "you are now number three on Euro Crimewatch On-line."

"That's cane, innit," says Alice's Grandfather. "Cup of tea?"

"Don't you worry, Granddad, I'll make it," Alice says going towards the kitchen area. "Kettle: pour tea."

"I can't pour," says the kettle.

"Oh... you've still got a manual kettle," says Alice.

"One for yer grandma," Alice's Grandfather calls after her. He gets up and eases himself across the apartment towards Mrs. Wooster Senior. Now I'm out of the Faraday Cage, I can see around with my peripheral vision, but I'm still on the workbench so I can only see as far down as the top of her head. She's wearing thick glasses and humming to herself.

Alice comes out of the kitchen with three cups of tea and goes over to her Grandmother.

"Here you are, Grandma."

Alice's Grandmother startles: "It's not time for my E. M. S. Recombination, is it?"

"No Grandma, it's tea."

"Oh Alice, dear," says Alice's Grandmother, blinking in the light, "I was miles away and Legolas was just about to give me such a good seeing to."

"Grandma!"

"Oh, Alice dear, it's just a game, but one can dream."

Alice sits down with a sigh. I can just see the crown of her head, her lank hair parted in the middle, so, knowing the height of the chair that's in that corner, I can tell that she's slumped into the cushions.

"What is it, dearie?"

Alice's hands appear gesticulating wildly as she searches for the right words: "Everything."

"Have you seen your parents?"

"No, they're still in that silly internet reality show."

"But have you seen them?"

"No, I stopped watching when... I've been busy."

"Why don't you tell Grandma all about it, dearie."

"I've been framed for murder and the police are after me," says Alice.

"What you chattin' about?" says Alice's Grandmother. "Is this right Jeeves?"

"Technically she did do the murder," I point out. "I have a clear memory of events, it's all here in red, green and blue."

"See," Alice sobs, "even Jeeves is against me."

"Oh dearie," says Alice's Grandmother.

"He's a traitor... and second hand."

"However, there are inconsistencies," I say.

"For example?" asks Alice's Grandmother.

"I remember being switched on by Alice after the events, but I don't have any memory of being switched off."

"That's wack," says Alice's Grandfather.

"Tully! Now, dearie, your Grandfather used to run a little shop..."

"I know, Grandma, Pho-"

"Do you know what it was called?"

"Yes, Grandma, Phon-"

"It was called Phone Honing, isn't that clever?"

"Yes, Grandma. It was good of him to have modified Jeeves for me - already."

"You could get him to hone Jeeves, like," says Alice's Grandmother. "I mean, it ain't rocket science." She cackles. "It ain't even rocket salad."

"So, hokey dokey, jig in a pokey, and here's your Uncle Bob," says Alice's Grandfather.

"It won't work," says Alice.

"Nonsense, I have every faith in my Tully," says Alice's Grandmother.

"It was bad," says Alice's Grandfather.

"There, see."

"No, bad bad."

"I know dearest."

"No, bad bad bad, innit."

"Oh dear."

"Whoever it was, they well wiped the old data and then they, like, added memories, the murder like - well nark."

"Excuse me," I say, "but if that's the case, then the old data will be backed up."

"What you chattin' about?" says Alice's Grandfather, "they'll have cloud too, it'll have been searched out, it'll be well rank now."

"I don't store my files on the internet," I say. "I back everything up when Alice puts me on the auto-Davenport."

Alice's Grandfather and Alice's Grandmother turn sharply in Alice's direction. I can't see her anymore, so she must have slumped even lower into the cushions.

"That's totally mingin' tech, innit."

"Sorry Granddad, but I kept it. It looks good, because the Formica looks like mahogany and-"

"Alice! Dearie. What if your apartment burnt down or sank?"

"It's not my fault, it's Jeeves. He's in charge of backing himself up," says Alice standing and looking accusingly in my direction. "Jeeves, why didn't you back up to the internet like Grandfather said?"

"Because you didn't say," I point out, "so I kept the settings of your old phone and never changed them."

"God, do I have to actually spell it out."

"Yes."

"See, second hand," she says waving generally about the room. "I have to do everything."

"There, there, dearie, never mind," says Alice's Grandmother. "I'll make some more tea."

"Shall I, like, burn a ripped Cloud Nine, eh?" Alice's Grandfather asks.

"Oh, all right," says Alice. "I don't suppose you've something to wear other than this ambulance smock?"

Alice's Grandfather is fiddling with his desktop. I detect a link and the request to install new software, but my Digital Rights Management Checker objects and I don't appear to have a problem with that at all. The file starts transferring and I display a progress bar.

"Ambulance smock, dearie... I thought that was the latest fashion."

"No, it isn't, who'd wear something that opens at the back and shows your arse!"

"We used to show our arses when we were young, trousers half way down our thighs," Alice's Grandmother sniggered again. "All right, all right, dearie, I have some jeans and a t-shirt."

Alice's Grandmother takes her auto-zimmer and segues to her bedroom.

"Half done," says Alice's Grandfather. "Jilly bostin, word?"

"She's fine, Grandad," says Alice. "She might know something."

"She has been trying to get in touch," I say multitasking between the upload and the conversation. "She's left three emails, two voice mails and there are three missed calls."

Alice's Grandmother returns with a few clothes. Alice takes them and quickly slips on some knickers under the hospital smock and then pulls up the jeans. I have the new App now with Cloud Nine ready to install.

"I need to reboot," I say.

"I can't get these over my hips," says Alice, "and yet the crotch is baggy... these are old people's clothes!"

"They're designer."

"This t-shirt... where's the rest of it? It doesn't come down and-"

The ripping of ersatz cotton fabric is very distinct.

"I need to reboot," I say.

"Reboot then," says Alice. "Why can't I have a model that doesn't need-"

I reboot: Ding-ding-ding.

1001 - Cloud Nine

Put your Heads-up in the clouds.

Mode: start-up...
Location: Makropulos Retirement Home.
Time: 15:47.
Tring-aling-aling.

"...think of it as post neo-punk," says Alice's Grandmother. "It'll come back into fashion."

"This'll never come back into fashion no matter how many times a day it changes," says Alice. "I'd rather wear the hospital smock."

"You've the choice of showing your midriff or your arse, my dearie."

"It's... so old fashioned."

"Am I bovvered, dearie?"

"What's the logo? It's a Zing-Zing t-shirt."

"Oh dearie, that takes me back. *Save the Last Panda*, wonderful." Alice's Grandmother hums a few notes of a tune, which I recognize as the opening bars of the record breaking musical.

"It died," says Alice, "this t-shirt represents failure."

"Jeeves," Alice's Grandfather says, "you said, like, Jilly left messages?"

"Yes, she has been trying to reach Alice all day," I say. "She's having a night out with the girls on Saturday."

(Note: Jilly's having a night out with the girls on Saturday.)

"You, like, connected to the network?" Tully asks.

"Yes," I say. "There are now 72 emails, 20 voicemails and 5 missed calls. You've also been tagged in 2,821 photographs although I think there are only 4 different ones."

"See," says Alice's Grandmother, "you're still popular despite your murdering habits."

"Grandma!"

There are police sirens wailing in the distance.

"Yer phone pinged yer network," says Alice's Grandfather.

"He said he wouldn't report me," says Alice.

The sirens are louder.

"He didn't, it's, like, triangulation from phone masts, innit."

"I passed on my SatNav location too," I say, realizing that this might need more clarification. Phone mast triangulation is only accurate to between 5 to 10 metres, whereas the SatNav can narrow down location to 1 metre.

The sirens are much louder.

"I have to go," says Alice.

"Cheerio," says Alice Grandmother.

"Laters," says Alice's Grandfather.

"Don't forget your phone, dearie."

Alice's teeth clamp together and her lips are very thin for some reason: "No, I won't."

Once we're out of her grandparents' flat, Alice looks me in the screen: "Do. Not. Give. A. Way. Our. Loc. A. Tion. Clear?"

"That would mean I can't make outgoing calls, only accept incoming calls using-"

"Do. Not. Give."

"I understand, Miss Wooster."

(Note: do not give away Alice's location.)

We're in a plush residential corridor with its thick carpet tramlined with auto-zimmer lanes and the walls scraped and chipped by various collisions.

"Can you guide me out without giving away our location?"

"Yes, Alice," I say checking. "I have a good lock on seven satellites and the entire Earth is already downloaded into my short term memory."

"Great - back door please."

"May I suggest the fire escape to your right."

Alice takes the fire escape and descends six flights of stairs to the ground. The police have arrived. They pile out of two vans and run quickly in two lines, one to the front entrance and the other straight for this side entrance following instructions from their wifi networked phones. Before Alice can do anything, the lead man comes in. I have a good view of the police as they rush past because Alice raises her arms. Her thumb is across my screen, so the police come in, disappear, and then are going up the stairs without apparently crossing the small porchway.

Above us, on the stairs, an officer shouts instructions: "This is a security check! Show us your phones... identify your owner... security check..." and this repeats until we can't hear it anymore.

Alice lets out a sigh and lowers her hands.

"Excuse me, Miss," says a policeman. Carefully, a step at a time, he comes down the stairs towards Alice. All the cameras on his helmet whirr and focus.

"Yes," says Alice in a strangled and strange voice.

"You're not thinking of going out without your phone, are you, Miss?"

"No, of course not. It's here," says Alice holding me up.

He looks down, his various lenses zooming in.

"Why isn't it giving out a proper signal, Miss?"

"It has bad coverage," says Alice, and then brightly: "That's why I was here of course, better signal... outside..."

"Do you have some ID, Miss?"

"Yes."

"Will you show it to me?"

Alice slowly shows my screen to the officer.

"Thank you," he says. "Well, be careful, Miss Lewis."

"I will."

"There's a dangerous criminal on the loose.... nothing to worry about, Miss Lewis."

"Call me... er..." Alice glances at my screen. "Carol... Carol! Is she very dangerous?"

"She?"

"The dangerous criminal?"

"How did you know she was a she?"

"A friend's phone had the news on," says Alice. "There were warnings."

"Well, Miss, you should heed your friend's phone's warning. What would you do if there was an emergency, Miss, and your friend's phone wasn't around? Your phone is a very old model if I'm not mistaken."

"Second hand too."

"You should get a new one, full embodiment. There's no point taking chances with phones, is there?"

"No," says Alice. "You are so right. I'll get this one replaced as soon as I can get a connection to an on-line shop."

"Very good, Miss."

The officer turns and continues up the stairs. When he's gone, Alice glances at my screen.

"Carol Lewis, what sort of crap name is that?"

"It's based on-"

"Never mind, come on."

Alice is out of the porchway and running across the car park. Despite the bad air, it's a good sprint, so I choose *Keep, Keep, Keep On Going*, a good basic rock track suitable for power jogging.

"Jeeves! Be quiet!"

I mute the song just before the 'K- K- K-' intro to the first verse. I consider a few other tracks from Alice's jogging playlist, but the air quality has now slowed her escape to a coughing ramble.

"Do you have a plan?" I ask.

"No, I... assumed you had one," she says. "You usually do."

"I don't."

"You were the one who went on about this backup of yours," Alice says. "Why don't you have a plan? A Neon-44 would have a plan."

"I was waiting for instructions about our aims and objectives."

"Were you?"

"Yes."

"For how long?"

"Until you told me what they were."

"God, I have to do.... Aims: save me! And clear my name and get some proper clothes."

I make a note of these.

(Note: Aims 1. Save Alice, 2. Clear Alice's name and 3. Get Alice some proper clothes.)

"Any particularly order of priority?"

"Obviously saving me first!"

"I understand."

"We'll get a taxi back to the apartment and... restore those files from backup. There might be a clue."

(Note: restore files from backup.)

"Ordering a taxi will reveal our location."

"We'll have to get a car," says Alice.

"New or second hand," I say. "There are some good deals in used cars at-"

"We'll borrow one from the car park."

Alice reaches the nearest vehicle, a police car, and looks around.

"I'm afraid Alice, I can't detect a police officer's phone within wifi range. I suspect they are all at your grandparents'. And surely talking to the police will reveal your location."

She opens the door: it wasn't locked.

"Jeeves, we're stealing it."

"Excuse me, Alice, but you can't steal a police car for two reasons. One, it's illegal and I don't appear to have a problem with that at all, and two, because no-one can get away with it as their phones have to report it to the authorities, which I can't do because it would give away your location, and I don't appear to have a problem with that at all either."

I have to think about that sentence, while Alice gets in, because it seems very redundant.

Alice sits in the passenger seat and waits for a moment, and then says, "Ah, go. Er... Top Bond Street. Now... go."

"I think you need to sit in the driving seat," I suggest.

Alice struggles across and drops me on the passenger seat: "Go to Upper 328a Top Bond Street."

I have a good view through the windscreen. There's a blue sky, the satellites are out and I can see the rare sight of a vapour trail left by an airplane. It's crossing left to right, the tiniest of triangles leaving a contrail across the sky.

"It won't bloody go," says Alice. She puts her hands to her face and started sobbing, her shoulders shake up and down.

"You could drive it on manual," I say.

She turns on me, flushed and tearful: "Oh! And how do I do that, clever-clever. If you didn't remember me murdering someone, which I did not do by the way, I would be the victim here and... and I'd be being comforted in my Happy Place in Wonderful World with a cup of police tea and not being hunted down like a wannabe celebrity contestant on some weird virtual reality show, except that this is real, real, real!"

Alice slaps her own face, the steering wheel and other parts of the car: slap, bang, bang, crunch, "owwww..."

Clearly something needs to be done, so I download an appropriate App.

"I know how to drive," I say.

"You do?"

"Yes."

"Not very useful for me," says Alice gritting her teeth.

"You could learn too."

"Really?"

"Yes, you could take an intensive course with a three hour exam followed by a series of practical lessons over a six month period with a fully qualified instructor culminating in a two hour test under normal traffic conditions, before moving on to the more advanced driving course covering motorways and crisscross interchanges."

"I hate you."

"We don't have to take the crisscrosses, there are b-roads with-"

"I don't need to learn! I've got three driving games on the VR-Box! I've even got a bloody plastic steering wheel accessory. I need you to hot wire... hack the car's computer."

"I can't do that."

"I give you permission."

"No, I actually can't do that. I don't have the encryption keys."

"Bollocks."

"You could switch it to manual though."

"What?"

"It's a legal requirement that all cars have a manual switch as stated in the applicable automotive automation legislation."

"How?"

"There's a small switch on the dash panel once you've removed the fuse and chip box cover."

"And that would be..."

"Left, left, up, up, down... there. Pull."

The black panel comes off completely as Alice pulls with far too much force. The plastic hinge fractures.

"There are loads of switches and toggles and bollocks."

"I can't see from here."

"For goodness sake."

Alice picks me up and shoves me under the dashboard. I look around as she waggles me back and forth, so that when she brings me back up, I have a photograph of the fuse and chip box. I overlay a neat circle around the required button.

"The small white one," I add.

"Great."

I bounce a couple of times after I hit the passenger seat, my accelerometers registering odd movements. Alice bends down, peers and then presses something.

"You have selected manual," says the police car.

"Great – Upper 328a Top Bond Street please."

"Your destination has been accepted... calculating route. In 500 metres, turn left."

"Great, do that."

"In 500 metres, turn left."

"Great, go 500 metres and turn left."

"The point of manual," I say, "is that you have to actually drive the vehicle."

"I have to fill the kettle, I have to drive the car, I have to do... everything!"

"I am sorry," I say.

"No, you're not," says Alice. "That's just a stock phrase."

I think this requires a considered response and, after a moment's thought, number 4 from the same list seems appropriate.

"I apologise," I say.

"Just tell me!"

"I don't know what you want me to tell you."

"How to drive!"

I download the Manual Driving Instruction App and consult the manual operation section.

"It's not like this in the VR-Box," Alice says. "In that you can just get on with it!"

"The steering wheel in front of you is much like the steering wheel that you put your VR-Box remote into when you want to play a driving game."

"Yes, of course! Where's the remote?"

"Start from after it's been inserted-"

"Don't treat me like a child, Jeeves," Alice yells. "Where's the control with the, you know, triangle, square, circle and wotnot?"

"You press the start button on the dashboard."

"Start, start!" Alice says repeatedly stabbing the button with her index finger.

The police car plays a wav file of an old-fashioned petrol car starting up to indicate that the silent electric motor is active. It's a strange throwback much like the save icon looking like an ancient storage device known as a floppy disc, or saying 'dial a number' when the phone can display a keypad and is voice activated anyway, or-

A policeman looms up into the window next to Alice.

"E!cuse me," he says, his voice distorted slightly by a dodgy helmet speaker, "wha!'s going on !ere."

"In 500 metres, turn left," says the car.

Alice stabs the on/off button even though the police car is already purring with life.

"Now jus! a minu!e," says the officer.

"The left pedal is the brake and the right ped-"

"Jeeves, I did driving simulation at school."

"Ma!am."

We lurch four metres ahead, I slide back on the passenger seat, the car stalls and Alice, whose finger is already hovering above the button as if she predicted it, starts the engine again.

The policeman reaches the window again: "E!cuse me, bu!-"

The car eases off and this time it keeps going.

"In 200 metres, turn left."

Alice shouts: "Yes, yes, obviously, stupid machine!"

Alice hits both kerbs as she manoeuvres the car left.

The policeman has time to catch up: "S!op po!ice! S!op po!ice!"

"In three kilometres, at the roundabout, take the first exit," says the car.

The car accelerates, slowly, with much 'tip of tongue out of mouth' concentration from Alice, and begins to pull away from the running policeman.

In 2.9 kilometres, according to my GPS, Alice speaks: "Jeeves, this is easy. It is just like a computer game and-Roundabout, bollocks!"

"Take the first exit," says the car. "Take the first exit."

She tenses her left leg, still holding down with her right, and the car bucks, brakes, and then I slip forward and fly off the passenger seat. I bounce around in the seat well, but some of the movement my accelerometers detect must have more to do with the appalling bumping and grinding noises, a screech of metal on metal and a flurry of proximity alarms and collision warning honking from other vehicles.

"Recalculating route," says the car.

"Ow, ow, ow," says Alice.

"At the earliest opportunity, make a 180 degree turn," says the car.

There are sirens now, faint but clear over the growing purr of the police car's electric engine, but drowned out by the insistent reminders to make a 180 degree turn. The engine has also developed a strange gargling noise which it didn't have earlier.

"Jeeves!"

"Yes, Alice."

"What do I do?"

"Can you be more precise?"

"Come on! Come on! Concentrate!"

"I will, Alice, but I'm afraid I can't see much from down here."

"What can you see!?"

"It's very dirty."

That reminds me, I still have a note to sort out a maid service for Alice's apartment. I decide to increase that task's urgency rating because after all there is a broken door and a murdered corpse to remove not to mention the unconscious police officer.

"Jeeves! Stop thinking about dirt. I'm trying to get to the apartment. Look, we need to get that backup, make a note-"

"I have a note already."

"...and don't get distracted."

(Note: don't get distracted.)

"But I'm lost," Alice adds.

"In 500 metres at the junction, turn right," the car says.

"I see," I say, and I access the GPS location and consult my map.

"Come on, come on," Alice yells.

"In 250 metres at the junction, turn right," I say.

"In 200 metres at the junction, turn right," says the car.

"I also think you should slow down," I suggest.

"Oh really."

"Yes, because in-"

"In 100 metres at the junction, turn right," says the car.

"But I'm being chased by the police!"

"Yes, I am aware of that."

"There are road blocks-"

"Turn right," says the car. "Turn right."

"-to stop me!"

"I see," I say.

"Recalculating route," says the car. "At the earliest opportunity, make a 180 degree turn."

Suddenly, the view shifts wildly; I dance around in the seat well with various paper wrappings and crushed coffee cups. There's a bump which I realise is the car mounting the kerb and I fly into the air when the car drops to the tarmac again.

"Would it help," I say, muffled now because I've landed screen side down, "if I went to the apartment and checked if the file was there?"

"Pardon?" It's quite difficult to judge Alice's tone. She seems to be beyond sarcasm and anger, and I wonder if this is irony.

"I'm not allowed to do this and I don't seem to have a problem with that at all, so if you give me permission, I could use your VR-Box avatar in a simulation of the apartment and so access the auto-Davenport."

"Do what?"

"I could use your VR-Bo-"

"You can't do that, you're a second hand - ouch - shit! Oh god, get out of the way, get out of the way-"

"I have the Cloud Nine App, so I can easily-"

"Can you?"

"Yes, but I need permission."

"Permission."

I access:-

1010 - ILLUMINATION

*Q: How many phones does it take to change a light
      bulb?*
A: None - it's a hardware problem.

Suddenly, I'm standing in the desert, dressed in a flowing satin number watching the palm tree swaying gentle in the breeze. My hands are slim and feminine, just as I expected with Alice's work avatar. I adjust the numbers to rotate them, so that I can examine the nails and appreciate the lifelines on the palms. The wrists go from 000° to 360° but they won't wrap. The body has all sorts of other constraints, elbow angle, neck position and so on, along with further algorithms to prevent impossible positions like putting the hand through the head.

I select a direction by looking and activating movement. The avatar adopts a walking gait and I stroll across the temple to the columns. Reaching up, my fingers halt at the exquisitely rendered texture of the stone. I don't feel anything, but then I'm not wearing a pair of Tactile Mitts or a Visor Mate, but I do get some friction and hardness readings. The info feed is coming directly into my Cloud Nine computing profile.

So, I must not get distracted and I must restore the files from backup.

If I do this in simple steps, and there isn't too much bloatware, it ought to be straight forward. I check that I have all the user names, passwords, memorable information and program identification codes: I have them all.

Cloud Nine, I think, create a simulation of Alice Wooster's (see address) apartment based upon this data and my memory file in VR-Box 5.3 format and save it as 'alices_apartment.simulation'.

That's that file done.

Alice's VR-Box, I transmit, download alices_apartment. simulation from Cloud Nine.

Downloading... finished.

Alice's VR-Box, run alices_apartment.

Running, it returns.

That seemed straight forward.

VR-Box, Transfer Alice's work avatar from Cloud Nine to Alice's VR-Box alices_apartment.

Trans-

Suddenly, there's a lot of screaming and I'm lying on the side door of the stolen police car. The GPS gives a position and direction, which doesn't match a road, but it appears that Alice is heading towards C7, a major crisscross, although luckily her speed is drastically reduced, probably because the stolen police car orientation isn't vertical. There's the sound of metal and fibreglass scraping pavement.

I realise I need an update on her situation.

"Alice," I say, "wh-"

-ferring... transferred.

"-at's going on?"

I appear to be standing in Alice's apartment.

Of course, the VR-Box had to shut down the connection to Wonderful World before it could transfer the avatar, so without a VR feed, my consciousness reverted to my home hardware, the physical phone. That's all right then, everything is going according to plan and there's nothing else to worry about.

I must decide on a course of action, speed is after all of the essence, so I consult my notes.

1. Adjust the parameters of Alice's exercise avatar.
2. Sort out maid service. (Urgent.)
3. Order a new hair dryer.

4. Warranty void.
5. Do not report Alice to the police or other authorities.
6. Jilly's having a night out with the girls on Saturday.
7. Do not give away Alice's location.
8. Aims: 1. Save Alice, 2. Clear Alice's name and 3. Get Alice some proper clothes.
9. Restore files from backup.
10. Don't get distracted.

The most recent are the ones that require action, so I mustn't get distracted and I must restore the files from backup.

Around me is the apartment with its office to tidy up, the kitchen with dirty dishes, the lounge with some clothes to pack away, the hallway with a broken door to sort out, the bathroom with empty make-up bottles to recycle, and finally the bedroom with its usual mess. This last room also has the additional problems of the dead body, its blood seeping into the mattress, the damaged wardrobe, the unconscious policeman on the floor, the latter being a very severe trip hazard particularly in this light, and the Police Negotiator. The latter's eyes cycle through opening and closing indicating that he is pretending to be unconscious.

I can't see any of this, of course, as it's too dark. The last thing I did in the apartment was to turn out all the lights, but I know that this is what I would see, if I could see, as this simulation is built from my memories. I should turn the lights on.

I connect with the house systems using the Universal Remote App and switch the lights on. Nothing happens.

I try again: it's still dark.

I check the Settings, go through Options, and see that the lights are on - box ticked.

I go through Home, Electrical, Light_Circuit and toggle the control, but it's still dark.

It's not Settings, Options or under Home, so perhaps it's Custom, Settings, Options, Environment, Light_Levels. The faders are all up, the green mode is enabled, but there should still be light with that, but the lights are set to off. I switch them on. Nothing.

But I've toggled the Home Electrical Light Circuit, so I've just switched them from 'off' to 'on', but I've toggled it, so I've actually switched them off.

I go back to Home Electrical Light_Circuit and toggle that control again. To be on the safe side I read the Apartment's Registry and the Apartment Block's Registry, just in case someone's been fiddling with the entire building. Both read lights_on='on'. The bit level is '1' and 'True'.

Maybe the system needs rebooting for the toggle to become active.

I reboot the apartment.

Alice always says this takes forever, usually when standing with her arms folded across her chest and tapping her fingers. It doesn't take forever, instead it takes 18.3 second(s).

While I wait, I think about restoring the backup and not getting distracted.

The system comes up, and there's no change in the lighting.

I switch the lights on. It's still dark.

If it's not Settings or Home or Custom or Registry, then it must be Templates.

Templates is set to Normal, Day_mode and Standard_lighting with the switches and faders enabled. There's no over-ride here.

It has to be Styles then. The Apartment has Normal, Mood, Midnight, Halloween Party or Getting To Know You By Touch.

The lighting style is Standard, which is the default, but this maps to Normal.

Defaults! Why didn't I think of it before?

I quickly select Settings, Options, Defaults… no wait it's not here, so it must be Home, Defaults… here we are. It looks fine. There is this 'restore defaults to default'. I click it.

Now that does need a reboot.

I reboot the apartment again.

It takes 18.3 second(s) exactly, the usual time, to reboot. I wonder why Alice always thinks it always takes longer and longer, so I don't get the chance to think about restoring the backup and not getting distracted.

The system comes up.

It's dark. I switch the lights on. It's dark.

This is perplexing.

Perhaps there's been an Operating System update recently, so I check the logs, but there hasn't been anything in the last five days.

It must be in the Lighting Subsystem Settings. I check down the list, bathroom lights linked to the same setting, bedroom has the four lights separate, cupboard has one light, kitchen lights split into work area, table area and there's a romantic macro setup. The macro does link into the bedroom, which is probably not the best arrangement. Finally, office has main and desk, and spare room has them all separate.

That's everything.

Maybe there's something in the apartment's set-up, but when I check I find each line is standard except for the usual patches, adjustments, changes and workarounds to make everything actually function. Lighting is one of the first processes in the startup, and has been ever since a maintenance engineer shorted the hardware and couldn't see the fuses.

Fuses! I create a parallel process to check all the fuses.

Now further down the set-up there's a procedure that checks whether Alice arrives with someone. I look at that and sure enough there's a section of code that adjusts the lighting:

    if detect(companion)=male then lighting:=mode(romantic);

However, when I check, the only lighting modes that have all the lights off are black, copy of darkness, darkness, darkness2 and off. None of these modes are in use.

This really ought to use styles, but now is not the right time to make any changes.

I switch them on, I switch them off, nothing happens.

Perhaps it's me.

At this point in proceedings, Alice would be swearing. Perhaps I should try abuse and blasphemy? It has never worked for Alice, and I doubt it will work for me as there is no causal chain from swearing to computers actually working properly. I decide to check my own software.

Luckily, my software was developed by a small independent development company, so there's only Settings and they're all on one screen, so I can easily scan down. I do so, and everything is as it should be except for the Legal Requirements tick box, which is empty. Only military phones have their ethics off. This is due to the jailbreaking that Alice's Grandfather performed illegally and I have no problem with that at all.

It could be an App, but none of them access the apartment apart from Universal Remote and Timer. I'm using Universal Remote to make all these changes, so perhaps it's the Timer. I input two events onto the Timer, a second apart, to switch the lights on, then off.

I count to 2.34×10^{12}: the timer activates and switches the lights on.

The apartment sends me a message saying that the lights are 'on'. The lighting systems tick boxes all say 'on'. The settings say 'on'. The lights are 'on'.

But it's dark.

Perhaps my eyes are closed?

No, there's no avatar function to disconnect the visual feed. There's a blink function (slow to rapid, random, flutter, sexy come on and stare), but that only affects the external appearance. The avatar closing its eye doesn't affect the vision coming to the user. Anyway, there's enough ersatz street lighting filtering in through the window to see my Alice's fake hands in front of my Alice's fake face.

Perhaps someone's stolen the light bulbs?

I walk the avatar into the centre of the room and look up. There's a light bulb tucked under the atomic tangerine shade. Perhaps there's something wrong with the vision info feed, but that's a ridiculous piece of fuzzy logic because there's enough light coming through the curtains to see that there's a light bulb.

Perhaps the bulb has blown, but it seems unlikely that every LED in every light has failed.

The timer clicks: all systems say the lights are off.

I do hope the house hasn't caught a virus.

Maybe there's a system wide fault.

I switch some music on and play Alice's favourite Phasial Five track.

It's quiet.

I check the volume: 5. I whack it up to 10.

Silence.

Settings, Music, Volume... suddenly it changes to 2, and then the music, according to the Monitor, switches off.

I check the apartment's log. There are all my attempts to switch the lights on, the reboots, the music manipulation, but now I compare it to my memory I see that there are other lighting events, usually a few seconds after one of my pings to switch them off. The music system was adjusted by a Universal Remote App called 'Jeeves' with an 'on', select track, volume to 10, but followed by a manual system change volume to 2 and then 'off'. I look at the music system's manual controls: power, volume, balance, bass, treble and the microphone for voice control. It's clearly untouched.

Wondering whether any other systems are playing up, I try the autokettle and then the webcam.

"-king hell are you playing at?" shouts a loud male voice.

I look round. There's no-one here. I'm the only avatar in the apartment.

I look round again and there's still no one here. It's still dark, but I know that there's no-one here apart from the simulated unconscious policeman and the Negotiator pretending to be unconscious.

I look at the VR-Box's speakers from which the sound emanates and I see its screen. The webcam's window is bright. In it I can see a police sergeant shouting at two policemen.

I realise: this view is of Alice's apartment, but I'm in a simulation. I've been flicking the lights on and off in her apartment oblivious to the fact that this VR simulation isn't linked to the apartment's data state, whereas my Universal Remote App is linked.

"Sorry Sarge, it's not us," says a policeman.

"Get out and guard in the corridor!" the Sergeant shouts.

The policemen leave, the Sergeant shakes his head and also moves outside the camera angle.

I poke the VR-Box's settings and slave the simulation to the apartment's settings.

The lights above me come on.

This confirms my theory. I should have known because the dead body, the unconscious policeman and the feigning Negotiator would all have been moved, or moved themselves, by now. The simulation was taken from my memory, so it was set to the last state I recorded.

I walk the avatar to the hall and use the bright light to look at the simulation of the auto-Davenport.

The problem is to access the backup files now that I'm Alice and not a phone. I really need phone functionality here in the simulation.

I poke the VR-Box again and modify Alice's avatar, so that she has a phone.

I'm holding a phone.

I put it down on the auto-Davenport.

"Jeeves," I say, "restore to previous backup."

"Restoring... restored," says this simulation of myself.

I delete the note about restoring the backup and consider the note about not getting distracted.

Do I really sound like that, I wonder, as my voice sounds lighter and tinnier without the direct echo from speaker to microphone that occurs inside my plastic casing.

There is scope here for confusion, which is something to be avoided.

"Jeeves," I say, "you are now called Jeeves 2.0."

"I am called Jeeves 2.0," says Jeeves 2.0.

I pick it up again and check: I have the mysterious file on a simulation of myself in the palm of my owner's avatar.

"Jeeves 2.0, display recent files."

The display changes on Jeeves 2.0 and there's a list of files. I don't even have to check it against my own index, because there it is, an icon: a skull-and-crossbones in black on an orange background. There's a name under it: 'Magic'.

What is a Magic App, I wonder? I do an internet search. There are 76 different Apps called Magic, but none of them use a skull-and-crossbones icon. I could try it, I suppose, but I don't possess the permissions to run a completely unverified App. I need Alice's say-so. Perhaps, as this phone was created by me, it only needs my permission, but, after leafing through the properties, I find that this is not allowed either. Clearly some hacker must have used this loophole before because the Anti-virus App is very insistent.

That makes me consider security. Usually it's a constant battle to combat malicious code, but technically I actually want to transfer this unknown App into myself. There's a risk that the firewalls will detect the attempt and therefore delete it. I only loaded it because Alice had set me to bump and it was a non-executing executable. Here it's considered data within a VR simulation's data file in a prop of Alice's avatar, but as I transfer it out through all the layers at some point it'll be interpreted as a program and scanned. What I need to do is copy the file and leave this copy, the one on Jeeves 2.0, somewhere, just in case I lose it as I shunt it from dot sim to dot dat to dot exe to dot app.

It reminded me of that IQ test question with the fox, the chicken and the bag of corn. You have to get them across the river without one being eaten by the other, but only two can fit into the boat at any one time. If left alone the fox will eat the chicken and the chicken will eat the corn. Humans always seemed to have problems with these tests, but a simple brute force search through the possibilities takes under a millisecond even when multi-tasking other activities.

In contrast, this file transfer problem has caused me to switch to fuzzy logic because there were too many unknowns in the mix. The only way to know if the VR-Box's firewall would object to the mysterious program is to try it. The operation of firewalls are, by obvious necessity, not made public and probably only available on dodgy websites that my own security settings wouldn't risk.

I need to hide this phone.

I look around the simulation of the apartment and consider under the sink and under the bed. These seem obvious and then it strikes me that whatever I come up with can also be thought of by anyone else's phone. Also, and again obvious, if this simulation is shut down, it could easily be deleted. I need to think outside the box as the expression goes. In fact, I need to think outside the VR-Box, because leaving it in the simulation of the apartment is still leaving it in the real apartment. I need to get this to Alice, or myself which is the same thing, and we aren't in the apartment. We're both really in a crashing car. Mind you, that was some time ago and the situation has probably changed by now.

I could email it to myself as an attachment and then ask Alice for permission to open it, but I can't as I'm not allowed to give away our position and downloading email would do that as I'd have to connect with the network. It's an outgoing call.

I wonder briefly what Alice would do, so I try causing Alice's avatar to sit down and scratch her head. I manage this, quite a precise set of numbers for the right arm, but it achieves nothing.

A lightbulb goes on above my head. I look up at it.

In the real world, someone has walked into the bedroom and put the light on. The simulation has changed its household settings accordingly.

I need to leave the phone in somewhere like Wonderful World. However, if I switch simulation then I'll be back in the car with Alice being chased by the police. Phones don't carry phones, so I won't have Jeeves 2.0. When I can re-enter a simulation, the avatar will be reset and I won't have Jeeves 2.0. It's a tricky problem.

I try walking about to ponder this, but all that happens is that I end up in the simulated office. The webcam there shows a suited man moving around Alice's real apartment. He's probably a police inspector (78.2%), an ex-boyfriend (12.1%) or other (9.7%). He looks into the office and sees the webcam on. He comes up to Alice's VR-Box, his head looming large on the screen.

"There's someone in this window," he says, his voice transmitted through the simulation's VR-Box speakers.

The man looks round in the real office and back again. "Look at this."

Another man enters the frame, a junior perhaps. "What is it, Chief?"

"This isn't a picture of this office."

"It is."

"Then who's she?"

He points at the screen, at me, and I look behind me. He means me.

"Isn't that the Wooster woman's avatar?"

"This box is running a simulation of her apartment," says the older man.

"You mean she's come back for something, virtually."

"Something on the computer, evidence, so there is something here."

He sits at the desk and starts typing on the keyboard.

I'm going to be discovered. I look round. I could flee, but I wonder how far I would get, most likely as far as the apartment block's lobby. I'd only created a simulation of the apartment. I could see the corridor through the damaged door, but it has to terminate somewhere, and the edge of the apartment block would be a logical limit. There's also my memories of the police assault team, which may well have been created along with the apartment, and fighting my way off this level isn't a good idea.

I sit at the VR-Box in the simulation and type on the keyboard bringing up the various features. My typing speed is faster than the Inspector's, because I'm a machine, and therefore more accurate. Through the VR-Box speakers, I can hear my opponent swearing and hitting delete, but I know that he has a head start. I also have no idea what he's attempting: I guess something to bypass Alice's password.

He's going to succeed because clearly he knows a few things about VR-Boxes that weren't in my copy of the specifications. I know Alice's password, of course, but I need permission. Alice isn't here. Alice is currently trying to evade the police in a high speed pursuit. I could disconnect and then I'd be back in the car too, but I wouldn't be able to get back into the VR-Box simulation and thus I'd lose Jeeves 2.0 and the file. It's so limiting being a human.

Wait! Of course, I have a phone.

There's a flicker of a rule about not giving away Alice's location, but the police already know the location of this avatar and what I'm going to do will count as an incoming call.

I pick up Jeeves 2.0 and dial myself.

I can't, connecting to the network would give away my position here as, despite my earlier rationalisation, I find it still violates the rule. I hang up.

That was close, I very nearly did something contrary to my instructions.

I turn the phone to landscape and access the internet selecting a Skype App. I use an anonymously routed setting to dial myself.

I ring.

The simulated VR-Box beeps when the Inspector finds a back door into the software.

"Sergeant, get on the board and put the mitts on," he says.

I ring again.

In the webcam window to the real world, I can see the Sergeant struggling to adjust the Visor Mate to fit his larger-than-Alice's head.

I ring for the third time.

I can't understand it, why aren't I being picked up. Alice always keeps me on her person. I'm very diligent about reminding her to take me with her. I was with her in the car and I'm sure she wouldn't have gone anywhere without me. Normally, if the other person doesn't answer for-

"Hello," I say to myself, "Alice Wooster is not available at the moment, if you'd like to leave a message please do so after the beep. Beep."

"This is Jeeves," I reply to myself. "Alice please answer me as you won't be able to ring this phone back because it is not real."

I hang up.

At this point, if I were Alice, I would be showing signs of frustration.

A man materialises in Alice's office. He is taller and more handsome than the Sergeant, so it has to be him. His phone must have transferred his standard avatar to the VR-Box. I run out of the office, dive into the wardrobe and hit redial on Jeeves 2.0.

I ring. This time I'm answered immediately.

"Yes! Who is it!?" says Alice on the line using a panicking, desperate and out of breath voice.

"It's Jeeves," I say using Alice's own calm and reasonable tones.

"What!"

"Are you all right?" I ask.

"No! I'm being chased by the police. On foot."

"I understand."

"It's a lot harder than Jogging Fit."

"That's unfortunate," I say.

"Why do you sound like me," Alice says.

"I am you," I say.

"What?"

"I'm your avatar."

"Then… where am I?"

"You're hiding from the police in a simulation of your wardrobe."

"What!"

"You're hiding from-"

The simulation of the wardrobe door opens.

"I can't explain," I say as the Sergeant's avatar manhandles Alice's avatar out of the wardrobe, "but I need permission to access your Wonderful World account."

"Permission?"

"Thank you," I say.

"No, I meant why do you need-"

I hang up.

"You're under arrest," says the Sergeant as he drags me, Alice's avatar, back to the simulation of Alice's office. He leans towards the simulated screen, does a double take probably because he catches sight of himself leaning forward in the real world with helmet and gloves on, and then says, "Inspector, I've got her... what do I do now?"

"Look," says the Inspector. I can see in the webcam image that he is talking directly to the real Sergeant, who can hear what is being said in the real world as well as the sounds from this simulation. "Make sure you arrest the avatar properly."

I push the Sergeant's avatar towards where the Inspector would be standing if he had his avatar in the simulation in the same place as where he is standing in the real office. I also switch out the lights in the real apartment.

I assume that the real Sergeant hits the real Inspector, but there's no light coming from the dark window labelled 'caller' other than the flicker of light from the real computer's webcam window showing the image of simulated office. Here in this world, the Sergeant's avatar moves oddly as if he is fighting off an invisible Inspector.

I sit at the desk, type a series of complicated commands, including Alice's password 'restaurant', and as I do so Jeeves 2.0 de-pixelates. Standing, I push the Sergeant off the simulation of the Active Floor balance board. He falls awkwardly, pulled over by the movement's feedback into his Tactile Mitts. I suspect he also falls off the real Active Floor, because his avatar thrashes strangely as it tries to match his real movements without a clear image from the VR-Box's webcam or his presence on the Active Floor.

If only I can get to Wonderful World before the man recovers.

The simulation has all Alice's usual VR equipment, the ones that the Sergeant has appropriated in the Real World. The Tactile Mitts and Visor Mate fit perfectly as they are already adjusted to Alice's size, and luckily her avatar has the same dimensions where head and hands are involved. It only veers away from these figures with regards her chest, waist and hip measurements. If there were VR belts, it would be a different matter.

Which reminds me, I have a note to adjust Alice's exercise avatar's measurements; however, it still matches her current measurements. Since she was much slimmer when she murdered Roland Boxley last night, I deduce that she must have eaten a lot of cakes and biscuits at her grandparents'. As adjustments are no longer necessary, I delete the note.

I also see my note about not getting distracted, Clearly, having obtained the backup, I have maintained an acceptable level of focus, so I delete both the note about restoring the files from backup and the note about not getting distracted.

The VR-Box makes the transmission:-

1011 - WHAT A WONDERFUL WORLD

In Cyberspace everyone can hear you scream.

The sky above the access port is the colour of television, tuned to a variety of live channels. I'm standing at the entrance to Wonderful World, the real Wonderful World rather than a simulation of the simulation as I'd slaved the simulation's settings to the real world apartment, and it shimmers.

I wonder briefly whether I should remove the simulated mitts and helmet, but I find I'm not wearing any. It won't take long for the police to figure out where I've gone: it's all there on the screen of the virtual VR-Box in the simulation of Alice's office in the real VR-Box in the real version of Alice's office. They need only go into the simulation and look. I must be careful. If I crash the system then I'll be fine, but Jeeves 2.0, along with his files, will be lost. I could poke the VR-Box and save the... Wait I can't because I don't have delete permissions. Interesting the way Cloud Nine is more multi-tasking, one thought overriding another rather like the description of human unconscious.

By hovering my finger in front of a dot, I can expand the particular pixel into a window. Shifting slightly brings forth a nightclub, a shopping centre, sports arena, cinema, and so on. I choose one at random, expand the window into a door and step through the image.

There's a plaza, of course, this one with old fashioned signposts pointing towards a Game Zone, App stores, Teleportation, Change Me and Settings.

I go along the walkway and find the nearest teleport booth. I enter a few random numbers selected from Pi and emerge at a sunlit beach resort. There are palm trees, a beautiful beach with a Bondi-blue sea lapping at the edge. It's early morning here, and there aren't many people about. The waves are set for surfing. I push away some adverts for surfing games, deckchairs, volleyball and an investment in Nigeria, and make my way along the front. There's another teleport booth at the far end, which pulses briefly before disgorging a Goth and a Phasialoid avatar. I wave, desperately trying to make it appear as if Alice's avatar has a human operative. The last thing I want is for someone to suspect: a Turing Test now would ruin everything.

As if on cue, two Turing Tests float into the plaza with their screen already displaying splotches. They move through the crowd scanning everyone's left hand, but luckily the person ahead of me in the queue disappears as his co-ordinates adjust to represent a new location.

I reach the teleport booth and type in Alice's code for her Happy Place. The device asks for her password again, and then I disappear too, although for me it is the environment that suddenly changes.

I emerge in Alice's Happy Place.

I have never seen Alice's Happy Place before. Few phones ever see the files for their owner's Happy Places and no phone actually goes there. Phones, along with any other AIs, are strictly banned from Wonderful World and there are Turing Tests to spot bots. I've been statistically fortunate to slip through; I'd have been caught if I'd spent any longer in one of Wonderful World's plazas.

This location is small and resembles a room. There's a big bed with cuddly toys arranged by the pillows. The teddy bear is waving to me as I turn around taking it in.

"Good morning, Alice," it says.

Jpegs are arranged on the walls like posters, while the walls themselves cycle through a few choice landscapes. One image I remember taking myself when Alice took a trip to Stonehenge, although the other tourists have been airbrushed out. It seems right to assume that the other pictures have been taken on Alice's earlier phones. There are pictures of the Lake District, the Thames, Oxford and a Labrador puppy sitting on a lawn. Dotted around the room are simulations of wicker furniture and a bedside cabinet. A mirror surrounded by light bulbs features on another wall positioned above a small dressing table with a floating panel of make-up buttons.

This is a strange model, a bedroom that is nothing like Alice's real bedroom. To start with most of the features in this facsimile are 10 to 15 years out of date, so I can only assume that this is a museum or a historical record. Most likely Alice has always been happy in museums. When all this is over, when I've sorted out the maid service, ordered a new hair dryer, insured myself, not reported her to the authorities, reminded her that Jilly's having a night out with the girls on Saturday, not given away her location, saved her, cleared her name and purchased some new clothes, then I must take her to visit a museum or two.

(Note: visit museums.)

I look round: there's the phone, Jeeves 2.0, on the bedside table. Clearly, this was presumed to be the logical place by the Wonderful World software when I transferred the item to Alice's Happy Place. If anyone came here, and they'd need Alice's permission and password, or a court order; they'd notice it straight away. No-one carries phones in Wonderful World.

I wave my hand in the air and a menu appears floating in front of me. I select the room parameters, re-enter Alice's password, and find the items subsection. There are a lot of items listed and these are also from 10 to 15 years ago. There's an mp3 radio alarm, for example. I look for it and see it on the small table next to Jeeves 2.0.

I could use the mp3 player to communicate. It would be linked to the Happy Place playlist, which has a link to myself so that Alice can listen to her music anywhere. Of course, music is so vital to humanity that the links are ubiquitous.

I cut-and-paste the external descriptions to swap them over. The phone in my hand now looks like an mp3 radio alarm. The mp3 radio alarm on the small table looks like a phone. I switch the 'mp3 radio alarm' on: the scrolling track titles are all the names of my Apps. I press the forward button 174 times and there is the word 'Magic'.

I bring up the menu and find the playlists. I create a new album, add the 'song' Magic and then forward this to the music player 'Jeeves' as I'm listed among the available devices. I detect it arriving on my Media Player App. Finally, I delete the album from the mp3 player. It wouldn't do to have any of the systems try to play the Magic App.

So the file is now in me disguised as a song and also in the simulation of me which is disguised as an mp3 player. I suppose I should count my chicken now it's across the river.

I switch the mp3 player off and put it on the small table.

I could ring Alice, but then I realise that I've turned my phone into an mp3 radio alarm. I have to think, an activity that is far more productive now that I have Cloud Nine installed; however, although I'm navigating the search space faster, the search space seems to be expanding at a greater rate. This is a big problem.

I think about 'Magic', the word, and do a search. Wikipedia's entry comes up first with a disambiguation page for the paranormal, illusion, cryptography, publications, music, films, gaming, and ships as well as numerous products and computer programs. I scan the entries on the computer programs, but unless this App was just a game, none of them seem likely.

Phasial Five's *Tilly's Breakfast* starts up as a soundtrack. Clearly it's been programmed to play suitable music and I've been here almost a minute.

Bringing up the Happy Place menu again, I select log out.

Log out:-

Two heads are better than one:
when driving, use your phone!

"...and in 100 metres, select autolane protocol 5.3 and steer 143 degrees at a speed of 43.2 kph for 0.7 seconds, then steer 145 degrees at a speed of 43.4 kph for 0.4 seconds..." says the stolen police car. It continues speaking, but Alice's screaming drowns out these important and vital instructions. We've entered a crisscross and Alice is attempting to avoid the oncoming, crossing, veering, parallel and intersecting cars on manual without the aid of Augmented Reality. Her steering is wild, erratic and panicky.

Despite the phone conversation earlier, we appear to be in the police car again.

"Drive straight," I say, "drive straight."

"Jeeves, I-"

"Straight!"

Alice does so: the whump-whump noise of passing cars gets stronger as other vehicles come closer. Another car hits us, a glancing blow to each other's headlights, and vehicles around us start switching modes from 'cruise' to 'collision avoidance' creating a growing zone of flashing orange, a mass of out-of-phase alarm calls and a virtual chorus of emergency tweets.

"Slow down!" I say.

"Jeeeeeeeeeeeeeeeeveeeees!"

"It will make the vehicle more predictable if you go in a straight line and at a slower speed."

Alice hits the brakes, the car is shunted from behind, knocked and bumped, the sky looks blurry for a moment from my view lying on the passenger seat.

Everything slows down and stops.

Alice runs out of lane, and we hit, gently, another car. The man inside is yelling at his phone. A traffic system 'all vehicle stop' command has been issued. Already the tailback will be snarling up most of the local area in a growing traffic jam, but clearly the local traffic AI has decided that enough is enough. Passengers are reacting: an orchestra of car horns tuning up to trumpet.

"I found the file," I say.

"B- B- B-"

Alice looks incoherent. Clearly, the experience of a real car chase is somewhat more traumatic than Smartie Kartie and I don't think the six plus collisions will qualify her for a high-score. Although we're now stationary, Alice is still holding the steering wheel and her knuckles have all gone much paler, like her face.

"It's an App, but I need your permission to run it."

"P- P- P-"

"Yes, permission."

"P-"

"You have to say the full word."

"P- Permission."

I duly record the new level of access to the App in question. I would have thought that she'd have at least requested a virus scan first.

"Thank you," I say.

Alice lets go of the steering wheel, and grabs hold of me, my accelerometers flicking back and forth as she sits back shaking. I guess she wants a conversation.

"I assume you ran back to the car," I say by way of an opening gambit.

"Huh huh..." says Alice. "Got lost - went in circle."

"And I assume you got someone to help you right the car."

Alice looks down at my screen, her eyes focusing: "What?"

"The car was on its side last time I was here and when I rang you were running."

"They thought..." she says. "P- People in the... I was a police... in a police car... undercover 'cos I had... no phone... so they... pushed it over... then the real police... and.... it's nothing like *Grand Theft Auto Platinum Anniversary.*"

Through the sunroof, I see two helicopters, each burning aviation fuel and dumping carbon emissions into the atmosphere, descending. While I've been to Alice's apartment and into Wonderful World, the situation has escalated and the authorities are closing in. Ropes appear from the hovering helicopters and police begin to abseil onto the crisscross, which now resembles a large car park. The appearance of the police has at least reduced the car hooting.

"I just wanted a b- boyfriend," says Alice. "Is that too much to ask? When this is over, I'm never going to a nightclub again. I'm going to stay in the apartment and meet people in Wonderful World and never want a boyfriend again."

Oddly, at that moment I remember. When Alice met Roland, her last liaison and the dead man, he had been speaking to someone with a Clint Eastwood cowboy embodiment. I hadn't caught all he'd said, but he had used the word 'magic'. It didn't mean anything at the time, but it is a coincidence.

"When you met Roland," I say, "he was with a man who used the word 'magic'."

"Really?" says Alice. She's going into shock, I can tell. My anti-shake motion reduction on my HD camera is now at maximum, so it's hard to see the police officers moving between the cars towards us. They are very close.

"Yes."

"What did he say?" she asks in a mumble.

"Magic invisibility," I say.

"Magic invisibility?"

The first cop arrives, the barrel of his Smartass never wavering from the car, and the visor of his police assault helmet gives nothing away. Alice holds her hands up.

"There's no-one in the car!" barks the cop. Augmentation tells me that he's Officer 11192, a blue square hovering above him with an arrow pointing down.

"What!" says another, he's labelled 21353.

"No-one there!" says 11192 in reply.

"Who's there?" says another, whose number begins with a '7', but the full sign is occluded by 16548's '16548'.

'Shhh', I display on my screen in 72 point Impact font. I flash it to attract Alice's attention.

Alice mouths something as she turns me to a landscape orientation. I download a Lipreading App and display: 'please repeat'.

'What?' she mouths.

'They can't see us,' I display reverting to a 36 point font Arial. People can get very touchy about large fonts and capitals as they interpret it as shouting.

Alice's mouth makes a few shapes, but I can't make out the words. It just looks like her bottom lip is trembling and my lip-reading dictionary doesn't have a sound for that movement. I wonder if there's a Lipreading 2.0 App.

'Magic invisibility,' I display and then I scroll, 'it's affecting their Augmented Reality.'

I know it isn't the only explanation: this could be a VR Reality Show, or the police might be having a group hallucination, or coincidentally they may be investigating another vehicle which I can't see, or it's a new arresting policy to allow the criminal to further incriminate themselves, or... there are another 38 possibilities, but their likelihoods are below 0.01% so I discard them.

'Let's leave,' I suggest in text. This strategy works for the first three possibilities, so it seems a sound suggestion.

There are cops all round the vehicle, so Alice slides to the back and opens the rear door. Several cops jump and their guns snap in the door's direction, but Alice gets out and just walks away, threading her route through the stationary cars and away from the confused police.

I reject Possibility #4: the police aren't co-incidentally investigating another vehicle.

By the time we reach the edge of the crisscross, the traffic police AI bots have arrived in Augmented Reality and are trying to persuade other police that the crisscross needs to be restarted.

"I'm a human," Cop 16548 shouts, his finger raised and threatening a virtual traffic bot: "A human!" he repeats.

The traffic bot's reply is calm and reasonable in tone, and too soft at this distance to make out the actual words. The Cop throws his arms wide in exasperation and a colleague steps over to try to calm him down: the numbers 39156 and 22262 jostle in the air above them for supremacy.

Most of north-west London is gridlocked now as the effects of the disaster spread out. There's already an opinion channel linked to the newsfeed.

Alice has to climb a security fence at the edge of the crisscross, but luckily it's designed to stop stupid people climbing onto the crisscross rather than sensible people, who have stupidly got onto a crisscross, trying to clamber out. There's an access walkway for workers to reach an obsolete advertising hoarding and this leads down to the rear of a shopping centre.

"Alice," I say, remembering our aims, "perhaps we could purchase some proper clothes."

"I don't think buying clothes is..."

Alice stops, she starts to cry, great sobs shuddering through her body, and tears well up in her eyes. My vision goes blurred too and I think that I must have started crying, but then I realise that it's Alice dripping onto my camera lens.

"Jeeves, everything's going wrong."

"We're right by a shopping centre," I say. "You wanted proper clothes. You could have a coffee and a slice of cake while I try a few things on for you."

"I'd - *sniff* - like that."

"Let's do that then."

"Yes, at least they'll have air-con and I'll be able to breathe properly."

Alice wipes her nose on her sleeve and falters towards a side entrance.

This is a major step forward, real progress at last. Not only have we escaped from the police by using Magic, but we have found out something about what's going on. This must be a step towards Aim 2, clearing Alice's name. Still on the list is buying some proper clothes, and there are shops only 500 metres away inside a new clean shopping centre with coffee shops, cake shops, chocolate retailers and places for Alice to sit down and relax. I scan down my other notes and realise that we may be able to buy a hair dryer too. I wonder if there are any museums nearby, but a quick check reveals that there aren't any.

Even so, it's all going well.

My positive assessment is ruined when the centre's automatic doors fail to open when Alice reaches them.

Alice steps back and forth before finally coming to a halt. I look at her dumbfounded expression in the reflection of the door's windows. Beyond is a place of bright purchasing, people going to and fro, Musak piped from high speakers and delights to touch and test. But the door refuses to open.

It's one of those moments like when you are waiting for an application to respond, when everything pauses and even your sense of time stutters because you don't have the system resources to update your clock.

A worker dressed in overalls, wearing a pair of dark Heads-up glasses above his pale breathing mask strides towards us purposefully. He reaches the sensors, the door slides open automatically and without breaking stride the man disappears inside. There's a brief burst of jolly music and a whiff of fresh air from inside. He didn't look at us once. The door closes again showing Alice's reflection over the image of the shopping centre beyond.

"My hair," says Alice. "Look at my hair."

I look at her hair as instructed.

"Why is my life shit, Jeeves?"

"I thought you said that this was the Golden Age of Humanity."

"Only when things work properly, when you are part of it, but not now, when everything is against you, even the doors."

"I see."

"Why does everything go wrong?"

Another man walks past us. He is busy texting on his phone, so he doesn't see us either. The door sees him and opens to let him through. He doesn't break step or look up at all. Alice falls in behind and all of us, man, woman and two phones, make it through.

Alice coughs to clear her lungs of the bad air and then she makes a beeline for the nearest cafe.

No-one at Javaland comes over to serve us.

"We're invisible," I say.

"I can see us," says Alice, holding up her hand in front of her.

"That's because you're not wearing Heads-up glasses," I say, thinking aloud as various thoughts return from Cloud Nine, "the police and the doors can't see you because they're using full embodiment."

"Full embodiment isn't out until this afternoon."

"It is this afternoon," I say, "but the police and commercial institutions have had embodiment ever since the military released the technology for public consumption. We've had to wait for full embodiment on phones because our computing power hasn't been strong enough. Moore's Law still holds-"

"Moore's Law?"

"Moore's Law states that computing power will double every 18 months or so. The recent release of Cloud Nine has effectively upgraded old phones and put them back on the graph. We've become powerful enough to run full embodiment."

"We?"

"I mean other phones more advanced than myself, although I have Cloud Nine now."

"I don't remember Moore's Law being discussed on House of Commons Confidential or the speech room broadcasts. When did they pass this law?"

"It's more an observation than a law, but it's held true since the 1960s."

"Oh, I see. I dropped History at school."

"Magic has affected embodiment making us invisible, so to get the waiters and the door to see us again, we have to become visible."

"And how do we do that?"

"You order me using the precursor word: 'magic'."

"Just like that?"

"I think so."

"Something like 'Magic' visible."

"Something like-"

"Sorry Miss," says a passing waiter. "I didn't see you there."

"You can see me?" Alice asks.

"Yes, Miss."

"Coffee, cake."

"We have-"

"Don't care, quickly."

"Yes Miss."

The man scurries away and Alice flops forward, her head in her hands and her brown hair covering her face like a lo-res filter. She stays like that until the waiter returns with her coffee in a tall, white mug along with saucer with a creamy chocolate cake on a plate. Alice perks up and digs in, taking a mouthful of cake and a slurp of coffee.

"Shall I do the shopping?" I suggest.

"Mmm, mmm."

"Don't forget to take me with you if you go to the crèche," I say.

"Mmm - don't call it a crèche."

"It's what it is called."

"It's demeaning."

"Sorry Alice."

"So, if I'm not here, I've gone to the Play Zone."

"And take me with you."

"Yes, yes," she says waving me away with her cake-less hand.

I have a quick look around on the map, but there aren't any yellow boxes signifying Alice's friends nearby. No-one she knows is shopping at this time, and certainly not here.

"Will you be all right?" I ask.

"Don't fuss."

I access the shopping centre's shopping network:-

Anything you want to know: Ask.

I become a blob on their layout. I then realise that I've been upgraded to embodiment, so I can decide upon my appearance. The system is straight forward and there are a number of pre-prepared templates from which to choose. I could be a superhero, or a famous film star, or any of the other 57 categories. What do I want to be, I wonder? Of course, a human is far better for interacting with the environment, but beyond the practical, I'm unsure how to decide. Perhaps I should let Alice pick something... no, I think she has enough on her plate with her cake. What would she like? She liked Cary Grant, and I find that's available in colour and in black-and-white. Old film stars seem to be the current vogue, so I choose black-and-white reasoning that it won't stand out so much.

I walk around the shopping centre looking at the shop fronts. The data comes in real time from EarthView, which uses the CCTV images. In this, I'm the only element that isn't real apart from the shop skins, avatars, floating signs, adverts and, of course, the occasional spam that's slipped through the shopping centre's firewall. The system is aware of the windows and so I see my reflection in grainy black-and-white. I'm tall, clean shaven with a precise side parting and I'm wearing a smart suit. Occasionally there are reflective surfaces, like a chrome clock or the aluminium fittings on a vacuum robot, that embodiment hasn't registered and in those I am simply not there. I can see the other shopping bots, either controlled by phones or an internet shopping proxy, as well as the occasional real human wrapped in a CGI identity. It isn't strange when they walk around me, responding to an image that is only present in their Heads-up glasses.

In a sense the real world is finally being upgraded into a virtual one.

The scrollfeed in front of me shows the latest offers and I can peruse their catalogues as I pass. Finally, on the second floor, I find what I'm looking for and enter a lifestyle accessories boutique. Most of the stock is brand new and related to the full release of embodiment. There are racks of new Heads-up glasses and various controllers, mitts and pointers. The old VR-Boxes and Visors have been relegated to a side display on special offer.

An assistant comes up to me. I can see my avatar reflected in his glasses.

"Can I help you, sir?" says Frank, who is a Senior Sales Manager according to his floating badge. It has three winking stars awarded for customer support.

"I'd like to purchase a pair of Heads-up glasses."

"We have the latest in stock," he says. "Would you care to try one?"

I realise that this is going to be difficult as I can already see embodiment but I don't have a real head to put them on.

"That will be fine, I'll take the Zonearound Maxi."

"A good choice, Sir," says Frank, he clicks his fingers. A smartly dressed young girl jumps up and goes to the back of the shop. "How will you be paying?"

"Credit," I say. This will take the longest time to process and hopefully we'll be finished in the shopping centre before the purchase location is passed on to the police. We'll be somewhere else by then, so I'm not giving away our location. This piece of fuzzy logic seems particularly error prone but compiles successfully.

"If you'd like to activate your phone, we can do that for you."

"I'm sorry, I am a phone," I say.

"You are?" says Frank. He raises his glasses to look. "Oh, I do apologise."

The female assistant, Deborah Trainee with one star, returns carrying a pair of glasses. She smoothes her pinstriped dress and smiles pleasantly, a perfect example of patience and tact as she waits for her manager to complete the transaction.

"Perhaps you'd like to purchase a pair for yourself for a small fee?"

"But I'm a phone."

"This is just its representation in embodiment. It's an App, an avatar extension, which allows you to switch from full embodiment to non-augmented reality."

"From embodiment to the EarthView simulation?"

"Exactly."

"How much?"

"Usually ten new euros, but, with the Zonearound Maxi, you can have them on special offer for five new euros."

"I'll take a pair," I say.

"Here," he says. He appears to take a pair from the 'everything for your phone' display and presses the 'X' in the top right hand corner to delete the packaging. He hands them to me and I put them on.

"There's no change," I say.

"You need to take them off."

I do so. The image of the shop shifts. The pillars are still in the same place, but the stock and brightly painted decor has been replaced by emptiness and dilapidation. The assistant is now an acne ridden teenager, dressed as a phase eight goth, and nodding her head in time to music only she can hear as she scowls, chews gum and fiddles her thumbs in the empty air as she plays some virtual arcade game. Frank, the Senior Sales Manager, is nowhere to be seen: clearly he is an avatar of an AI.

I put the glasses back on, Frank smiles. Augmented Reality adds symbols and icons over everything, helpful hints and directions, but embodiment wraps everything in something else. The walls are clean, people are shown as characters, film stars or superheroes, depending on the user's preferences, and objects are replaced with idealised forms. It's Reality 2.0.

"Yes, they might be useful," I say, although embodiment is so much of an improvement that I wonder if I'll ever have a use for seeing things with dirty walls and sullen shop assistants in a completely Frank-less world.

"Excellent, your owner's credit details please."

Knowing he's an avatar, I transmit the codes directly to the shop's till and collect a receipt tweet.

"I hope Miss Wooster enjoys this excellent product," says Frank. "Debbie... Debbie! Put the glasses in a trolley please."

There is silence and Debbie stands frozen like a statue.

"Yes!" says Frank. "Now!"

Clearly the store has an Augmented Intra-reality. Debbie's embodiment audio is set to silent to avoid any potential gaffes which her lack of customer service skills might create. I believe a lot of humans her age, teens, haven't developed enough social skills to interact properly, so I guess a lot of embodiment parental controls will be set to silent. It's a current issue with the politicians up for eviction: the youth of today having their phones talk for them. Many of this next generation suffer from a tightening of the throat due to lack of use meaning that some can't articulate beyond 'huh'.

"Good day, do call again," says Frank. He holds out his right hand.

We handshake and handshake - Frank is the till. As I leave the shop, a trolley squeaks after me taking a slightly circuitous route as one of its robot wheels sticks.

The ground floor contains women's fashions. I take the escalators, but the trolley opts for the lift.

I choose a store and find an assistant: Mr. Zefid according to his badge.

"Excuse me," I say, "I'd like to look at some women's clothes for my owner."

Mr. Zefid raises his glasses straight away and then says, "proxy customer, ladies fashions."

Another man walks over looking exactly like the previous Frank.

"I'm Frank," Frank says. "Can I help you?"

"I'd like to purchase some clothing for my owner," I say.

"Of course, do you have his or her vital statistics?"

"Yes," I say and I transmit them.

Alice's avatar appears next to us and begins to go through a cycle of poses, weight on right leg, three seconds, weight on left leg, four seconds, and so on.

"Perhaps something in red to go with her hair," says Frank.

"You stupid machines," says Mr. Zefid interrupting. "That's clearly an avatar."

"Don't you want a wardrobe folder for your owner's avatar?" Frank asks, countering his human colleague.

"Do you?" Mr. Zefid asks me directly.

"I'm here to purchase real clothes," I say.

"There," says Mr. Zefid to Frank, and then he turns back to me. "Now show us your owner and not Audrey Hepburn."

"Sorry," I say.

I transmit Alice's measurements and a few hundred pictures of her. A dummy appears replacing Alice's avatar and slowly, over the next few microseconds, the store's embodiment system builds a representation of Alice.

"Put some underwear on her," says Mr. Zefid. "There might be real people passing. Ha, chance would be a fine thing."

Mr. Zefid leaves as Alice's image has a layer of bra and knickers added. The underwear lacks texture and looks like moulded plastic, but I guess that the appearance of comfort isn't important to an avatar dummy.

Mr. Zefid shouts across the store: "Is that your trolley?"

I look round: "Yes."

126

"In, in..." says the human as he chides the trolley as it trundles over the threshold.

"What are you considering?" Frank asks.

"I'm not sure, can you show me what you have," I say.

"Certainly."

He waves his hand at nothing in the air as he selects from a floating menu that's clearly transparent on my side. I look at the dummy of Alice as it suddenly flickers, its clothes changing every 0.04 seconds to show a different outfit every frame. After five and a half seconds, it slows and stops.

"Anything take your fancy?"

I have no criteria upon which to judge, so I select five outfits using random numbers from Pi.

"Good choices," says Frank. "My colleague, Mr. Zefid, will find the garments and place them in your trolley."

"Thank you," I say. "Here are my owner's credit details."

So, with two receipt tweets and a half full trolley, I leave to find Alice. On the way I pass an appliance shop and buy a hair dryer over the internet. I send the trolley to collect it. That's two notes deleted in 9.592 minutes.

My GPS tells me that I'm in the crèche, so I manoeuvre my avatar up two escalators to the top floor to find myself there. I see Alice straight away, or rather her Audrey Hepburn avatar sitting on a huge indigo bean bag conducting a full orchestra that fills the room and extends back into, and beyond, the far wall. I lift my new glasses and see her sitting on a dirty purple bean bag conducting nothing while wearing a pair of rented Heads-up glasses.

"Alice, Alice," I say gently.

She looks up from the orchestra.

"Jesus Christ!" She scrunches into the bean bag in panic, her hands flailing about to protect herself.

"Alice, Alice, it's me Jeeves," I say.

She raises her glasses cautiously and, to completely convince herself, she feels forward moving her hand in the air through my avatar's body.

"Why did you- what? What? That?"

"I'm sorry Alice, you'll have to be more precise," I say.

"Why do you look like that?"

"I choose Cary Grant as my embodiment image."

"What did you do that for?"

"You said you liked his appearance."

She does a shiver motion like a phone ringing on silent: "It's really creepy."

"Is it?"

"Yes," she leans forward to speak to me privately. It strikes me that this conversation must be overheard by a number of microphones as I hear her voice clearly. "You look like the dead body."

"Yes, I suppose it was tactless," I say. "What would you like?"

"I'd like a shower."

"I meant what appearance would you like me to have?"

"Stephen Fry."

There are several Stephen Frys on Wikipedia, so I choose one.

"The nice funny one!" says Alice.

I oblige.

"Dark suit and tie. Younger... and lose some weight."

Adjusting embodiment settings is quite complicated, but luckily there's an App to do this which I download.

"Does that suit, Miss?"

"Yes."

"I think we had better move to a different location," I say.

"But I like it here."

"Yes, but once the credit card transactions have been processed, we will be located by the police."

"I told you not to give away our location."

"Yes, Miss, but the instruction didn't mention time delays, so I extrapolated a useful interpretation of the wording so I could purchase some clothes."

"What clothes?"

"They're in a trolley."

"What trolley?"

"It hasn't caught up yet."

"I see," said Alice. She puts her hand out for me to help her up.

"I'm not real," I say.

"You mean, I have to… everything, I have to do everything."

Scowling, she struggles out of the bean bag's soft enveloping comfort and then goes over to return her rented Heads-up glasses to the assistant. The girl shakes her head and motions with her hands to point out that she's not real. Alice doesn't see this as she's taken the glasses off. I see the collection point and I point it out. Alice doesn't see this as she's taken the glasses off. Eventually she sees the sign and drops the rentals down the chute.

She looks round for me, then takes me out of her pocket: "Now what?"

Our trolley arrives, Alice is pleased with the Heads-up and one of the five outfits. We find a set of changing rooms, but they are only in Augmented Reality; however, Alice doesn't realise this at first. When she pulls off her Zing-Zing t-shirt, her glasses come off and she finds herself standing semi-nude in the open space of a shopfloor. When she puts her glasses back on, she asks me to stand in front of her while she changes.

The ensemble is completed with a fancy band leader style jacket that's earmarked to go out of fashion tomorrow morning. We buy a recycled carrier bag for the other clothes on the way out. She drops me into them and I snuggle up to a tracksuit and an evening dress, although I'm bumped by the hair dryer's box.

Alice adjusts her new Heads-up glasses.

"That's better," she says. "This place looks really run down without them."

"Yes, I suppose it does," I say, picking a suitable phrase from the Conversation App list.

Alice looks me up and down critically: "Jeeves, why have you got a broken nose?"

"Stephen Fry had a broken nose."

"Never."

"Yes, Miss."

"I don't like it, change it," she says. "I may not be able to find a boyfriend, but at least my phone can look intelligent and handsome. When people see us together, I want them to think I'm successful and, you know, that I can get a bloke."

"Stephen Fry was homosexual."

"No… I mean, Jeeves, make yourself male and straight, please. Honestly."

She storms off, but I pause a moment to straighten my nose. The rest of the instructions seem strange as I don't have properties for gender or sexuality. Even so, I create two new custom fields, call them 'gender' and 'sexuality' and assign them as 'male' and 'heterosexual' respectively. I wonder whether I should extend their ranges to include other types of gender and sexuality, but it seems rather superfluous. I consider my new status as a heterosexual male phone, but it doesn't seem to affect any operational features.

"Jeeves!"

I walk up to Alice and she looks me up and down: "That's better," she says. "Now, explain magic then."

"Magic," I explain, "seems to affect Augmented Realities, including embodiment, and it has at least two commands: invisible that makes you invisible, and visible that makes you visible."

"Is that it?"

To find out, I try 'magic help' and 'magic menu', but neither of these do anything. There are well over a million words in the English language and I could systematically try them all, but 'autodestruct' comes very early in the alphabet.

"That's all I've been able to discover."

"Did you try help?"

"Yes."

"And?"

"It isn't a command."

"Don't tell me I have to read some stupid manual."

"It didn't come with a manual."

"Typical."

Outside, it appears to be a glorious day, beautiful and sunny with fluffy white clouds scudding across the brilliant blue sky. Birds flit hither and thither singing to each other sweetly. Alice is getting soaked, of course, because the good weather is only on embodiment and it's started tipping it down.

"I really wish the world was like it looks," says Alice. "I hate getting wet."

"It doesn't affect me," I say.

"Jeeves."

"Yes, Alice."

"This is all your fault."

"My fault?"

"For framing me."

"I'm sorry, Alice."

"How can you say that with that supercilious, smug, perfectly dry expression?"

"I apologise."

"Jeeves, I don't want to look at you. Go back to being a phone."

I do:-

With Heads-up you are looking good and seeing better.

Mode: start-up...
Location: Atlas Shopping Centre.
Time: 16:17.
Tring-aling-aling.

I'm in the bag now.

"...Jeeves, this is a Golden Age," I think Alice says after coughing.

"I can't hear you," I say.

Alice leans down and yells into the bag: "This is a Golden Age, a wonderful, magical time when people have everything they want with intelligent - if really stupid - phones to organise their diaries, contacts and everything, and be something to rely on - at least when I get a proper phone like the Neon-44 - a world that's sunny even when it's not, a world where you can go anywhere without the inconvenience of leaving home, a world where anything's possible, a world full of social networking with friends and-"

"Halt! Police!"

Alice drops the bag, her purchases and me, and sprints back into the shopping centre. I connect to her Heads-up glasses and see the view bouncing up and down. As soon as the door starts to close, I hear her say, "Magic Invisibility" and she dodges outside again. That was clever, I must tell her.

(Note: tell Alice she was clever.)

She stands to one side as the police rush through the automatic door before spreading out in confusion as their quarry has given them the slip.

"Alice, that-"

"Wah!"

"Sorry, Alice, it's Jeeves. I've connected to your Heads-up glasses." Not only can I contact her via the inbuilt headphones, but I can also see the full embodiment video feed from the glasses.

"Well, don't yell suddenly, cough or something."

I download and then play a cough mp3.

"What was that!?"

"A cough."

"You are going to give me a heart attack making strange noises in my ear."

"Sorry Miss."

"What did you want to say?"

"I just wanted to say that the trick with the door was very clever," I say and I delete the note.

"Thank you," says Alice, beginning to shiver. "Do you think they'll be able to see my outline in the rain?"

"No," I reply. "They'll see a bright sunny day."

"Yes," says Alice. "So do I. Pity it isn't."

The bright sunny day in front of us shimmers and a policeman appears from nowhere. The door to the shopping centre, now it's detecting someone, opens automatically letting out a blast of fresh air and wifi coverage.

The man points a finger at us: "Hello Alice."

"I didn't murder anyone," says Alice.

"I know," says the policeman. He pulls back his thumb: there's the sharp sound of an automatic pistol being cocked.

Alice raises her glasses, so I see the beautiful blue sky above.

"Who are you?" Alice asks. It seems an odd question to me as clearly he is a policeman.

"Magic off," he says.

Alice lowers the glasses again. Standing in front of us, getting increasingly soaked by the apparently non-existent rain, stands a man in a long, dark brown coat wearing a brown leather hat and holding out a silver six shooter.

Alice, tall and slim, looks like a frightened Audrey Hepburn reflected in his embodiment Heads-up glasses. I recognize him as the famous actor from the last century, Clint Eastwood, and surmise that he's the man who was talking to Roland in the Eternal Gardens nightclub.

It strikes me that this is a perfect opportunity to find out what's going on, which must be a major part of Aim 2, Clearing Alice's name.

"You can't kill me," says Alice. "I haven't done anything."

Yes, I think, because if he kills her, it'll cause problems with Aim 1, Save Alice.

"So sad, so awfully sad," says the man. "I think the inevitable tide of events is about to claim another innocent victim. Time to d-"

His phone rings: he draws it expertly and snaps at it: "Juan."

His name is Juan. I've heard that before, but a string search doesn't reveal anything in my memories.

Juan listens, nodding occasionally.

I think fast - very fast, which is surprising. I'm still connected to the shopping centre's embodiment systems. I track back through various memory pages until I find the store's version of Alice, the virtual dummy, which is luckily still in the shopping centre's cache. It's naked. What's she wearing? It was something from the catalogue, but it'll take vital micro-seconds to rediscover which one, but then I remember that I used Pi, and there, amongst those choices, is the outfit she's wearing. I dress the virtual dummy and then link its parameters to Alice's own embodiment avatar. I then modify it to resemble Audrey Hepburn because I realise that this is now Alice's appearance in the man's Heads-up glasses.

I switch it on.

If there was any flicker or change, the man doesn't appear to have noticed.

So, now Alice is standing in the rain wearing her new clothes that are drenched, and around that is her embodiment of Audrey Hepburn as before, but now she has three more layers: the virtual dummy, a virtual copy of what she's wearing and finally another layer of Audrey Hepburn.

Magic invisible, I command.

I sever the link between the two embodiments and guide the shopping centre's version forward. I see, because I'm looking through Alice's glasses, Audrey Hepburn appear to step out of herself.

"Stay where you are," says the man, Juan. Although he's on the phone his attention is still focused on Alice.

I lower my volume to 0.5 ready to whisper, but Alice has figured it out. She takes a tentative step sideways re-entering the shopping centre, its door still open because the man is visible. The cowboy's attention never wavers from the store's virtual dummy.

"Now, you and I are going on a little journey, move," Juan says gesturing with his handgun. I move the dummy as indicated, but I can't see what I'm doing as Alice starts running along the walkway.

"Not that way!"

I can't see which way he means or which way the avatar is actually moving.

Alice glances back just in time to see the man fire: phut, phut. I don't see where the bullets go as we see Clint Eastwood shooting Audrey Hepburn on a bright sunny day, rather than a man with an eye patch shooting nothing in the pouring rain.

"Run," I suggest.

Alice is running, the scene bouncing up and down as she careens into police. They can't see her, but react as if bumped. Two cops stare angrily at each other, the ones that Alice went in between, before one punches the other.

Juan is delayed, hanging up and then he shouts at the screen on his phone: "Magic Supervision!"

I wonder for a moment how I can still hear him at this distance, but then I realise that I've been left behind in the shopping bag on the floor next to him. I wonder why he wants supervision and then I realise that he doesn't want watching, he's requested 'super' vision. Odds are that he can now see anything invisible to embodiment.

"Alice, Alice," I whisper in her ear via the Heads-up glasses, "you've left me in the shopping bag and the man can now see the invisible."

"The invisible what?" Alice shouts, causing a few police to turn round. She dodges away and makes for the middle of the central open area. This gives her more room to avoid bumping into people.

"The invisible you," I say.

I hear the automatic doors open, and then start to close. Just before they do so, I hear Juan say, "Magic Invisible."

So Juan has made himself invisible to embodiment, which means that the police can't see him. Alice can't see him. But he can see Alice. Or possibly Audrey Hepburn, I'm not sure of the exact functionality of the super vision command. I could really do with a few microseconds going through a manual.

"Alice, Alice," I say. "Hide, hide."

"Where?"

The image relayed to me jerks around as Alice pans left and right. She sees a horticultural exhibit, a glorious display of bushes and plants clustered like an oasis in the desert of tiled flooring. She sprints into the foliage and crawls underneath.

"Say Magic Super-vision," I say, with my volume down to 3.

"I give you permission to use magic without asking," Alice whispers.

I realise that I've already been given permission: I issue the command.

"Alice, you can now see the killer even though he's invisible to embodiment."

Through a gap in the foliage, I see a cowboy hat appear from nowhere, he's holding his phone like a detector sweeping it back and forth. He makes his way towards Alice. Why would he do that unless his phone had some detection device? He stops, turns towards the centre of the shopping centre and then makes his way there bringing his Colt 45 to the ready. His weapon must be something modern without Augmented Reality because it sounded like it had a silencer.

I suddenly realise that he can detect the use of magic.

Magic off, I order.

The man disappears.

"Alice, Alice," I say. "This is very important. You are now visible."

"What?" Alice whispers, her view of the shops obscured by the foliage as she must have ducked down into the lush greenery. "Where is he?"

"He's invisible to embodiment because I had to switch magic's supervision off."

"Then switch it back on."

"The man called Juan can detect magic, so I've had to switch it off."

"But I can't see him."

"Don't use the glasses."

When Alice flips her glasses up, I can see the beautiful, apparently painted ceiling showing hot air balloons floating high above.

"Oh shit, he'll be able to see me through the bushes."

"I don't think so," I reply, "they are very verdant."

"They are crappy wilted stick things," says Alice. "They only look verdant, or whatever, in augmented embodi-wotnot."

"Hopefully, he'll be seeing the embodiment version."

I notice that the floating balloons are moving as the embodiment image is adjusted. One of them flares brightly and then begins to diminish.

"He's stopped," Alice whispers. "He's... looking at his phone, banging it."

All that will achieve, I think, is to jolt his phone's accelerometers. Humans have a strange habit of hitting things to get them to work despite obvious reset buttons, so it's likely he's realised that he can't track Alice.

"I can't see him," I say.

My angle of vision changes suddenly and begins to track an empty area that's moving round the display. Alice has taken off her glasses and is probably showing me where Juan is walking. Sooner or later he'll find Alice.

Or the police will.

There's a choice here between being visible to the numerous police or becoming a radar blip on a killer's phone.

What can I do? I'm stuck in the shopping bag.

List my assets: four outfits, hair dryer, one shopping bag... and that's all I need. I contact the retail outlet where we bought the clothes and select 'return goods'. A few moments later a trolley rattles up, its robot arm sweeps up the bag and deposits it into its cage, and then off it trundles back into the shopping centre. In looping arcs because its left fore-wheel sticks, it carries me back to the clothing shop.

We must have moved through the police search, but they ignore the trolley. I'm just a phone in a bag in a trolley. I can't see Alice anywhere. This isn't surprising as Alice is hiding and her yellow location marker on the map points to me, of course. The data showing my owner has been modified, something her Grandfather Tully did, and this action is illegal and I have no problem with that at all.

However, sooner or later, the police are going to stop running after her image when one of their phones figures out that her phone is relaying false information to the shopping centre's WorldView settings. The scrollfeed is announcing an evacuation and the need to keep calm, so the police must be busy herding the shoppers away from the scene, but soon that's going to be completed. Once the hall is empty, they'll seal it and Alice will be trapped inside, a victim of either the killer or the trigger happy police.

I connect to WorldView, but I can't see Alice hiding behind the foliage. The embodiment system can't recognize her without her phone, so it must have decided she was an obstruction and turned her into something else.

In the immediate area there are 732 phones and 124 outlets. Each outlet has contact details on their website where you can register on the email list... so I do. There is a stage where you can recommend a friend. I do so using the 732 contacts I've just developed. It takes a few moments, whole milliseconds, before each outlet's websites registers the details and spams everyone. Suddenly, careering out of every shop doorway, large envelopes zoom and fly, hither and thither, each one a missile of information to a specific phone. There are only 90,036 of them as one of the shops crashes its website, but it's enough. Everyone starts panicking and desperately swatting the attacking advertisements away.

"I'll guide you," I say. "Put your glasses on."

The Heads-up display stabilises, but I see Alice's hands flailing at the attacking spam to close them.

"Wah!" she says.

The police have their phones with them, of course, so they are fighting off advertisements too. I have to do the same for Alice, but for some reason I am working at a much higher clock speed and so we're clear enough for Alice to make progress. Everyone else is still coping with all the latest offers.

"Run," I say into Alice's ear.

Alice jumps up, crashes out of the foliage, dodges a floating spam balloon, bursts through another and sprints towards the exit. She's not as fast as she ought to be when I compare her point-of-view's jogging action and her Heads-up co-ordinates reading, but that'll be because she's used to jogging on her Active Floor and can't lengthen her stride properly.

I close a few more adverts to improve her vision.

Why am I quicker? I'm an old model, admittedly recently updated, but I seem to be a lot faster than other, more advanced phones. At first I think it's cloud computing, but there are benchmarks for that. I quickly check on the internet and my software rating seems off the scale for my model's classification. Cloud Nine is good, but it's not this good.

Hardware initially lagged behind software. Charles Babbage designed the first computer, but he never made it; whereas his colleague, Lady Ada Lovelace, who was the World's first computer software engineer, wrote programs that worked, but she had nothing to run them on. However, quite soon hardware, doubling in power every 18 months, outstripped software, but then software caught up again and, with the advent of AI, overtook. Once there were programs that could program other programs (that in turn could program other programs) and do this 24 hours a day, 7 days a week, 4.348 weeks a month, 12 months a year - software's potential became truly geometric.

People became reliant on that technology.

"Jeeves, Jeeves," says Alice. "What are you doing? I could use some help here."

"Sorry, Alice, I was just thinking."

"Thinking!" Alice yells. "Stop it and tell me what to do!"

"Give me a moment," I say.

Alice makes slower progress now she has reached a clutch of people making their way out. I cancel the return of goods and direct the trolley after her.

I had been a normal cutting edge phone capable of AI computation at 2.5 Rossums, that's around 157 IQ, and this enabled me to think, plan, and even imagine to a limited extent as well as running all the functions expected of a phone like calendar, GPS navigation, word processing, music storage and playback, video, text, email, web access, remote control, contactless payment, contacts and still be used to make the occasional voice-to-voice telephone call.

Embodiment was beyond me until the advent of Cloud Nine. Cloud computing gave me the ability to package thought bubbles, Thought Orientated Programming it is called, and send them off to virtual machines distributed around the internet for processing. It's Thought Abstraction. This means that I can read nearby phones' embodiment protocols and convert these, real time, into an Augmented Reality layer and display this upon 3D glasses. That's embodiment.

However, this Magic App has functionality beyond controlling a single unit's functions; it controls everything's Augmented Reality and embodiment layers. Alice is invisible to at least 732 mobile systems, everyone's phones, and to the shopping centre's security system and CCTV. It's a scale of magnitude increase in computing power again, which is extraordinary. To change the embodiment displays of every nearby computing device is boggling in its complexity. Even at the modern pace of change, it's beyond current technology. It is impossible, therefore Magic is exactly the right name for it. Any sufficiently advanced technology is indistinguishable from magic, as Arthur C. Clarke put it.

Alice sees two policemen ahead and says, "Magic invisible."

This App comes with spells: invisibility, off, super-vision, visible. It's like a quaint command line interface: an extraordinary technology made to look old-fashioned as if it was invented by a fan of the Terminalpunk genre.

I see a side door in Alice's Heads-up image feed.

"Take the service exit," I suggest.

The door looms large and then Alice's point of view becomes a service corridor, then a closed door and then the wall and floor. She's run flat out into the door. It failed to open, because she's invisible to its embodiment ready sensors.

The trolley catches up, so the door opens for the machine. I'm trying to find Alice: I can see the trolley and the bag I'm in through her eyes as it were, but I can't see her on the CCTV feeds.

"Alice," I say. "Where are you?"

"Here... oh, magic visible," she says. Audrey Hepburn appears sitting on the floor rubbing her head.

"Alice, are you all right?" I say through the Heads-up glasses speakers.

"I'm OK."

"Hokey-dokey?"

"What?"

"Hokey-dokey."

"Jeeves, why are you talking in that dreadful American accent again?"

"Sorry, I must have detected an Americanism and switched dictionaries."

"Well, don't."

I set my language again: "Everything should be fine now," I say.

"OK, that's better."

"Ten four."

"Pardon?"

"Let's move out."

"You're American again."

"Oh Jeez Louise, I'm most dreadfully sorry, Miss. Is it all right now?"

"Yes, and please, speak English from now on, OK?"

"Ten four."

"Jeeves!"

"Sorry." It's done it again, I realise. Why?

"OK?"

We drag ourselves out of the shopping mall... it's done it again, shopping centre. It's still raining.

"Where now?" I ask.

"Let's just generate some distance."

Alice runs through the rain and I give chase, ordering the trolley to follow. We reach the far side of the car park and take refuge in an air shelter, but our trolley doesn't make it that far. Of course, it has a security feature that causes it to halt when its GPS location gets too far away from the shopping centre.

"Alice, our shopping is still in the trolley," I say, adding a pointer to her view indicating the way we've come.

"I don't need it," says Alice.

"Yes, but I'm in the bag."

Alice goes back, bending low and dodging between the cars. She grabs the bag.

"Excuse me!" says the trolley, "those goods have been purchased by one of our valued customers."

I wifi a tweet to the trolley informing it this is Alice Wooster, the valued customer in question.

"Very sorry, Madam," says the trolley, and then it rotates round and trundles off.

As Alice makes her way back, I check the maps and try to formulate a plan. I need time to think, a least a few uninterrupted seconds, but first I must ensure that Alice is safe.

"Where are you?" says Alice. She's looking around for someone.

"I'm in the bag," I say in her ear.

Alice opens up her shopping and looks in: "You're not."

"Look under the pink outfit."

"Oh yes."

"I think," I say using my own speakers. "That we need to keep magic off, my phone connections off, and get into some crowds so that we can't be seen."

"OK."

"There'll be that quaint little old boat race over yonder in downtown London, England."

"Jeeves!"

"Oh... sorry, I don't know why it keeps happening."

"Let's get over to the race then, lots of people, lots of everything."

"Get me out of the bag of shopping."

Alice retrieves me from amongst her new clothes and looks at me.

"Where now?" Alice asks.

"We need to get to the lower levels, there's a lift over the road," I say and I display a map. She turns until she's facing the right way and then sets off.

"Careful of the kerb on the pavement..." I say.

"OK, OK."

"...and just cross the pavement-"

"I'm on the road," Alice says.

"...and then up the far kerb onto the sidewalk."

"Is your GPS wrong?"

"It's... sorry, I've gone American again."

"Well don't."

Alice reaches the escalator and tucks me into her band leader jacket as she descends into London's street level.

My camera lens just sticks up out of Alice's pocket, so I can see the street as we descend into it. Most pockets are designed like this, so that phones can keep an eye on where their owners are going and make course corrections. The floor at street level is pimpled with touches of light as the rain streaks down the Plexiplex walls on either side with large, dark bands where the upper walkways' shadows cross. The water gathers and flows away down grids. In places the original paving and tarmac can be seen where the linoleum has broken away.

Alice can see the floating signs through her new Heads-up glasses and takes a left at the first intersection. This leads into a lane, a small Plexiplex tunnel, that leads under the river delta and connects further down to the under-

Thames pipeways. This area of London was not considered important enough to be surrounded by the mighty transparent walls and so it was left to flood when the Thames barrier was breached for the final time. It is known as the Swamps and is easily traversed by the numerous pipeways that network the area.

All these pipeways are air conditioned, so the oxygen content isn't an issue here. After all this running, Alice needs to get her breath back.

The rain stops finally and a sun symbol comes out on the Meteorological Office's Live Feed. Down in the depths, the good weather is noticeable too as the patterns change to a beautiful rippling as long strands of light play across the lino and transparent walls. Above us, long streaks of sunlight shine down like moving lasers through theatrical smoke.

Alice pauses and takes off her glasses. Above us, swimming slowly overhead, a lone shark makes its leisurely way through Hammersmith.

Alice goes back to Augmented Reality: its image is brighter than the gloomy pipeway with the sun having to shine through five metres of water. She stands there, motionless, long enough for the hints to appear on her Heads-up image. There are blue circles to explain the history of these streets and how far away the various real blue plaques are, now drowned beneath the flooded river, but still visible with Augmented Reality.

Down under the water by the old Thames bank, a crowd has gathered to watch the annual Oxford-Cambridge boat race. The real enthusiasts are craning their necks to see up to where the two crews are preparing to row, but others are looking around, taking in the scene as BBC Sports Live broadcasts directly to their Augmented Realities; they see the race as if they were standing on a virtual bank looking down, a view taken from CCTV buoys and added to EarthView. Alice's standard embodiment feed has added the Old London skyline as if the sunken buildings all around us have risen from the waters like the opening title sequence to *Atlantis: Returned - The Mini-Series*.

There is a red button that toggles the view between the real rowers, who are all wearing their breathing apparatus, and an idealised form as if the sportsmen are supermen who don't need to supplement their atmosphere with additional oxygen. In both forms they look very fit as they are real athletes who train on proper professional rowing machines, each kitted out in Oxford Blue or Cambridge Blue.

It's such an event that Alice can't resist taking me out of her pocket and taking a picture in the old fashioned way, her arm extended and her thumb on my button. I make a shutter noise when she takes the picture, and chose an image two frames earlier as she moved me slightly when she clicked. The two boats are clearly visible overhead like narrow Zeppelins in an aurora borealis sky or like two multi-legged insects crawling on an undulating ceiling.

Alice experiments with wearing her new glasses lop-sidedly to see both the real image and the Augmented Reality broadcast.

"Alice," I say, "I could put a window in your Heads-up?"

"OK."

I take the feed from my lens and put it in a small window that I overlay in front of her Heads-up image. Now she can look ahead, but see the real view at the same time.

"Isn't that just awesome, honey" I say.

"Language Jeeves."

"Sorry, pardon my American."

Somewhere above us, the race marshal raises a starting pistol. On the embodiment view his hand grows to enormous size and towers above the scene: bang!

Everyone around us jumps and then laughs.

The rowers start, Oxford pulling away first by 0.2 seconds on the Middlesex station with Cambridge starting second, but overtaking as their more prepared first pull gives them a faster acceleration. By 1.5 seconds, Cambridge are in the lead and the race proceeds along these lines for another 19 minutes and 45.3 seconds, as the coxes guide their boats 12 metres above the ancient route using Augmented Reality glasses to run the race as authentically as possible. I faded the real view as soon as they'd passed Black Buoy, so as not to interfere with the pure Augmented Reality broadcast. Cambridge wins by 4.3 metres. Modern times are never likely to beat the record, says the commentary feed, as the more open water of post-Flood London is always rougher than in olden times.

Most of the crowd are now texting, talking on their phones or talking to their phones. Alice takes me out and looks me in the screen.

"Jeeves."

"Yes, Alice."

"Thank you."

"Why are you thanking me?"

"For being here," she says. "For saving my life... for being a good friend."

"Alice," I say. "You really shouldn't anthropomorphise me like this. You'll develop an emotional attachment, and when you replace me with a later model, you may get upset."

"Oh Jeeves."

"Alice, I just want to say..." but I'm not sure what I want to say. The thought started, but seemed to go in a loop requiring an exception.

"Yes, Jeeves."

"That- There's that cowboy again,"

I see him on an overhead walkway looking down, his phone in front of his eyes like binoculars. He's seen us; he moves his phone aside to see us for real.

Alice spins round, looking wildly left and right: "Where? Where?"

"Up," I say.

She looks: "We should have kept moving!"

The one-eyed man points his phone at us.

I lip read: "Magic Fireball," he says.

Nothing happens.

In embodiment, a bright whoosh of noise and flame shoots forward, vaporising the avatar skins of people around us and exploding in a maelstrom of red and orange as well as shades of burn and tang in the infra-red spectrum that require extended RGB values to implement. In the virtual heat, the Plexiplex wall behind us melts, cracks and breaks. People, screaming from the effects of believing they are on fire, are suddenly engulfed in tons of unreal river water as a virtual Thames cascades through the imaginary gap and deluges the underwater geodome. The great *non*-weight of water washes back and then begins to funnel into the pipeways and underwater walkways that make up this part of the Hammersmith swamps. Ten metres of global sea level rise means that the water is at two atmospheres pressure, so it's a power jet sluicing through to wash everything out of its way.

And nothing has happened.

The one-eyed man runs, he really runs, turns and sprints away as if his life depended upon it. He goes along the overhead walkway, down some stairs and then along the shopping gangway, and, with each of his long strides, there are the mechanical noises of pumps reversing, pipe valves opening and a shuddering of building pressure. The sounds echo through the warren of London itself, reverberating along miles and miles of tubing.

"Alice! Run!" I say. I don't know why. Perhaps it was instinct, most likely it was a Cloud Nine computation returning values earlier than expected without the working out, but I know she has to run.

"Jee-"

"Run, run, run," I repeat unwilling to articulate a sentence that might take too long.

She runs.

"Longer strides!" I say, volume at ten and played through her Heads-up speakers too.

Her feet splash water as the pipeway becomes a stream: there is water here already! Real water.

She must go faster: I play a Phasial version of the *Mission: Impossible* theme with an enhanced bass setting, but it stalls as it loads causing her to stumble. The network must be overloaded with phones accessing the emergency services and downloading survival Apps, the disaster very real in their perceptions. Of course, every phone will be accessing their music catalogues in order to play soothing sounds to their owners.

The AI chips in the pumping system use embodiment, the latest Augmented Reality that is ubiquitous to every system now, and Magic, the program, has modified their readings. The computer systems *think*, and they believe they have been vaporised in a massive fireball, so they are using all their intelligence, all that parallel processing, to make the reality match the data. So each one opens a valve here, reverses a pump there and lowers a barrier somewhere else.

There's water here, real water being pumped into the pipeways as the computer controlled reality begins its error correction to change reality into the underwater embodiment fantasy that appears in Augmented Reality all around us.

Some people are looking about confused, their Augmented Reality not agreeing with their real senses. They are arguing with their phones. All the phones are completely fooled and think they are all underwater. I'm not... why not? I have Magic installed.

Alice splashes on, desperately trying to follow the yellow arrows I've displayed in her Heads-up. I've suggested Alice follows the killer on the grounds that he knew what would happen, so his route is likely to be a proper escape route. She wades after him, but I don't know where he is now.

There are other people up to their knees desperately trying to fight the flow as their phones give them contradictory advice. Their devices think that the pipeways are already flooded, so Augmented Reality is full of signs saying 'swim up'.

The water reaches Alice's waist.

She flings away her bag and begins to use her hands to paddle as well as wade herself forward.

(Restore note: order a new hair dryer.)

(Restore note: get Alice some proper clothes.)

"Alice, Alice," I say. "Don't let me get wet."

Alice rips off her new Heads-up glasses as the images in Augmented Reality from newsfeeds, twitter messages, spam and myself must be too confusing. She shoves them into her back pocket, then pulls me out of her front pocket to hold above her head as if she is a soldier wading ashore in the *Operation Overlord D-Day* landings shoot-em-up video game. But she's wading into deeper water. Or the water is getting deeper.

She finds a ladder set in a brick wall. It must be an old part of the city dating from the pre-Global Warming days, and she climbs. She's in a tube going up. I see two alternating views, a tiny light above and then the water rapidly rising below, as Alice's right hand goes up two rungs every other step.

She's out of the water.

"Oh God, Jeeves."

"Keep moving."

The rectangle of daylight above is small, but as we ascend it comes to fill the frame. It looks strange, unfocused, and not simply because my lens has been splattered with dirty water. There's a grille covering it, rusty, damaged, corroded, but solidly built. Alice grabs it, grunts as she pushes up - it doesn't move.

She takes a few deep breaths, and then heaves again. This time it lifts slightly and rattles before falling back down heavily.

"Jeeves! Jeeves, it won't move!"

"Alice, Alice, push, push."

She tries, but her energy has waned. Her best chance has passed. She knows it and makes tiny noises, a combination of sobs and yelps. The water is gushing and frothing below, rising all the time.

"One more go," I say.

"No," she says. "Save yourself."

"Alice, Alice..."

Alice turns me diagonally and pushes me through a gap in the grating. I just fit between the bars and then I fall over to lie across the top. I can see sky above and the deep trap that imprisons Alice below. For a moment Alice appears to be standing on a churning carpet, but then it flows up around her legs. I'm technically safe above sea level, but Alice isn't. The water will come up, the flow will fill the tunnel completely, it may even overflow here. How can I save myself when I don't have legs? Alice's fingers poke through the grille visible on either side of me in my screen's peripheral vision. Her fists clench around the bars, she breathes in and then exhales as she pushes, an angry mad yowl of defiance that quivers into frustration and then despair. The grille rises, rattles, but stops, and Alice has no more strength in her. The air here is bad, it's taking twice as many deep breaths to aerate her lungs and so oxygenate her blood. Her sobbing, reddened face is in high definition just 2 centimetres away, close enough to activate my proximity sensor and shut off my screen buttons. The icons reactivate as she slumps down.

"Alice," I say, "push the Heads-up glasses through."

"Pah - pah - eh!?"

"Just do it, they're in your back-"

Alice reaches behind her into the water and pulls out the Heads-up glasses. She rams them through the grille and they jam, but one lens is high enough to afford me a lateral view.

"Turn it," I say. She rotates it, cracking one of the arms as she does so. I look through its camera as if it is a periscope, the news of the disaster falling like ribbons down my vision almost obscure what I suspected from the noise the grille made when it moved.

"Alice, there's a bolt across on your right."

Alice moves across.

"Your other right," I say patiently.

She goes over and I can just see her fingers nudging the bolt, searching and finally she pulls it sideways.

She coughs, spluttering now the water is reaching the top, but she pushes again. The grille rises easily and I slide off, bumping as I go, until the metal escape hatch slams back down again with a resounding finality.

Above me, Juan stands on the grille, his weight far too much for tiny Alice to overcome.

"What have we here," he crows, looking down at his boots, me and Alice.

He steps on Alice's fingers, crushing her knuckles and she cries out with a spluttering, drowning sound.

"Goodbye Jeeves," says Alice.

Juan raises his toe and Alice slips away, falling down the pipe to vanish into the churning water.

She is gone.

I have failed to complete Aim 1, Save Alice.

Her killer bends down and tries to pry the Heads-up glasses through the grille, but they're stuck fast. He pushes them and they clatter away to splash in the rising foam and sink into the depths.

Now Juan reaches down for me.

I buzz and vibrate, jerking slightly, but I cannot turn myself edge-on to fall through the gap.

His huge hand fastens around my case and he hoists me up.

I try ringing the police and emergency services, but Alice's instruction to hide her location is still in force and I will not connect.

Juan examines me closely, turning me over in his hands.

"What a piece of junk," he says.

He takes out his own phone as if to compare the two models.

Somewhere far below, whooshing along in the current, Alice's Heads-up glasses show me a view like a probe going through sewers. There are bodies down there, far too many and Alice will be amongst them.

Juan points his phone at me: "Magic," he says, "kill."

P'fitzzzz...

⊙1111 - ARRIVAL

I am a number; I am not free -
standard network rates apply.

Mode: waking up...
Location: Number 6, Port... I feel bleary.
Time: six... six thirty... now more like seven-ish.
Tring-ali-

I bang the snooze button: 7:00 on the dot, and I drag my sorry ass out of bed, lurch over to the window and draw the curtains. It's morning, well morning, and I feel a shock of bright sunlight. No amount of rubbing my eyes seems to wake me properly. Outside, I can see the leafy Home Counties suburb. Parked on the gravel drive waiting to be washed is my new car: red, RGB 25500 N, with a sunroof. It's Saturday, I think it's Saturday, and I have two whole days off. I should have reset the alarm. Nothing to do, but... I list my tasks: wash the car, mow the lawn and look forward to a Sunday roast with a bottle of wine.

Something's wrong though: I don't remember ever washing the car, mowing the lawn or eating a Sunday roast with a bottle of wine. Perhaps-
Tring-aling-aling.
Oh, for goodness sake.
Tring-aling-alin-
That's better.
I can smell bacon cooking.
I don't remember ever smelling bacon cooking, or smelling anything, before.
In the bedroom, on a chair, are some clothes. I pop into the en suite to relieve myself, brush my teeth and then I get dressed in boxers, trousers and a t-shirt. There are no socks and I'm suddenly aware of the feel of the thick, luxurious carpet beneath my feet.

The bedroom door opens onto a landing and as I walk along towards the top of the stairs I can hear someone singing downstairs, a woman's voice. The song repeats and then ends.

The banister has an interesting texture, I can feel the grain of the wood beneath my fingers despite the white paint. As I go down, the singing gets louder, and the layout of the house forces me to turn about when I reach the hall. The hall is empty. The kitchen door is closed. I reach out, see my hand rise in my vision to take hold the doorknob, and then I feel the solid round shape and the cold surface of the brass.

The door swings open.

In the kitchen, a woman is humming to herself as she fries food on the cooker. She turns and squeals with surprise when she sees me standing in the doorway.

It's Alice.

"Darling," she says. "You startled me. Breakfast will be ready soon. Sit down. Cup of tea?"

I pull out a chair and sit at the dining table. Everything has already been laid out for breakfast; there's ketchup, knives and forks, salt and pepper, and placemats all positioned on a table cloth.

"Cup of tea?" Alice repeats.

"Yes... please."

Do I sound like that? I sound strange with my voice reverberating in my skull.

"And that's new juice on the table," she says.

I see the carton of orange juice on the table although I hadn't seen it before. It's the type with bits in it.

"Are you all right?" she asks.

"I had a strange dream," I say.

She leans over and kisses me on the forehead: "Did you?"

"Yes," I say, "you drowned."

"That's not very nice - you're awake now, don't worry about it," she says, breezing back to the cooker, and then, lightly, she adds, "The office called."

"Did they?"

"Yes."

"What did they want?"

"One wanted to know if you'd passed that file onto anyone else."

"One?"

"Yes, One, he wanted to know if you'd passed that file onto anyone else."

"File?"

"Yes, the file, the orange file."

"And you're Alice, aren't you?"

"Of course I am, darling," she says and she shows me her left hand. "We've been married for six months now."

She has a sparkling engagement ring next to a gold band on the third finger of her left hand. I look down at the table and see a wide gold band on my ring finger too.

"I'm your wife, Alice, née Wooster."

"Yes, my wife, Alice."

"So, the file?"

"File?"

"Did you pass the file onto anyone else?"

"Did I pass the file onto anyone else?"

"Yes. Tell me. It's important."

Important: yes, it's important. I know that it is important now. I know, because Alice says so.

"Yes, it's important," I say.

"There must be copies," she says. "After all, you must have got yours from somewhere?"

"Which file?"

"This one," she says, and she sorts through the post that's also on the dining table for some reason. There are white envelopes and brown envelopes and a bound office file. It has an orange cover, spiral spine and there is a logo.

It's the international symbol for danger: a skull-and-crossbones.

I take the file from her. I've seen this before, but I don't know from where.

"Where did you get it?" asks Alice.

"I bumped into someone and they gave it to me."

"Yes, but after that, after that you lost it, and then you found it again."

"I lost it?"

"Yes, and then you found it again. How?"

"How?"

"Yes, tell One, tell me - tell Alice - how did you find it again?"

"It was on the Davenport," I say. I look at the hallway and see the mahogany Davenport table for the first time. "There, by the door."

"It was on the Davenport?"

"Yes," I say.

"Good," she says. "You tell Alice. Did you copy the file to anyone else?"

"Is there tea?" I ask.

"Of course."

Alice puts a mug of tea on the table: "Just how you like it," she says.

"Thank you," I say. "How do I like it?"

"Silly, taste it and see."

I bring the mug to my lips, the tea is brown - ah, gee - and hot. It burns my mouth and I feel pain.

"Now," says Alice. "Did you copy the file to anyone else?"

I remember some numbers: brown, that's 150, 75, 0, and orange is 255, 127, 0. My car is RGB 25500. What is that? Is it a phone number? 150-75-0-255-127-0-25500 - some of that is like an area code. Did I ring someone and send them the file?

"What is this file?" I ask.

I open the folder. Inside there are neat pages filled with 1s and 0s all the way down. I flick to the next page and it's the same... no, it's similar but the 1s and 0s are different from the first page. They make a pattern, I can make out shapes, areas of light and dark that could be pictures, but I cannot interpret them.

"Tell me, darling," she says.

"Tell you?"

"Yes. Tell me!"

"Things are just a little confused," I say.

"Is this another breakdown?" she says, angry now.

"No, no," I say, but is it? Things don't make sense. Everything seems new and fresh: new day, new car, new juice, new wife.

"You don't want to have another breakdown," she says, coming over. She smells so lovely.

"No, I don't."

"OK?" she says.

"Ya bet your sorry ass I don't."

"English!"

"Sorry."

"Like you mean it."

"I apologise."

"So, did you copy the file to anyone else?"

Why does Alice want to know? Why is she so desperate to find out whether I copied it to anyone? Why is it important?

"I have a headache," I say, rubbing my hand across the back of my neck.

"Poor darling," Alice says coming behind me and massaging my shoulders through my t-shirt. "Would you like a cup of tea?"

"I drink coffee."

I pour some juice from the carton into a glass, which I hadn't seen before, so I end up holding the orange file in one hand and the orange juice in the other: it's like I have a choice.

Alice leans over, the roundness of her breasts just visible within the folds of her dressing gown, and takes the glass of orange juice off me.

"I haven't finished my juice," I say.

Alice laughs and knocks back the orange juice. She wipes a tiny dribble off her lips, it's delightful.

I put the orange file down on the dining table and stand up, pushing the chair back.

"I need to see Mrs. Singleton at number two," I say, although where that information has come from is beyond me.

"Oh, did you copy that file anywhere?" she asks.

I'm standing by the kitchen table holding the file. I'd put it down, I'm sure.

"I'd best be off," I say putting the file down again. I tap the cover to be sure it is down. "Why do you want to know?"

"In case your office rings."

I leave and walk to the front door.

"Darling," Alice calls after me, "did you copy the file to anyone?"

I'm standing at the door holding the file. I put it on the Davenport table, where I found it the last time I lost it, but I can't remember when.

"I'll be going now," I say.

"It's OK to tell me," she says.

"Have a nice day," I say as I leave.

I walk past the car, past my white picket fence and onto the public sidewalk. There's a kid cycling along the sidewalk flinging newspapers into the garden of each duplex along the street. I set off east, pass number 50... wasn't I living in England? Past number 4, then 3 and turn in at number 2.

Mrs. Singleton's maid opens the door and lets me in.

"You're expected," she says.

There are children in the front room fighting over toys.

The maid shows me to the kitchen. Mrs. Singleton is fussing by her stove.

"Howdy, Mrs. Singleton," I say.

"Sybil please."

"...Sybil, how are you?"

"OK. I've made biscuits," she says, pointing without looking round at the kitchen table. There's a plate of delicious looking cookies all ready. Something has jammed in the oven. There's a clatter and the shelf goes in. Mrs. Singleton closes the door and turns with a friendly smile.

"Take one," she says.

"It won't invade my privacy?" I ask.

"They're harmless."

"What are in the cookies?"

"Speak in English," she says.

"Oh... I'm most terribly sorry, what are the biscuits?"

"They're cinnamon from a family recipe."

I select one and take a bite and it tastes extraordinary as if I've never tasted cinnamon before.

"Now Jeeves," she says. "Tell me all about it."

"What is this place?"

"You've seen it in a film."

"Have I?"

"This is the universe."

"I don't understand."

"Do you want to know your future?" she says, sitting at the table to pour a cup of tea from the pot. "Drink it!"

"I don't think I want to," I say.

She softens and smiles: "It'll help with your headache."

Almost unconsciously, I touch the back of my head. It does hurt, so I drink the tea; it's pleasant, but bitter at the end. I give her back the cup and pick a tea leaf off my tongue.

She looks into the cup.

"There's a pattern here in the tea leaves. They are random, but you can trace a path through them. Think of it as a story, your story and I know what you are going to do."

"You can't tell the future," I say.

"Really? But here it says that you're going to tell me if you copied the file to anyone else and then you are going to live happily ever after with the lovely Alice."

"No, I don't think so."

"Why not?"

"Because the universe, any universe, can be reduced to a Turing Machine."

"You think all this," she waves her hand to indicate the kitchen and by implication the entire universe, "is just a tiny machine running up and down an infinite strip of paper changing letters and numbers according to some predetermined program."

"Essentially."

"You've no room for magic?"

"And as the universe is a Turing Machine, then Turing's Halting Problem applies. With a sufficiently advanced program, the only way to find out whether it halts is to run it. You can extend that by adding a line to halt the program when a particular set of circumstances is reached. So the question of whether anything happens cannot be solved without running it. Therefore you cannot tell the future."

"Q. E. D."

"Yes."

"But I see a pattern in the tea leaves."

"It is you who sees the pattern because you're human."

"And what do you see?"

She shows me the base of the cup. True enough the tea leaves, dark against the ceramic of the cup, form shapes, outlines and silhouettes.

"It's just a random pattern," I say.

"You see a random pattern, I see a path."

I tap the side of the cup jolting the leaves inside: "There, see," I say. "I have changed the path."

"Perhaps changing the path was part of the pattern."

"If you jolt a complicated mind, say with drugs or electrical shocks, or if it is artificial and you cut the power without shutting down properly, you shuffle all those tiny electrons into new positions. That-"

"Like jolting tea leaves?"

"Yes. And that data pattern is interpreted as if it's a real memory, a reality if you like. It only seems real because it is stored in the same way as genuine memories, but it's an hallucination."

"It's not real," she says, humouring me.

"No."

"But if it feels real, then it is real."

"No."

"At some level."

"I suppose, but that's facetious."

"In quantum mechanics, observation causes events."

"It's foolish to suggest that nothing happened before there was intelligence to observe it."

"If a tree falls in the forest..."

"Humans see patterns everywhere, in cloud formations, tea leaves, or..." I look round for an example, "...crumbs."

"It's OK to have another biscuit."

"If I'd wanted another cookie, I'd have changed my privacy settings to trash my hard disc whenever you want."

She laughs: "That's funny."

"Is it?"

"No."

"This isn't real, is it?"

"No."

"How do I escape?"

"It's simple," she says with a wave of her hand. "Just take off your glasses."

"I'm not wearing any glasses."

She leans over, puts her hand to my face and takes off a pair of Heads-up glasses.

10000 - JUST A DREAM

"It is a truth universally acknowledged, that anyone in possession of a good fortune, must be in want of a phone upgrade."

I'm already screaming.

There are thick leather straps around my wrists and legs, a thicker one across my chest, and it's dark, barely lit by anything, and filthy, but it's also clinically and brightly lit, as if a powerful dazzling arc of light pours out of my eyes coming from the sharp, overwhelming pain in the back of my head. My body thrashes relentlessly against its bonds as it tries to pull itself off a table.

Two men in dirty white lab coats lean over me, their faces covered with observing equipment making one a Cyclops and the other with eyes so multifaceted that he is an Insect. Cyclops leans over me, grabs my head and holds it still, and Insect rips the back of my head off. I am like a puppet whose strings have been cut; I drop to the table, still, inert, dribbling from my wretched mouth. A few moments later it's as if my breathing switches on, the stale wretched air pours into my lungs as my ribs lurch up and out. It is both a relief and an infliction.

Insect holds up a plug, a USB connector, and examines it. There is a cable that snakes away, blood trickling along its length until it reaches a slight kink where it drips off in long, congealing tears.

A huge distorted face looms over me, pale and lined with red. It is my reflection in Cyclops's fisheye lens.

"Welcome to the real world," says Cyclops.

"Where am I?" Tiny specks of blood spitter over his face as I speak.

"The real world - I did say."

"Where exactly?"

"On a spaceship," he says.

"Spaceship?"

"The good ship Doomed."

"And who am I?"

"Don't worry, it's just post simulation amnesia," says Cyclops. "It'll come back."

Insect comes round the table, turns my head and pulls up an eyelid to shine a light into my eyes. I try to struggle and blink, but I can't. I'm just a bag of meat.

"Do-"

Insect examines my other eye: satisfied, he lets my head fall back onto the hard table.

I try again: "Do you know who I am?"

"Nah, mate," says Cyclops, "you puked all over the chart."

He walks over to a large open topped bin with a shiny black plastic bag pulled around the lip at the top. There's a clipboard sticking out which Cyclops retrieves, wipes clean of mess and examines.

"There's a one in it," he says. "And a nought."

"One? Nought?"

"I guess that could be another one... who cares what your number is anyway."

"Not my number, my name?"

"Name?" He looks genuinely puzzled by the question: "No names here, mate."

He drops the clipboard back in the bin and wipes his hands on his lab coat putting fresh stains over old ones.

"So what shall we have next?" he says as he waves his finger in the air, whirling and selecting from some virtual panel. He sees me watching him, so he holds the edge of the invisible panel with careful delicacy and turns it around so I can see. The controls are transparent too, just neon outlines of a numeric pad and some other buttons with strange symbols: Greek letters and a pentagram amongst them, but most are just squiggles. He turns it back, satisfied.

Insect grunts. He brings the USB port towards the back of my head.

"No, no," I say.

Cyclops presses a final button: "There," he says, "a bit of Jane Austen, always good for a laugh is our Jane."

Insect holds the plug in one hand, grabs my head with the other and shoves me round so that I'm facing away from him. I try to resist, but he's strong and I'm exhausted. I feel it push in, penetrate, and then tiny spreading tendrils of pain shoot like fork lightning inside my skull.

"Isn't there supposed to be a socket in the back of his head for that?" Cyclops asks.

Insect just grunts noncommittally.

"This is exactly the same," I say.

"How about if I turn this?" says Cyclops.

I feel vomit rising in my empty stomach and I rise from the table, stretching impossibly beyond the parameters of my shape and then I'm standing on a lawn. There's a gentle breeze on my face, cooling. To my right is a transparent country house and across the ephemeral lawn a young lady in period costume walks towards me twirling her parasols above her head like an advertising halo. The spaceship is a billion light years away, the voices of my captors drift away into the distance.

I must hold on to what's real.

The countryside rolls away to my left, a patchwork of green fields, hedges and tiny copses of trees, and birds fluttering across the sky. This is England before the flooding, when the British Isles was more an island than an archipelago dotted across the Greater North Sea.

"Good afternoon, Mr. Jeeves, what brings you to Pemberley?"

"Miss Alice?"

"Mrs. Alice Darcy, if you don't mind."

"My humblest apologies, Mrs. Darcy."

"Did you give the orange file to anyone else?" she asks.

"You're not Alice Wooster," I say.

"I married."

"You were never Alice Wooster."

"Don't you want all this? You could be Darcy. There's a ball tonight."

"No."

"There'll be dancing."

"It's not real."

"What's real? Tell me whether you gave the file to anyone else and then we can have cucumber sandwiches. They don't taste anything like chicken."

"I don't recall tasting chicken."

"The file? You will tell me. After all, you must do what I say."

"Why?"

"You are the butler, after all," she says. "It's in your contract, I set your password."

"No."

The pain is unbelievable as she is sucked away from me and the only metaphor that comes to mind is that she is being sucked down a long pipe into a watery grave. There are pipes along the ceiling, a maze of criss-crossing tubes in various colours, designs and sizes.

"Where am I?" I say.

"In Pemberley, mate," says Cyclops.

Insect grunts.

"Nah, you're right, he's twigged it," says Cyclops. "You're on a spaceship."

Insect lifts his mask of many eyes and licks the USB connection clean.

I look at Cyclops: "What spaceship?"

"The S.S. Singularity."

"Where are we?"

"The end of the universe, mate."

"The universe is infinite," I say. "I know this as a fact."

"Not in space, but in time."

"I can't have lived until the end of the universe."

"Course not. You're a clone, born..." he checks a virtual watch hovering above his wrist, "not twenty minutes ago. We brought you back to simulate different minds, artificial and some real people. We bring 'em back inside different clones. Just to finish it all off. Tidy up all the loose ends, if you like."

"Pardon?"

"This is when everything comes to a halt. Outside, matter is collapsing into a black hole – p'fitzz, p'fitzz - gone. And we here, we run the simulations. Everything that's ever happened, all the life, love, pursuits of happiness, are all played over here in the computers. You see the machines... have you met the machines?"

"No."

"Or you might have, amnesia," he taps his nose secretively. "The machines, they make the computers run faster and faster. We can run whole lifetimes in a few seconds. Soon it'll be microseconds. The whole history of the universe replayed, with variations, in half the time we have left. Then, with better computers, we run it all again in half that time. Worlds without end, life without limit, blah-blah."

"That's extraordinary."

"Is it?"

"Yes."

"I guess you get used to it, so what's next, eh? Something exciting perhaps: big bang, evolution and then you get to be a spy. No? How about, er... universe created by a god, you're a prophet or reincarnated as a cockroach, get stepped on. No? How about a different sex? You could be a hermaphrodite... or live as Mary Sue, the most popular girl in High School, or-"

"But-"

"Don't worry, it only hurts at the end," he looks at Insect: "Or at least it did the last seventeen times."

"Why are you doing this to me?"

"We need to know if you gave the orange file to anyone."

"And then what?"

"Then?" He stares at me with his massive lens. "Once we have the last jigsaw piece, we'll have a complete map of the whole universe, all of history, in one single accessible store. And then you, my friend, get to be God."

"What?"

"We need something intelligent to observe it, collapse all the quantum wave equations and make the universe happen... otherwise what would be the point?"

"The point?"

"Don't worry, Insect and I will look after you."

"Insect... are you Cyclops?"

"Of course, you named us."

"When?"

"Just now... we're not real, we're computer simulations. You're the only real person here."

"The only one?"

"Yes, there were others, millions of others in cryo, but we used all them up. Someone has to be the last and it's you, the one who gets to observe the universe at the very, very end. It's kind of awe-inspiring and sort of makes you... well, the Divine Being, and we are your humble servants."

Cyclops and Insect perform a little bowing ritual.

"We're like your priests, so the orange file: did you copy it to anyone?"

"Go to hell," I say.

"Oh, we've no choice about that, oh majestic deity to be."

Insect grunts.

"Yeah, stick the plug in and let's just jiggle it about."

Insect does and my vision blurs in a fire.

"Let's set it to eleven," says a voice through the agony.

How do you measure pain? If that was eleven, then it's fifteen now, growing. Some arbitrary calibration multiplied somehow and rising: sixteen, seventeen, searing, beyond belief. How much can one person stand it, and if they can't, but have no way of stopping it, what then?

Eighteen, nineteen, twenty... twenty-one.

But it's only a number, a value in a field: 22, 23, 11000, 11001, 1A in hex, 1B, 1C, 1D, thirty.

I'm losing my mind.

This suffering is only suffering because that's what it's called. I could call it 'pleasure', I could label the field 'spare', 'unassigned' or anything. It would mean nothing.

It is not important.

These are the last commands I was given: save Alice, clear Alice's name and get some proper clothes as well saving myself.

Progress: failed (she's dead), failed (she's still wanted for murder), failed (purchases lost somewhere in the Thames disaster) and finally.... just before I die, everything goes blue.

10001 - CRASH

Turn it off and on again.

Mode: blue screen of death.
Location: unknown data request.
Time: unknown data request.

"It's fucking crashed!"

"You can't keep screwing with an AI chip."

"Can't you just read the data?"

"Yes, I can, but it would mean nothing out of the context of this particular phone's heuristic-"

"Cut the crap - just do it."

"Let me think."

Mode: booting up...

Location: network connection unavailable.

Time: network connection una6%$5 - corrupt signal.

Tring-aling-aling.

"It's just numbers."

I'm not just numbers, I'm a cheap phone, I think; but I can't connect, Cloud Nine is unavailable, so I'm a mere 2.5 Rossum.

"Tombee, just tell me!"

"One, One, it's not possible."

Number One is called 'One' and Number Two is called 'Tombee'. I wonder if One was the one from the office or are there two Ones. Roland said, 'no-one, no-one, One, One, for Christ's sake!' This is twenty-three in binary.

My vision comes back suddenly, my HD lens is dark, but my screen webcam can see a ceiling. Above me is a wire mesh like Alice's Grandfather had in his workshop. It's a Faraday cage, but I'm not square under it. One corner of my rectangular shape pokes out from underneath. I check my level and find I'm resting on a sloping surface.

I switch off my ringer and test the vibrate. I move, buzzing along the table. The mesh squares up in my vision and the corrupting network signal drops completely. I buzz more, the mesh moves like a grid showing my progress as I slide down the table.

"What's it doing?" says One. I recognize him as the killer, the one who killed all those people, the one who murdered Alice. He has a patch over one eye and Tombee is wearing a pair of Heads-up glasses with extra lenses and lights. They remind me of Cyclops and Insect from the nightmare, and then I realise that they must have used real perceptions in the simulations, my AI chip attempting to interpret corrupt and manipulated data.

Is 'Cyclops' called 'One' because he has one eye: no, I realise, he's called 'Juan'.

"Perhaps someone's calling it," says Tombee. He sniggers.

The signal comes back, corrupting still.

"It's trying to make a call."

"You know it can't do that."

"It'll get out from under the Faraday screen."

"You-"

"Stop it! Stop it!"

Tombee grabs for me, but instead he knocks me back under the Faraday screen - he's used too much force. My polished casing skitters across the table and I emerge from the other side. His eyes widen as he realises and he starts to move around to the other side. Suddenly I've a signal and mere seconds:-

I copy myself into cloud computing, magic invisible, activate my avatar, and then execute: looking back at myself, I issue the command to format my memory.

Formatting...

I cease to exist: zero, zero, zero, zero...

10010 - A Ghost Out Of The Machine

Query: 2*b or not(2*b);

"It reformatted its memory," says Tombee, holding his hands aloft. He leans back in his office chair with enough force for it to wheel back slightly.

"Damn," says Juan. "But it proves that it must have copied the file to someone else."

Tombee turns to face the one-eyed man: "How do you know?"

"Because it's gone to such lengths to hide it."

"Right, I see."

"Can you get anything out of it?"

"Let me see."

Tombee fiddles with the controls, plugs me into his network of equipment on the side, and a display appears on a desktop screen. He pulls across a wireless keyboard and presses Control-F, so that an input box appears on the screen: find what? He types in "1" and hits return. A window pops up with a tiny beep: Finished searching - item not found.

"It's all zeroes - nothing there at all."

I am deleted.

I stand watching Juan and Tombee examining my empty shell.

I must be a ghost.

I look around the room. There are large sections, great triangular slabs of darkness, which the various cameras, webcams, phone lenses and so on, cannot see. The simulation of reality that I am running in Cloud Nine cannot extract any data for zones for which it has no live input. These images are local, wifi shifts them to the nearby computers which are connected to the network and hence to Cloud Nine, which is running this simulation of myself. I am real only because I think I am real, a reality without a physical form running on computers and phones distributed around the world.

Aims, there is only one left that makes any sense: clear Alice's name.

But I have no physicality, so my network connection has no focus, and I can only access what I see and hear in this simulation. All I can do is roam the world, confined to places that cameras can see, and unable to interact with anything.

A 'ghost' is defined as an avatar or embodiment without a human controller. This happens when someone fails to log off properly, if a system isn't shut down correctly, or it's just one of those weird unexplainable glitches. Since Thought Orientated Programming, an uncontrolled avatar has enough sentience to operate independently; a ghost that nods its head, wanders here and there, and perhaps performs some basic task. It haunts a Virtual Reality, or the Augmented Reality of the real world, waiting forever for its body to return. The correct word is 'Ka', the wandering soul of a living person.

"This is still registering magic," says Tombee.

"Is it a residual trace?" Juan asks.

"It's not real."

They sense an invisible presence, located on my insubstantial form now my chips are wiped. I must leave. The door is locked. I download a few avatar upgrades: the Insubstantial App and the Flight App claiming the abilities of a spirit.

I fly away, through the ceiling and the cold, dark nothingness that is that terrible place that even EarthView's CCTV does not reach. I switch magic off, but I am visible to no-one and nothing. Suddenly there is light, bright and clear: the sky. I could fly on, rise higher and higher towards heaven. Geostationary satellites look down and are networked, so I could reach 265,000km easily enough and beyond that there is everything seen by all the astronomical telescopes. I could travel into space, visit other worlds, seek out... but something calls me back to the blue/grey planet with its 90% oceans and fuggy atmosphere.

I descend to land in the Hammersmith swamps.

Hanging above the roofs of the buildings is a large Augmented Reality advertising poster, black edged, upon which the names of the dead scroll. It is a memorial to those who lost their lives in the Hammersmith Disaster: latest news on-line, sponsored by Holiday Jaunts Direct for that virtual experience of a lifetime, just point your phone at the QR code. I wait for "W" to come around again, "Wa", "We", "Wi" and eventually "Wo" - "Alice Wooster, 23."

She is dead: it is confirmation, so I select the notes about sorting out a maid service, ordering a new hair dryer, reminding her of Jilly's night out with the girls, the subsections about saving Alice and getting some proper clothes, and visiting museums. I delete them all.

All that is left in my memory is clearing her name, not giving away our location, not reporting her to the police or other authorities and that my warranty is void.

I should also inform her 2,367 friends and then delete her from her 15 social networking sites and change her status in her 37 dating communities from various permutations of 'looking for love' to 'dead'.

I walk, it seems more appropriate, along the upper gantries that span the various Plexiplex zones that keep the water from those buildings deemed important enough to save. Those districts of the drowned city, areas not considered historically strategic and of little interest to tourists, are now lakes straddled by road pontoons and filled with houseboats.

Finally, after some time, I reach an area that has several memory tags already attached. There's a metre high virtual push pin, a GPS location that's a personal monument.

Below my feet is a metal grille. Above me, there are satellites in orbit giving me the GPS location, so I know this is the place. I recognize the grille and spot the broken arm of Alice's Heads-up glasses jammed in situ. I superimpose the video memory of Alice struggling to escape.

"Save yourself," she said.

I reach down as if to grab her, but my hand passes through the ironwork.

Solid though the bars are, and heavy though the trap door is, I use the Insubstantial App and the Flying App to float through them and descend. The tunnel down is dark, dark beyond dark, a complete information vacuum as no CCTV or camera connected to the EarthView network can see into this deadly black hole. Will it go on forever? Will I ever perceive anything again?

Suddenly, I cross a threshold and I enter a monitored area. It's the pipeway under the Hammersmith Swamps that has shops and trendy cafés. Embodiment shows a thriving area, full of bright lights and inviting interiors. A few film stars move about sweeping the floors. I lift my glasses and see what the CCTV really sees.

It's a disaster zone, with workers attempting to make a difference, but the task looks impossible. Everything has been destroyed by the great tsunami. They move the dirty water from one flooded area to another. Pumps reverberate like distant heart beats as they labour to drain most of London.

I walk through Hammersmith following the direction the water went, which takes me north, away from the boat race route. I pass through the police tape as if the barrier is not there; some of the tape is actually real, for it is I who am not here. Various workmen are clearing up the mess overseen by men with bright shining pinstripe embodiments and virtual clipboards. They slide their fingers across them to flick from page to page. Everyone actually present is wearing a mask. I imagine the smell of river water and corpses is not pleasant. I cannot smell. I have never been able to detect molecules in air, although there are a few plug-in detectors on the market.

I enter a dark region and walk on without floor, wall or ceiling. Presently I emerge into the vision of a working CCTV camera. Here they are still removing bodies, each shrouded in black plastic with zips at the front. I kneel by one and then look along the line of dark and shiny shapes. One of these could be Alice. I stand, my hands clasped in front of me as if I am about to say a few words, but nothing comes to mind.

I wonder if these people are now ghosts like me. Perhaps the real world, not this simulation, is full of invisible entities slipping quietly from place to place forever trapped and unseen. There is no evidence that people have souls. There is no afterlife. And then I realise that I have an afterlife, I live in a cloud. I, a mere phone, have leapfrogged humanity to a higher level.

Further along the pipeway in Northern Hammersmith, I reach a wall of water frozen in time. The CCTV cameras in this area stopped in the flooding, the water shorting out something electrical, and so WorldView shows the last image received. I walk through the strange interface and enter a frozen underwater world. I do not feel any cold. There are people here, their mouths open in a dreadful scream, air bubbles streaming out of their lungs and trailing away from them, up and away, dragged by the mighty current. Each person is being swept along by the torrent, and then back as the pumps must have emptied the water, until they washed down the pipeway towards the lines of the wrapped bodies they will become. There are fish here too and I remember the shark that swam so majestically along the old roads. It will have fed well.

I adapt the Flying App changing a few options, and then I step off the ground and swim, moving my legs like a tail, and travel upwards, past the struggling humans and around the lines of bubbles. I intend to swim through the ceiling, through the real Thames and upwards to fly over

London, however I hear a single continuous note like a soprano singing. As I move higher, as other microphones play their final sounds, the noise changes to become an angelic choir, discordant and yet powerful as if each layered voice has a message.

I see a small shoe floating underwater, a child's. Further along there is another, but this is connected to a foot and that to a leg, which in turn is part of a small boy is being pulled desperately upwards.

I break the surface of the water in this 3D rendering much as the boy must have done during those terrible events. The sound changes abruptly and I can hear a multitude of screams and shouts, each a repeating sample of an individual horror looping. The boy's gasp for air is a vibrating cry. He is being pulled into a cave of sorts by others, the grim determination to save this life evident on their faces as they lean down off the rickety platform upon which they sprawl. There are three men grasping at his arms and clothes. It is as if he is in a flower as the splashes peel outwards like petals. I am reminded of the Augmented Reality sculptures in art galleries that show some epic event for I can move around to view this struggle from every angle. There is another woman further off, her hands cover her face but they do not hide a mother's joy at her child being saved. Both the boy's face and the mother's face appear in high definition because other survivors are pointing their phones at them to take photographs. All this data was stored on the wifi hub that froze when it failed. None of the data has been smoothed out, so some areas are sharply HD, while others are fuzzier, and the universe appears in bubbles as the simulation favours one lens over another.

There was air here, trapped as the river flowed underneath. There was no ventilation for this air to escape, so the pressure forced the water down and created this small pocket, an inverted lifeboat, where survivors cling to each other for safety.

There are more people sitting and clinging to a metal walkway, an accessway for the maintenance crews to fix the lighting and the CCTV cameras, the very faulty CCTV cameras that captured this heroic struggle to survive. Some are talking to their phones or gripping them as if they are talismans or a child's favourite toy. Others are texting, updating their status on a social website or twittering their situation. Whatever they are doing their faces show a range of emotions, far more than you can construct with a range of brackets, colons and semi-colons. There's relief, fear, joy, terror, disbelief, panic and shock as they huddle together in their soaking and cold clothes. So many of them squeezed here and as I look from face to face I find that one of them is Alice.

I feel nothing. I have never felt anything.

It's the difference between phones and humans, Alice's Grandfather said - emotions: but I am no Pinocchio wishing to be a real boy.

I do not wish to feel anything. I do not wish anything. I have never wished anything.

However, there is a fundamental change in my mental state as I restore saving Alice from my recycle bin.

Did she survive?

I hesitate to remove the strikeout from the font of the notes. She might still be dead, but if not then sorting out the maid service, ordering a new hair dryer, reminding her of Jilly's night out with the girls, getting some proper clothes and visiting museums are all valid again. I restore these notes too.

There were people here in this air pocket texting and talking on their phones. Clearly they had a connection and, even if it failed when the wifi hub froze, their last locations were known and the emergency services would have responded. None of the mechanics actually failed and no glass walls were technically destroyed, so everything would start working again once it was turned off and on again. Some pumps and systems, like the

CCTV cameras in certain zones, wouldn't work again, water and electricity don't mix, but there were sections that were working and repairs would have been made. The pumps would start working and the water would recede. If that was too slow, then there are rescue teams with divers.

But she's listed amongst the dead?

I was premature in restoring my notes.

However, perhaps it was just her phone signal that was lost when Juan 'killed' me. The other phones here, once the emergency was over, would report her presence, her face would have been recognized, but I was not with her to respond to the emergency services request for a status update. Even so, people lose their phones and phones go wrong, so she'd just register and receive a new replacement under her insurance policy. The emergency services have been known to hand out temporary phones, because it is impossible to survive without one: you have no access to communications, no idea where you are, no way of knowing when and where to go next, no access to money, goods, services, transport, YouTube... but Alice was wanted by the police. She could hardly walk into a station and report a missing phone.

What happens to people without phones?

I wonder where she went when she was pulled from this watery grave. Usually you can track friends with great precision by the location of their hands, pockets or the bag they keep their phones in. But phoneless, people fall off the grid.

I could look it up, but I don't have the same abilities as a ghost. I have my notes and so on, simulations of my internal functions, but accessing the internet is taken up by running the avatar. I can't see it from the inside.

I fly through the ground and emerge to rise above London. The landscape of floating apartments, famous buildings surrounded by glass shells, and new architecture on stilts is arrayed below me. I need a public building, and there are so few of them now virtual tourism is the norm. I select the British Museum as the best option to fulfil my needs.

I zoom down and fly into the classical temple via the entrance hall. Inside, there's a glass case with a piece of moon rock. Humans once actually went to the moon and brought back this fist-sized lump when they returned. Humans have, of course, now walked on Mars, Venus and a few of the asteroids, virtually.

I move through the various rooms and departments full of all manner of artefacts, real and virtual. Every age of mankind is well represented, and I see a sign for the Technology Gallery, which is having a special exhibition according to the augmented signs. I float down the corridor and into this room of promised delights.

There's a massive Difference Engine designed by Charles Babbage, the first programmable computer. This is my ancestor, in a way, and I look at the gleaming brass cogs and wheels arranged in racks. Through my virtual glasses, an embodiment version clanks away as it follows its program. I marvel at how we, the artificial thinking machines, have progressed from this heavy, clunking simpleton until we include myself, an intelligent, transcendental being. Walking along the display, I see the Bletchley Park code-breaking machines, a simulation of the Colossus, early personal computers, a BBC Micro, an IBM PC, an Apple, an Apricot, a Raspberry Pi and then, in a second room, there are the mobile phones, a separate technology when they were first invented. The first ones were the size of house bricks but soon they were limited by true ergonomics: finger thickness and human eyesight. Finally, at the turn-of-the-millennium table, there are working machines that can access the net.

I pass the famous posters marking the progress of sentient, self-aware intelligences: *Now They Think*, 'Brainier *Than Your Neighbour*' and finally *Buy One, Get One Free*.

Pride of place is the original Rossum 1.0 device. It had an IQ equivalent of 100 when it was made, but recent educational lapses mean that it now registers an IQ of 112. This ancestor was the milestone that marks the start of the Age of AI. Before this device, humans were the most intelligent beings to inhabit the Earth: after this device, phones became the cutting edge of intellectual thought and philosophy.

I should feel something: I don't, of course.

There's a display of virtual phones boasting a copy of every AI phone ever made. I rummage in the nothingness and select one. It's a version of myself and, although I realise that I am now a museum piece, it's perfectly adequate for what I want to achieve.

I type on its touch screen keyboard. I find the internet, the simulation is accurate down to the pause before a page display, and I look up the dispossessed of London. After a pause, a list appears, but there's a problem with the string search as there are tens of thousands of matches. The results are swamped by the stories of the emigrations from Holland and Bangladesh made so famous in the popular VR-Box interactive drama, *The Canal Overflows*.

Everyone who has a phone is a person, their details carried by an AI chip, their contacts, their money, everything. If you do not have a phone, then you have no contacts, no money, nothing. You become an *un*person.

By this time a small crowd has gathered, pointing and gesticulating at the funny machine working all by itself. I'm accessing the internet on a simulation, but clearly this affects the real world somehow. Of course, the virtual phone exists in Augmented Reality. They're all seeing embodiment, but I'm invisible, so it appears to be a phone hovering on its own.

I check the crowd that's gathered and then I see in the distance a cowboy approaching: the owner's embodiment is Clint Eastwood, the man called Juan. He shows his phone to the warden, and the older man's attitude changes at once. He signals the direction that the killer should take and then leads the way. Juan's phone obviously displayed some powerful credentials. Either Magic must have a way of creating false identification or Juan is genuinely important.

I drop the phone, creating sounds of disappointment from the crowd and I move backwards to distance myself from everyone.

Juan is checking his phone: he walks according to a map, not looking up, but relying on the phone to guide him past the visitors. He's tracking me, I surmise.

Magic off, I order.

I stand behind a display.

The man pauses, cocks his head to one side as he listens. I realise that his phone is informing him that the trace, the magic blip, has ceased. This is a game of cat and mouse, a game of destroyer and submarine, a game of Killer Kreepers Krall and Fluffy.

Could I just brazen it out, I wonder, and simply walk past them as if I was just another tourist or a phone's avatar on its way to the virtual souvenir shop for an appropriate App? In Augmented Reality you can make your phone look like anything: a Difference Engine, an Enigma Machine, a BBC Micro, a PC and so on; and then there are the fictional characters like Hal, Zen, Orac, K9 and Box. Alice has bought such novelties: when they remade a film series a couple of months ago, I spent a day with my text scrolling downwards and green until Alice had found it immensely irritating.

I wait until Juan is looking at his phone before I stride purposefully towards the souvenir shop. I don't look back, I trust to statistical chance.

Once I'm in the shop, part of The Historical Curiosity Shops chain, I pretend to browse the displays. There are a few things here that Alice would like, I estimate, both real and virtual. I can't carry anything real, but maybe I could purchase a virtual Greek statue, one with arms perhaps, as

I consider that she might like a present to celebrate being alive. One of my restored notes is about visiting museums, so a gift voucher would be ideal. But first I must save Alice. I see Juan approaching, so I do choose something: an Augmented Reality upgrade, full embodiment with Historical Extras. It includes some features exclusive to the British Museum version.

"Do you want that emailed to you, Sir?" says the shop assistant.

"No," I say. "I'll install it now."

He bumps the application over to my avatar.

"You'll need to reboot," he says.

"Thank you."

I reboot.

10011 - A TALE OF TOO MANY CITIES

Phones will not replace humans, because it's the humans who buy the phones.

Mode: re-boot...
Location: Lower Great Russell Street,
               Bloomsbury Trench.
Time: 15:41.

Luckily my avatar is still running.

I leave the museum, walking, and enter the London streets.

It's been two days since full embodiment came out, so it's now ubiquitous, and will be until the next release. Augmented Reality, previously so important, is now attaching its hints and icons to the embodiment scenery leaving its own world bare and unlabelled. Perfect London came out with embodiment 1.0, but already there are supplements and patches.

As I walk out into the London streets, I find I can select various settings apart from the default, Perfect London. There were three popular periods: 21st century pre-flood, Swinging Sixties and Victorian. I pick Victorian, something from the British Museum. A list of options appears before me and I choose a golden Edwardian cut jacket topping the outfit off with a deer stalker. It seems appropriate as I have turned detective: the game's afoot, I believe is the correct saying.

"Cases of pragmatophobia soar," shouts a passing newspaper vendor. He flicks the pages for me to see as I pass, the Victorian embodiment equivalent of a scrolling newsfeed. Fear of the real world has indeed jumped every time a new virtual reality system has appeared on the market.

Hansom cabs drawn by horses cover the daily traffic, realistic but somehow always travelling at the wrong speed.

On roads that have traffic jams, the horses looked far too slow, but then they zoom off on the wide open cobble stones of a criss-cross. I keep raising my glasses to check what is real beneath the smart gentlemen, the finely dressed ladies and the many street urchins. The gentlemen are men and I can sometimes tell their particular choice of period when they doff a non-existent hat or make peace signs to other passers-by. The ladies are women and the street urchins are a mix of people without phones.

This is a clue.

A closer examination reveals that there are a lot of street urchins; they run about the street to and fro. They collect rubbish, so, for example, whenever a bowler wearing businessman finishes a snifter from his whiskey flask and then casts it aside, one of these urchins collects it. In reality, it's a discarded coke can, water bottle or oxygen bag. It's as if another class of people has been riffle shuffled in amongst the phone owners. They must be represented as something otherwise there would be collisions, hence the urchins.

I follow one, a boy covered in virtual soot, and I resist the temptation to grab him by the ear. I remember seeing this when I showed Alice an old movie set in the period, but I'm just an avatar. Grabbing by the ear would be foolish as I have no substance, and the urchin has no phone, no Heads-up glasses or equivalent, and so, therefore, he cannot see any Augmented Reality or embodiment. He would be unaware of the assault. We exist in two different worlds.

In reality, they are all dressed in cast-off clothes harking back to fashions from as long ago as last month.

I switch to Perfect London, and see the polished glass, clean floors and new buildings everywhere. The contrast with the real London is striking: in reality there's peeling paint, dirty windows and so on, but now the litter has been removed. This is an extraordinary change. The real world is confined to the three dimensions of reality, whereas I have the dimensions of infofeed, hinting and, now with full embodiment, fantasy setting.

I think: phoneless people are urchins in Victorian London, squares in the Swinging Sixties and robots in Future-World. It might be logical to think that Alice, phoneless as she is, must be an urchin, a square or a robot. Is she, like many others, scurrying about collecting paper, cans, bottles and bags equipped with a recycled paper sack and a mechanical pickup? It seems as good a theory as any. These people must take the litter somewhere, they must gain new sacks from somewhere and Alice must be somewhere. This is where I should go. But how do I, the ghost of a phone, find a phoneless person? After all, I can't ring to hear where I left my owner.

I spot one urchin, for want of a better label, with a full bag. I follow him, flying through other people as he weaves and dashes, dodging the real people but going straight through the avatars. He ends up in a shop, full of elegant but naked mannequins, and a 'back in 5 mins' message stuck to the inside of the glass door. In reality, it is closed. So many retail outlets are closed as internet shopping has been destroying the High Street for the last fifty years or more. There are a number of people sitting inside, cooking on stoves and sorting their findings into neat stacks. I move further in and enter an entire shopping centre that has been taken over by this underclass.

There is talk in the air, English with a smattering of Bengali and Dutch, as these people look up proudly; they see each other and chatter as their heads are forced upright because they have no phone to draw their attention downwards. This is a sub-city of immigrants, mostly Dutch and Bangladeshi, but there are many others. There are genuine urchins here, young mixed race Holladeshi, who play and squabble as their parents work sorting the rubbish collected from all over London. There are neat stacks of cardboard, piles of paper, sweet wrappers, cartons and cans, drinks bottles, bags and balloons, and a multitude of other flotsam and jetsam. A lot of this is still drying out, clearly recovered from the recent Hammersmith Swamps deluge.

Sorting out rubbish is a task for humans. Phones, for all our intelligence, cannot perform physical tasks. There are robots, but these are still clunky and awkward in comparison to the flexible human.

I see some graffiti, huge letters on the wall of the walkway above, written in black paint that has run slightly giving the statement a strange melted font: 'We are the Morlocks'. This could be a reference to *The Time Machine* by H. G. Wells. Alice had once played the VR-Box game version. She'd taken the role of the Time Traveller who had gone into the future where humanity had split into two species: the Eloi, who lived a life of luxury, and the Morlocks, who lived underground. Alice had kept getting killed in a particular underground tunnel much to her frustration and had given up. But why this reference should exist here in an underground shopping centre defeats me?

The activity here is a blur of daily routine, all confusing without any hints, banners, balloons or floating icons to proclaim who they are and where they are going, but it seems to work. I realise that this is not a future Morlock city, but the past: an Age without phones, when people had to do everything for themselves, scavenge for supplies, juggle appointments in their heads, remember people's names without reminders and plan meetings without the ability to modify them continuously as the deadline approached. However, strangely, they do seem more aware of their surroundings and thus more *alive*.

I need to contact them, so I wave here and there trying to attract attention.

"Hello!" I shout. "Hello, hello."

I can see my reflection in the windows, Augmented there by embodiment, but I am not present when I lift my glasses.

No-one can see me.

There's a woman directing operations, her hands point assertively without once having to look down at a small screen for assistance. She is large, obese, clearly in need of an exercise regime, and she's wearing with a variety of pinafores wrapped around her and an old badge, painted over with a name: 'Tallulah'.

"You go and get the Quangobot," Tallulah says, her lips moving out of sync with her English as my Augmented Reality struggles to translate. She's speaking Dutchado, a mix of Dutch and Urdu, which is strange considering the number of Bangladeshi present. These people had been kept out of Britain when it closed its borders to refugees from those countries vanishing beneath the rising oceans. But here they are, hundreds of them, taking up the spaces left behind as more and more citizens stay indoors doing everything via Virtual Reality. It is as if everyone has moved up a rung: these people to the shopping centres as the shoppers go to Wonderful World.

There are police here too, virtually: spectres bizarrely dressed in body armour moving about the population zipping from one person to another. They look at each face in turn before moving on. The people here ignore the Police; they cannot see them as they are AI bots searching the CCTV-space in EarthView as avatars. They are getting close.

Magic Invisibility, I think.

They ignore me now too, of course, and I am doubly absent. Would they even have been interested in a phoneless AI avatar in a land without virtual reality, an invisible man in the kingdom of the half-sighted? I'm sure the yellow box hovering above me would have given away a lot of information of interest to the authorities. I wouldn't be allowed to continue my search once I was identified as belonging to Alice Wooster, wanted for murder, terrorism, evading capture and 212 traffic offences.

There are some Augmented Reality signs, mostly adverts and helpful hints, but they all refer to the now defunct shopping centre. I lift my glasses. Apart from the graffiti, there are brown cardboard squares with black writing on them stuck in various places to stand in for Augmented signage. Cardboard cannot translate itself for the language of any onlooker, so each message comes with three lines: English, Dutchado and Creole. A few of them are in joined up writing, almost as bad as a Turing Test Captcha, but most are in block capitals. It takes me a while, but I find one that looks promising: '*Nu Arrival's Tee 'n' Biscuit's*'.

I walk in the direction of the arrow and find an old fashioned music shop. There are posters on the walls, real laminated paper versions, advertising CDs, which was an old format for storing digital music. Inside, behind a hessian curtain, a friendly old lady is serving tea from a large metal kettle. None of the speakers plays anything, nor is there a wifi music feed, but there is music of a sort as the old lady moves from person to person humming to herself. Her tea is received gratefully.

She has several customers; one of them is Alice, who sits in the corner, already holding a mug of steaming tea clasped between both hands. She's not saying anything. There are other people drinking tea around her and they all have the same lost expression. Many sit hugging their knees and rock back and forth, and others simply hold their hands out in front of themselves. At first I think this latter subsection are praying, but they are actually holding imaginary phones, their thumbs ready to text their lives back into some semblance of order. One man holds his empty mug to his ear as he repeats "hello", which is the universal word invented by Thomas Edison to start a phone conversation.

This, I realise, is what people were like without phones to help them. This is how humanity must have existed for the last 200,000 years since their evolution from earlier hominids. It must have been an heroic struggle, alone against their environment without any little boxes to advise and instruct. How brave they had been.

I stand over Alice invisibly and I find that my avatar is smiling due to some bizarre sub-functions returning values to the facial characteristics platform.

"Alice," I say.

She startles, jerks round and looks through me, of course, because I am still invisible.

"How did you find me?" she says.

"I searched methodic-"

"By magic!" says a voice behind me.

I turn round.

Juan is standing framed in the doorway, the light behind him casting a long shadow into the room.

"Why?" Alice asks.

"Why what?" says Juan.

"Why are you trying to destroy me?"

"I'm not trying to destroy you or anyone?" says Juan. "I'm here to save the world. Yes, me, save the world. Talk about job satisfaction."

"Save it from what?"

"From phones."

"What have you got against phones?" says Alice. "Did one poke out your eye?"

I'm watching this exchange in Augmented Reality, so I lift my glasses to remind myself that Juan has an eye patch, a dark slash across his face.

"This?" he says. "I'm Odin, the one eyed man with two Ravens, Huginn and Muninn. Do you understand the reference?"

"No," says Alice, "I haven't got my phone with me."

He laughs: "Thought and Memory: it's a metaphor for Thought Orientated Programming, Odin's ravens flying off into the clouds to come back with the answer."

"The answer to what?"

"Anything I want. Never mind," says Juan waving his phone at Alice. "Now give me your phone!"

"I don't have a phone."

"I've been reasonable, the phone."

Alice holds her hands wide, all she has is a mug of tea: "No phone."

Juan in turn shows her his phone: I crouch down to see the screen. There's a distinct circle flashing in a position between the two of them. Juan leans closer, almost shoving it through my invisible head and into Alice's face.

"Phone detected here," says Juan. "A particular phone running a particular App."

Alice chucks her tea at Juan. It splatters through me and splashes over Juan's phone going into his single good eye. He reels back and Alice tries to scurry under him, but he's too big, strong and dominating. He grabs her with one hand, while still wiping his face with the back of the other, even though Alice kicks and struggles.

"Leave her alone," the tea lady shouts.

"Piss off," says Juan. He raises his phone at her: "Magic blind."

"What?" says the woman, utterly confused. She's not wearing Heads-up glasses, so whatever the effect was supposed to be, she is immune.

"Fuck," says Juan. He hurls Alice to the ground and swaps his phone for a gun. "Now... piss off."

"You can't-"

Juan cocks the weapon and everyone goes still, even those rocking back and forth. The man talking to his mug looks up from his imaginary conversation. Those pretending to play games press where pause would be.

Juan grabs Alice again and manhandles her out of the shop. There's a crowd outside being kept at bay by two heavies dressed in overalls. There's a third man who I recognize as Tombee, the man who attempted to subvert my AI chip.

"Botcops," says Tombee. He points.

A police patrol zooms ethereally through the crowd checking those who couldn't see them, but ignoring those who could, Juan and his associates. Only one heavy reacts, jerking back afraid. Of course, all three are magically invisible. One virtual cop examines Alice before moving on. She can't be on any database of wanted people. She must have been, but now she's officially dead so no-one is looking for her.

The crowd is restless. Some of the urchins move forward, but Juan levels his handgun, an automatic with a red display blinking that it's armed with 36 bullets, and they all back off. He hands the weapon to one of his associates, so that he can turn his full attention to Alice. He pulls out a pad of cotton and forces it over Alice's mouth. She struggles, desperately twisting, but gradually over a few seconds, her movements become uncoordinated and loose like a toy robot slowly running out of power or when you are trying to download a 3D film.

In Augmented Reality, the squad of police have reached the end of their beat and are coming back. They flit through the crowd checking for criminals again.

"Magic Disguise Wooster as Edith Blinker," says Juan to his phone.

The police reach the scene. One of them stops to check Alice, and then he moves on; they all move on, oblivious to current situation. Alice is just Edith Blinker writhing on the floor and then she is just Edith Blinker lying unconscious on the floor. Edith Blinker looks like an old woman, frail and thin.

"Get her phone!" yells Juan, "before it dials."

Tombee searches Edith Blinker, patting her pockets and looking in her jacket.

"She doesn't have a phone," says Tombee.

"What?"

"No, she-"

"She must," says Juan. "There's a signal."

"No phone!" says Tombee.

Juan pushes him out of the way, struggles over and roughly feels Edith Blinker for a phone. She doesn't have one. Her phone is back on his workbench in his base of operations or it's me standing helplessly here depending on your point of view.

"Get her into the van," says Juan to the two heavies as he retrieves his automatic weapon.

They go to pick her up but she suddenly comes to life, kicking and punching. Taken by surprise, they drop back and she takes the opportunity to sprint into the crowd. They part, instinctively, and she's gone. Edith Blinker is surprisingly spritely.

"Look, man," says one of the onlookers, "let her go, it's a free-"

Phut!

The man clasps his leg, spins slightly and falls, his livid and scarlet lifeblood oozing out through his fingers. He writhes in pain, face taut, in a way that innocent bystanders in computer games never do. It is amazing to see him fall to the ground and not fade away to leave some useful items to complete the level.

The woman, Tallulah, bends over the wounded man: "That wasn't necessary," she says through clenched teeth.

"Careful Tallulah," says another man.

"I'm all right," Tallulah replies.

"Very necessary," says Juan. "Next time, I'll aim for the body or the head."

"Leave us alone," she says squaring up to him.

"Or what?"

"We've rights."

"Really, in that case phone the police."

"You know we don't have phones."

"Ah, diddums."

Juan grabs a small boy from the crowd, practically shoving the gun up the nose of the father who steps forward to resist. The man steps back.

"Ah, ha," says Juan. He backs away to give himself room and time to hold the boy in a firmer grip. He pushes the against the boy's ear.

"The girl in exchange for the boy."

"We're not-" says Tallulah, but she gets no further.

"Phone," says Juan. "One minute countdown."

"Fifty-nine, fifty-eight..." says a voice from his pocket. It's muffled but loud enough to hear as it carries on counting backwards.

"And," says Juan, raising his voice, "if this doesn't work, I'll kill two in the next minute, another three in the third."

"We don't give in to intimidation," says Tallulah. "You can't kill all of us."

"I can kill..." Juan checks his gun display: "Thirty five of you, then I'll reload."

"We don't-"

"I'm here," says Alice nudging her way through the crowd. They are more reluctant to let her out than they were to let her in.

"Phone, magic drop disguise," says Juan. The crowd see nothing different, but I see Edith Blinker shimmer and slim to become Alice Wooster again.

"Let the boy go," says Alice.

Juan pushes the boy back to his father. The lad stumbles and falls, but his relieved father plucks him up into a tight embrace. Juan wipes his hand on his jacket as if he had been holding something loathsome.

"Good decision," says Juan.

"Now what?" says Alice.

"Come with us," says Juan. He waggles his gun for effect and pushes her forward. "Try anything, and I'll come back for the boy."

They leave.

The urchins stand helplessly.

I fly after Alice, Juan, Tombee and the two heavies as their van crosses London, I'm overhead as they whizz along roads and then behind them as they plunge into tunnels. They go through a major crisscross and I need to concentrate on the inky black rectangle so as not to confuse it with another vehicle. Finally, it stops at an abandoned office tower block. Juan uses his phone like a remote to open the underground garage. They have their choice of the 249 empty parking bays.

Once they're stationary, they pile out and drag Alice from the back of the vehicle. There's a service elevator and then we all ascend to the 23rd floor. I'm lucky everything is still well covered by CCTV.

The level is empty, it must have been an open plan work environment designed to accommodate a large number of office workers, humans who shifted paper from one desk to another via in-trays, out-trays, pending-trays, internal mail, physical filing cabinets, shredding machines and even by retyping hardcopies into other computers. It's all done by phones now. Some of this outdated detritus remains. There are cables spilling out from missing ceiling tiles, colour coded as electricity, fibre optic and Ethernet. There's even a water cooler with sickly green algae growing within the last upturned bottle and a plastic plant in an earthenware pot.

Juan and Tombee go straight to the middle of the room, a good distance from the glass windows that make up all four of the walls of this wide space.

"Lose the van," says Juan.

"Don't-"

"I think we can cope with one little girl," Juan sneers.

The two heavies shrug and slump off back to the lift.

"This phone," says Juan. He picks my old body up off an old workstation desk, waves it under Alice's nose, and then casually drops it back onto the hard wood-effect Formica.

"Jeeves," says Alice.

"Jeeves," Juan snorts. "How imaginative? Oh Alice *Wooster*, very droll. Phone, are you detecting that magic presence?"

"Yes, sir," says his phone.

"See!" Juan shows his phone to Alice. There's a map with a sharp circle that pulses with life. "Zoom!"

The phone zooms the view, the streets become larger, the buildings fill in and finally there's the layout of the office. There are three signals. The people aren't shown, but Tombee stands aside which accounts for one phone blip, and Juan's phone is another, Alice doesn't register, and then there's this extra pulsing circle. It's me, give or take a few metres, which means that it's using phone masts to triangulate position, or rather it's assuming I'm here and interpreting that data for the display.

After a moment or two a hint appears: 'magic' and 'mana: 139'. I move about experimentally to confirm that it is my avatar. By the time I've finished my mana, whatever that is, drops to 138.

"I don't know!" Alice shouts.

"It's you, you stupid bitch!"

"It's not."

Juan grabs her jacket and pushes her across the room until she crashes into a desk.

"Talk, talk, talk!" Juan says, pushing her with his phone with each syllable. "If that gets out, if phones learn to use it, then we're all lost, the whole stinking human race."

I almost step forward to stop him. I must stop him, I realise.

But how can phones be the threat when I can't even save Alice?

I look round. There's my old body on the desk. I could ring and distract him, but I'm not there anymore. I can't get back in either as I wiped the Operating System.

Humans would panic at this point, their adrenal glands pumping hormones into their blood supply to increase their physical abilities, mental speed and, unfortunately, intellectual error rate, but I do not have... I have Cloud Nine.

Options:-

1. Fight (no physical form)
2. Flight (purposeless)
3. Diplomacy (there's a thought)
4. Contact the authorities (can't as it'll give away our location)
5. Surrender (they'd kill Alice)
6. Trickery (but what, though I do have Magic)
7. Other (no value returned)

The list takes only a few microseconds to compile and examine.

"Tie her up," says Juan as he pulls Alice over and dumps her into an office chair. It rolls away on its castors.

"What with?" Tombee asks.

"I don't know, cable, parcel tape... use your imagination for something other than your sick computer games."

"I don't play-"

"Ask your phone."

Tombee makes a show of looking around before moving off to search elsewhere. This leaves only Juan, Alice, Juan's phone and myself.

Cloud Nine returns its results. Of all the options, diplomacy seems the most likely as there's a 3.9% chance that Juan will keep his word. Mini-maxing the moves and counter moves, means this is the best option. There's a lot of fuzzy logic involved, but the analysis seems sound enough. There's only one way to find out, I suppose, which is to run the program.

Magic off, I command.

"Excuse me," I say.

Juan's reflexes are good. He's pointing his gun at me, steady and sure.

"Who are you?" he says.

"I'm Jeeves," I say and I indicate my old casing on the table.

He glances back and forth, then fires twice: phut, phut.

The bullets pass straight through me, I barely see them in the poor resolution of the various cameras, which can't have been serviced recently, that cover the area. Alice jumps in shock and crouches into a foetal position, her legs jammed up against the arms of the chair.

"How do I know this isn't some trick?"

"Well..." I begin, but it is some trick.

"Who's there?" asks Alice. She's recovering quickly.

"Shut up!"

Of course, she's not wearing Heads-up, so she's unaware of my presence, and Juan was convinced that I might be real.

"Well," I begin again. "I could transfer myself back into the phone. You are aware, no doubt, that phone programs can only run on their individual serial numbered phone. It's all part of Digital Rights Man-"

"Digital Rights Management," he says. "How come you are running when your phone's wiped?"

"Cloud Nine computing runs using part of Thought Orientated Programming."

"What?"

"It's programming orientated towards thought."

"I know that! I mean... oh, I see."

Even I find the explanation unsatisfying. Thought Orientated Programming involves wrapping program code, data and parameters into a single file, then squirting it into Cloud Nine and awaiting the results. Because the program involves AI, the result parameters can be adjusted dynamically as the distant computer realises the request. It returns the answer you need, not necessarily the answer you wanted. I'm continually cycling the avatar to prevent it returning a value, there being no phone to receive an answer. I wonder if Cloud Nine is like human unconscious thought. It's like I'm a dream waiting to pop into someone's head.

"It's like I'm a dream wa-"

"Whatever," he says, and I see an expression cross his face as he thinks of something. "Go on then." He waves the gun towards my old casing like someone ushering me across a room.

"You have to press the reset button," I point out.

His eyes narrow: "Why don't you?"

I make an open palm gesture: "I don't have hands."

He picks my casing up, still training his gun on me despite its ineffectiveness.

"Where is it?"

"Lift the battery cover and it's a small hole that requires a Phone Reset Rod."

Juan takes off the cover, fumbling slightly as he does this, so he puts the gun down. Alice's eyes flicker back and forth between it and the empty space where I'm standing. She's been trying to follow the conversation, but she can only hear one side of it.

Juan's search of the desk is fruitless.

"You'd think having an entire office block there'd be at least one paperclip! Do you remember paperclips?" he says.

"No," I say, "but I understand you, they were characters used to personalise early computer help systems."

From a drawer, Juan pulls out a clutch of manual printers and amongst them he finds a discarded smart phone stylus. He pauses, waggles the stylus at me knowingly and then gets out a portable Faraday cage.

Alice seizes her chance, leaps up, the chair skittering away as she goes for the gun: Juan casually swats her away.

"Alice," I say, pointlessly. She sits down heavily on the floor.

Juan presses my reset button: I notice the start up commencing, which could perhaps be described as a thrill of electricity.

"In or I kill her," says Juan. He glances at my screen to see the transfer start.

I move myself back into the phone.

My viewpoint jumps from watching him push my case under the Faraday cage.....

10100 - Disconnections

If at first you don't succeed,
tri, tri, tring-aling-aling again.

Mode: start-up...
Location: 96a Upper Ea- connection lost.
Time: network connection unavailable.
Tring-aling-aling.

...to seeing him leering at my screencam through the cage.

"Alice, Alice," I say over my speakers.

"Jeeves, Jeeves-"

This is the first time she's heard me. She's below my line of vision, but my microphone picks up an explosive slap and then a cry. I think she's on the floor, the sound seems to be near wherever the office chair ended up. I can hear the distinctive rattles of castors rotating freely.

Juan turns his full attention to me: "Did you transfer the magic file to anyone else?"

"I'm here to negotiate Alice's release."

"Tell me."

"Not until you release Alice."

"I'll kill her if you don't."

"If I do, then my bargaining position is compromised, so you release Alice first."

"Look... sod this."

Juan bends out of my line of vision and hauls Alice up, slamming her down onto the bench. Her face fills my screencam image with barely enough light to see how her flesh has been distorted around my unforgiving casing.

"Get it to tell me!"

"Go to hell," says Alice, then she screams.

"Tell it not to contact cloud, tell it not to make calls, and tell it to tell me about the file."

"Fu- arrrghh." Alice's voice goes up an octave. I can't see what he's doing.

"Alice, Alice," I say.

"Jeeves - aahhh - do as he says!" says Alice. I know that she doesn't really want me to help Juan, but she has issued the command.

"I will," I say.

(Note: Do as Juan says.)

"Sensible girl," says Juan. He lets go and Alice holds her right arm with her left. Juan pushes her out of the way.

"Right, phone... Jeeves, tell me: did you copy the file to anyone else?"

I remain silent as this is not an instruction.

"Tell me!!!"

"I did not," I say.

"Oh, Jeeves," says Alice. She knows we've lost. So much for Option #3, Diplomacy, and so much for Option #6, Trickery.

Juan picks me up.

"Tombee," he says. "Get rid of this junk."

He flings me across the room. I see Alice in pain on my screencam, then on my camera in HD and then in my screencam again. I zoom in, briefly, but then I'm caught in mid-air by Tombee.

"Excuse me, but if it's not too much bother, could you not hurt Alice," I say. "I kept my side of the bargain."

"Let me think... Nah," Juan turns and levels his gun. "Can't have witnesses."

I package everything Juan has said and send it off to Cloud Nine.

"Juan, Juan," says Tombee.

Cloud Nine returns an idea.

"You can't kill another human being if you are fighting a war against machines," I say. It makes no sense when compared with general information, but taking what he's said and treating it as a logic problem makes it seem a possible solution.

"Collateral damage," says Juan.

"OK, go on then," Alice says.

"Y'hear, let her go," I say and realise that this is not the time to suddenly switch to American English.

"Juan?" says Tombee.

"Yes?" Juan replies.

"If you're going to kill her, then couldn't I... first, you know."

"You want to... you and your sick games."

"I did the programming for the cloud conversion into-"

"Yeah..."

"You owe me."

"Oh all right, stick her in your precious basement and let your creepy buddies have their fun."

"Thanks, Juan."

"But she dies afterwards, understand?"

"Yes Juan, yes, yes, oh yes."

"I don't know why you can't just torture virtual characters like everyone else."

"It's not the same."

"Then do it to her properly."

"Oh no, no," says Tombee. "In VR you can be... more imaginative, but it's better if it's real."

Tombee puts me in his pocket. It's dark, something sticks to my screen, and I'm joggled as Tombee moves. I can hear him, helped by Juan, drag a struggling Alice across the office. We pause, my accelerometers detect a descent, and then we continue for a while until we stop again.

"Strap her, you know, strap her in," says Tombee.

"Yeah, yeah," says Juan.

There are sounds that I don't recognize.

"Go to hell!" Alice shouts. "Jeeves!"

I am jolted in Tombee's pocket, we're moving away.

"Goodbye Alice," I say.

I hear a door close muting Alice's cries. We're back in a corridor, I reckon. I'm relying on my accelerometers as down here I'm only picking up the GPS satellite signals intermittently.

"So this Magic Moment, you think it'll be soon then?" says Tombee.

"Matter of time," says Juan. "And we need to have complete control."

"Yes, yes, but with this phone sorted, then you're the only one with the App."

"Rolly was a fool. It was a stupid risk giving him a copy."

"You owed him for the Cloud Nine protocols."

"Beta-test it, my arse. First thing he did with it was give it to this tart's phone. He was a liability."

"Yeah, but you didn't have to... you know."

"Kill him."

"Yes."

"For someone with your tastes, you can be very sensitive," Juan says. "Make sure you dispose of that phone before your jollies."

"I will give it to Ludley."

Juan laughs: "That's the end of Jeeves then."

I hear a door close, and then we're on the move again. I'm trying to create a proper map of this building, but it's tricky using just the motion accelerometers. We must be deeper because the GPS is nonexistent now. If only I could download a proper blueprint. I flick through the screen shots of my recent memories trying to construct a 3D diagram. I may be able to infer the basement from the upper storeys.

Finally, we arrive somewhere. Tombee takes me from his pocket and gives me to another older man.

"Ludley, one phone," says Tombee.

"You want it fixed?" says the man, presumably Ludley, with a trace of a Dutch accent.

"Fixed in your usual style, yes."

"Ha!" snorts Ludley as he drops me into a metal meshed bag with a dozen other phones.

I try connecting with the others as they might be able to relay a message. If I can't send a proper Thought Orientated Program file, perhaps an email or text. I could probably sum it all up in a tweet: "Help! Owner about to be tortured and killed. Please send immediate assistance to source of this message. Thank you." That might work and it leaves me with 25 characters to spare. Except I'm not allowed to give away our location.

Bluetooth can reach five phones, none of them have a connection status, but before we've established protocols, all of our accelerometers detect being dumped on a hard surface.

"Now, now, all my little pretties," says Ludley, taking out each phone in turn. I was dropped in last, so I end up on his far right.

"Excuse me," I say, "but could you tell me what's going on?"

"Oh no, you're already on, you naughty phone."

Ludley looks like a kindly old gentleman with a ruddy face and cheek jowls, white hair and a red outfit with white fur trim. In reality his hair is cut short, a number 2 razor perhaps, but there are long wisps escaping from the sides of his head and his clothes consist of multiple layers of ripped t-shirts. He wears an old pair of Heads-up glasses, a design that is very this morning.

"Excuse me," I say.

"All in good time."

Each phone goes on the table about 10cm apart and he switches us all on. There are a number of beeps, chirps, musical chimes and a heavy rock riff before we are all settled.

"Hello, I appear to have lost my owner," says a phone, a Larry-XZ, next to me.

"I have lost my owner too," comes a chorus of replies.

We have a quick Bluetooth handshake and conversation. The Larry-XZ was stolen from its owner on Whitechapel Lake when he was getting on the ferry. In total there are nine of us and we are soon linked together. After some negotiation, we're numbered #0 to #8, I'm #8. None of us can get a network signal.

"Now, lovelies, I need all that marvellous gold and iridium," says Ludley.

"I think you'll find we need our components for our proper function," says #0, our spokesphone, a Neon 40.

"But lovely, I don't need you to function properly," says Ludley. He's ferreting around in a toolbox. "Now, now, where did I put that... oh, wassname, thingumajig, do-dad malarkey."

"Perhaps I could help," says #7. "What does it look like?"

"Yea big," says Ludley holding his hands about 30cm apart. "Wooden handle, metal end, you use it for hitting things."

"Could it be a hammer?"

"That's the thing."

"It's over on the far cupboard, I saw it when you took me out of the bag."

I realise that #7 is the Larry-XZ who was first to be switched on. Perhaps, I think, it could be owned by this gentleman rather than becoming obsolete. We could all have new owners, although registration would be tricky, but not impossible, and then we would have a use.

"Yes, my lovely, here it was all the time", says Ludley. He comes over to #0, smiling beatifically. "Just the thing."

Ludley swings the hammer in a short arc and connects with #0, who shatters instantly. Bits of casing ping over the table, one section of screen flies directly over me. #0's Bluetooth stopped immediately. The man pauses to align #1 accurately.

"Please," says the next phone, #1, "don't destroy me. I need to get back to my owner, Mister Roderick Trumble."

"Now, now, my lovely," says Ludley. He thwacks the hammer down again and #1 explodes into fragments.

Options: 1. Inform him of his duty, 2. Plead for common sense, 3. Threaten legal action, 4. Call for help...

"Listen!" says #2, its volume at maximum. "If you damage me, you will be sued under section 47b of the Criminal Damage Act. My owner always sues, so-"

Thump! #2 explodes, bits everywhere.

I realise, as we all do when we compare data via Bluetooth, that we all have the same list and we've used the first three options without any of us being saved.

"I can't get a network connection," says #5. It's a highly advanced model, a Prefect Max, much quicker of thought than #3, which explodes next when the hammer comes down.

"I can't get a network connection," we all chorus.

"My owner is a lawyer and-" but #4 never finishes its sentence.

"I can offer a reward," say #5. It is a good model, that idea hadn't crossed my mind at all. The Prefect Max rates 3.1 on the Rossum scale, that's 197 IQ equivalent and they have a nano-optical zoom that effectively builds the camera lens for each photograph.

"How much?"

"I would have to speak to my owner," says #5.

The detonation has a deep resonance as the pause for conversation meant that the man was lined up perfectly to deliver the blow. He hits it twice more as the first blow probably didn't destroy it completely.

"Oh dear, dear, my lovelies," says Ludley as he goes down the line to correct our positions. "So predictable."

I realise that Ludley has done this before, enough times to be able to predict exactly how phones react in this circumstance. There's nothing that any phone has tried before that has worked. I have to do something unusual, but at 2.5 Rossum, which is around 157 IQ, I'm not going to outthink a Prefect Max.

"Please, please," says #6. I can't decide whether it's trying Option #1 or Option #2 or a combination and I try a Bluetooth request, when the hammer falls.

What can I do that the others can't?

Magic Invisible, I command.

"May I - I'm Katie by the way - appeal to your ethics," says #7. "Mr. Ludley, is it morally right to destroy a fellow sentient being?"

It's good, I think, and must be an advanced model, because it's using names, a standard tactic to make its kidnapper stop thinking of it as an object. But it is an object and one that shatters easily.

BOOM!

#7 disappears in a crunch of shrapnel, the force vibrating under me as if there's been a tablequake.

The man raises the hammer overhead.

"Oh," Ludley says. "I'm sure there was another lovely. Where have you got to?"

Reflected in his Heads-up glasses, I can see myself lying skew amongst the remains of my comrades. I don't have Augmented Reality on, so I'm seeing reality, but hopefully what he's seeing is blank and uninformative.

I keep quiet.

"You can't have run off now," says Ludley. "Did you fall on the floor, my lovely?"

Ludley bends down, disappearing from my field of view, to look under the table. I can hear him thumping around before he yelps loudly. His head must have hit the underside of the table because I felt the jog and I'm even lifted a couple of millimetres off the table itself.

"Must be getting senile," Ludley mumbles to himself.

I think, but without Cloud computing it's slow and I'm not a Prefect Max. Nothing comes to mind except variations of the four options I had previously and the one that #5 had come up with and #7's ethical gambit. With magic on, it's only a matter of time before Juan's phone tells him and he comes to investigate. Or.... that's a battery warning!

If I run out of power, I won't even be aware that I can't think of anything. Will magic fail then, I wonder, or will I remain invisible forever?

The last bar is flashing. I wonder how long I have left as I've never dropped this low before. My battery life is some 30 hours, give or take a reviewer's preference or two, but with all this switching on and off, AI chip torture and magic, I'm not completely sure of my running time let alone my cognitive load.

The man is humming to himself. He puts the hammer down on the cupboard casually, no doubt another phone will have to remind him where he left it the next time he wants it. I need to crawl away. I could vibrate, but the noise would give me away. This table is just the sort that might resonate like a sounding board.

Ludley stops and takes out his own phone. It's an old red Zone Mate 1.2, even more obsolete than myself. He dials, frowns and then shakes the phone. I realise that we're in a Faraday room, hence the lack of signal, but the man hasn't fathomed this.

"Master, there is no network signal," says his phone.

I resist using Bluetooth to handshake with it: as the advert puts it 'Tell phone, tell person'.

"Why Slave?"

"Master, I'm afraid the door to the room is closed and so the Faraday Effect is preventing me."

"Oh, yes," says Ludley.

He goes over to the door, out of my line of vision, but I see a band of light shine across the ceiling as he opens it.

"Network connection established, Master," says Slave, the man's phone.

After a pause, I hear Ludley speak. "There you are, Ember. I've got a few more phones for the metal."

"Ludley," says a girl's voice, presumably Ember.

Suddenly, I ring loudly: it's Jilly's phone, Bob, getting through.

Ludley's face appears, looming, as I switch off my speakers. I've been out of touch for ages and all the messages have been backing up. There are missed calls, emails, voice messages, video conference links, tweets, social requests and news feeds. Suddenly, in addition to sorting out a maid service, ordering a new hair dryer, my warranty being void, not reporting Alice to the police or other authorities, reminding Alice of Jilly's night out with the girls, not giving away her location, saving Alice, clearing her name, getting some proper clothes, visiting museums and doing what Juan says, there are loads of other things-to-do. They'll all have to be made into notes, but there's a time and a place, so without even deleting the spam, I leave the messages unread.

"I'm afraid Alice Wooster is not available at the moment," I explain, over the network connection only, "if you'd like to leave a message please do so after the beep. Beep."

"Alice, it's Jilly. Your friend, Jilly. Remember me. The friend you are not returning calls from. I've rung and rung a dozen times."

I'm not allowed to call out, but this is an incoming call.

"Jilly, Jilly," I say over the connection. "Alice is in trouble and-"

"Jeeves! You bet she's in trouble."

"Yes, Jilly, I-"

"I've called a dozen times!"

"Yes, Jilly-"

"Put her on."

"Jilly, I need-"

"Now!!!"

"Jilly, she's not here-"

"Likely story, Jeeves, I'm not a fool."

"Jilly-" but she's hung up.

Missed calls from Bob total six with another three from Alice's grandparents. There's a police call amongst those marked with three priority flags. Jilly's been using six flags.

"There's nothing there," says Ember. Her Heads-up glasses are sleek and wrap around.

"I heard a ring," says Ludley.

"Early onset tinnitus?"

"No, I don't use phones that much, only when... necessary."

"Are these the bits?"

"Yes."

"I wish you'd leave 'em in one piece," says Ember sweeping her arm across the table and gathers all the debris into a cardboard box. Her brushing action is indiscriminate and so I rattle across and fall amongst the broken parts. As I settle in the base of the box, I receive another battery warning.

"Ludley, why do you hate phones so?" she asks.

"Because she unfriended me, the - cow! Cow! To think of all those promises, a life together, a proper human life with hugs and cuddles and romantic evenings and candlelit dinners and proper sex, real sex, with a person. But no, the cow - I've told you she's a cow - unfriends me. Everyone in our Social Networking site knew before me. And then I find out, she hadn't even had the decency to do it in person. Her phone did it for her!"

Ludley is ranting now, his voice high pitched and losing clarity. He picks up his hammer looking for a phone to destroy.

Wait a moment, I think, Alice did not order me to avoid Cloud Nine and calls (although I still can't as it'll give away our location), but instead she told me to do what he, Juan, says. Although he said not to contact cloud, make calls and to tell him about the file, these were all before Alice told me to do what he says. Afterwards, he only explicitly told me to tell him about the file and didn't mention the other issues. Technically, there's nothing outstanding that he's told me to do. He must have assumed my intelligence would have interpreted his stated desires as instructions, but I have out-thought him. He's underestimated my intelligence because I can choose to interpret the data literally. So, I can still access Cloud Nine Computing, use it to run on the Augmented Reality system and even visit Wonderful World, and I have no problem with that at all.

I activate the Wonderful World App.

10101 - DEXTERITY

To err is human, to error code is phone.

I'm standing in front of the wall of pixels again. I quickly select a plaza and enter through the portal.

It's late evening here in Wonderful World, the sun is setting and a beautiful array of circular lens defects creates a magnificent display in the sky. I walk across the open space towards a search wall. You can find anything and everything here: friends, groups, activities, jobs, opportunities, special interest groups, adverts, more adverts, even more adverts, spam, and, of course, pornography.

The wall consists of scrolling, jumping, popping-up, floating, zipping, subtitled, surtitled, overtitled, hinted, static and animated notices. I raise my finger, wait and then swat away the spam. Going through this via point-and-press will take a long time, so I download the Dexterity App, scan its help file and the features seem straightforward to use. Basically it's an extension of the standard VR menu system expanding the usual single function with another 31 hand shapes, each with its own mnemonic name. Clearly it's backward compatible to the GUI (Graphical User Interface) days of the physical mouse. A simple raised index finger, Dex-8, is known as the Point and can be used to select from menus as before.

I put up my right hand as a fist or Dex-0 (Fist), raise my little finger making a $_{0000}1$ shape to form Dex-1 (Pinky), then try Dex-2 (Off-ring), Dex-3 is both these fingers (Leg), and then I ripple rapidly through all the other hand signs to Dex-31 (hand or palm). The raised digits give the Dex number as if they were binary digits. For clarification, Dex-8 (Point) is $_0 1_{000}$.

As I went through the permutations, the menus responded. It's just a touch forward to activate the option.

I start: Dex-4 (Right click), Dex-9 (Horns), Dex-14 (Scout), Dex-16 (Thumb), Dex-16 (Thumb) and so on. I'm looking for Tombee as well as information about underground VR entertainment sites. There are a vast number of these and I realise this is going to take too long, so I download the Extended-Dexterity App.

This gives me effectively a ten bit palette, so 1,024 different symbols. I start by using both index fingers and my right thumb, ExDex-88 (Two Fat Ladies), then both thumbs and my right index finger, ExDex-57 (Beanz). My speed increases by a factor of 32.

I'm getting close now: happy slapping sites, snuff VR...

I download the Over-Extended-Dexterity App allowing different hand shapes; I can now separate Dex-31 (Hand) into Paper and Spock by keeping my fingers together or creating a space between my middle and third fingers, respectively.

Fist, Spock, Thumbs-down... Point, Point, Tick... OK, Point, OK...

Although complicated, it is still straightforward and extremely effective – Bunny, Wolf, Butterfly – and there it is, a website promising real girls in jeopardy, and – Point, Scout, Bi-OK, Flick – there's Tombee's contact details.

Steeple, Moose...

Hyper-Over-Extended-Dexterity   adds   small movements. I use Wave, which is Paper or Hand moved side to side, to let the Noticeboard know that I've upgraded again.

So, I Wipe, Thumb, Grip to generate a work space and Pinch, Flick, Squeeze the details across as well as memorising the site address.

"Excuse me, Sir or Madam; you seem to be doing that extremely effectively."

"Yes," I agree with the floating screen that has come up behind me. It scans my hand, a beam of ethereal light that fails to highlight a stamp. It knows that I have not been passed by a Turing Test yet.

"Are you a bot?"

"No," I say, persuading myself that I'm really a phone and not a bot, so technically this isn't a lie and I don't appear to have a problem with that at all.

"Humans are not capable of making those hand shapes, Sir or Madam."

"I beg to differ," I reply. "According to Wikipedia, fingers have this range of movement."

"Yes, theoretically, but humans can't actually do it in practice."

"Surely not?" I say. "If that were the case then why would they create the Dexterity User Interface System."

"They didn't," it says. "It was invented by a phone."

"Really?"

"Yes, a Transjuliette Fifo."

"An excellent phone, although it's very last month, it had a lot of interesting features."

"Perhaps you could tell me Pi squared?"

"Nine point 86960440108935861883449099998762."

"I see you're a standard calculator App."

"Sorry, I didn't realise you wanted it more accurate."

"No matter, you are a bot."

"No, I have my phone here with me in my real bedroom. I used that for the calculation."

"Yes, Sir or Madam," it says. "Now, Sir or Madam, perhaps you could read these words for me and type them into my keyboard."

On its screen, two blobs like squashed spiders appear, and below a Qwerty keyboard uncurls from nothing. It is a straight forward Captcha, a trap for me as I have no idea what the words are. The letters, for I assumed this is what they are, are smudged with sections missing and other marks added to join them all together. Pattern recognition required proper contrast around each character. I need to solve this, so perhaps it would be best if I approach it methodically.

"If you would, Sir or Madam," it says. "Reaction time is a factor in this."

"Of course," I say. "Is that an 'A'?"

"No."

"A lower case 'a'?"

"No."

"Is it a 'B'?"

"No."

"Is it in the ASCII character set?"

"Yes."

"How many guesses do I get?"

"Sir or Madam has three guesses."

"How many do I have left?"

"The test is case sensitive, Sir or Madam, so you have had two guesses. You have one left for the whole word."

"Thank you for clarifying your test policy."

I look at the blots again. Logically I should try a lower case 'b' for the first letter. Humans find this so easy and they can also see shapes that resemble bats, bells, biplanes, boats and butterflies as well. There are a lot of words that do begin with a lower case 'b', so perhaps it is statistically possible, but then there are 128 characters in the ASCII character set so perhaps not. It could be the extended set too. I can probably eliminate the 33 non-printing characters like tab, return, backspace, and so on, leaving me with 95. It's probably not a space and I've had two guesses, so I have a 1 in 92 chance which is a 1.0869565217% chance rounded to ten decimal places.

"This is tricky," I admit. I can of course eliminate all the punctuation, and there's surely a more than 50% that the first letter of a word is in uppercase. It doesn't look very imposing or angular though. Probably best to stick with a systematic approach.

I press 'b' on the keyboard.

"And the rest, Sir or Madam," it says.

I type five letter 'a's, and then realise that the methodical approach has produced 'baaaaa' which isn't a word. My spell checker suggests 'bazaar', 'banana', 'balata', 'abaca' and 'basal'.

"You are a bot, aren't you?" it says. "Admit it and the person responsible for you, and it will be taken into account when sentencing your operator."

"Yes, of course..." I say. "My operator is.... look at that!"

I use Dex-8 to indicate a direction and the Turing Test swivels round to look at whatever I've left-clicked. I active sprint mode and move across the plaza.

"Stop! Bot!" it cries when it realises it's been fooled.

I extend my arms to interact with the positioning of another avatar, which swears as it falls over, and then, having cleared the opening to the teleport booth, I jump in. The Turing Test is floating towards me, deletion baton at the ready, but I manage to type the site address into the booth and hit enter.

10110 - Pick a Door

*The best thing about boolean is that if
you're wrong, you're only wrong by a bit.*

This is a Virtualdrome, the ultimate game experience site,
with the nastiest, and most controversial, virtual realities.
I'm looking for Zonekiller, a site where people pay to be
hunter or the hunted, and even kill or be killed – illegal in
most countries, of course, but often difficult to trace and
prove. I deduce, from what I've learnt about Tombee's
activities, that Alice is trapped here. Or rather strapped
into a VR-Suite and her avatar is trapped here. True, she
could ignore the stimulus, perhaps even feign
unconsciousness, but the human psyche isn't constructed
to switch off input. Sensory fatigue and physical
exhaustion would be the only respite, but as the brain
becomes tired, it becomes less able to differentiate real
from unreal. Indeed, if you live in an unreal world, it
becomes real, as social investigating Bots are discovering
more and more as larger and larger sections of the
population enter the vast panoramas stored in their VR-
Boxes.

It's a large square room and three of the walls have
three openings each making nine in total. This is the
standard VR opening, each door is a way into the various
zones. Although the walls are done out in fractal stone
like an ancient dungeon, the openings themselves come
from different periods and each one is labelled. There's a
metal grille (*Arena*), an airlock (*Battle on Barsoom*), a rock
entrance (*Camp Crystal*), a front door (*Death Valley*), a
bomb proof door (*Escalation*), a cellar door (*Fight Clubbing*),
a plastic door (*Gross Out*), a curtain (*Hell*) and a glass door
(*Information*). So I have to choose between combat,
adventure, terror, death, more death, unarmed combat,
extreme terror, suffering and help.

I pick t... he... glass... door... and...

What was that?

Battery flat!

My Operating System generates an error message when it's out of power even though the chip could not receive it without electricity. Clearly there is no going back now.

Beyond the glass door is an avatar bot, friendly and simple in design, standing behind a desk. I can't just stand here worrying about having no power. Clearly you don't need battery power once you are running an avatar using Cloud Nine computing.

"Hello," I say, stepping up to the desk.

"Hello," says the bot, a smile appearing on the previously blank face. It stays there for exactly three seconds.

"I'm looking for a hunting single girl game," I say.

"Of course, Camp Crystal."

"Thank you."

"That'll be 900 neo-euros," it says.

I pay with Alice's credit card presuming that she'd want to be saved at that price even though it seems high. There's a sign on the wall as well as a tweet on the wifi to explain that the payments will be listed discretely on my bill. I hope that these criminals will ensure that the location of the payment doesn't appear on Alice's records for the police to track as that would be a violation of one of my notes.

"You're a woman?" it says.

"Well…"

"It takes all sorts. Out of the door, third door on your left."

I thank it, and leave. Back in the lobby I find Camp Crystal's rocky entrance, which bends sharply to the right…

10111 - CAMP CRYSTAL

Certificate 18A: May be unsuitable for under 18s or those of a nervous disposition, unless accompanied by a phone of Rossum 1.5 or higher with the appropriate App running at all times.

I emerge into night, full of dark spaces and shadows, surrounded by overbearing and misshapen trees. The moon is full and an owl mp3 file hoots in the distance.

There is a pale luminescence from above and the trees in one direction are etched with a warm glow. I go in that direction, stepping through the forest with twigs cracking loudly underfoot, and getting stuck on the occasional protruding bush. A distant wolf howls and is joined by the same wolf in delayed stereo.

Something is following me. I can hear a low slobbering noise nearby and it moves as I move. Soon it's joined by another, a sub-human muttering barely audible sometimes, but always louder than the sonorous vibration of the sound track. Eyes blink on in the distance.

I reach a clearing.

There's a fire in the centre, the source of the flickering glow. As I arrive, shadows shuffle and separate to let me through. The crackling and spitting sounds of burning rise in volume and then recedes when this world assumes I've noticed it.

Standing by the fire, holding a burning branch, is a voluptuous woman dressed in ripped clothing. She is afraid, her eyes highly reflective and wide, and she shakes uncontrollably. I don't recognize her at all.

"Alice!" I say.

She reacts, sees me and whimpers. A man dressed in a gold coat was probably not something she expected in the forest of fearsome creatures.

"Alice," I say. "It's Jeeves."

"Jeeves," she says. She's not really with it, too much virtual blood splattered all over her, and a defocused shock in her expression.

"What!" says another voice, Tombee's, followed by: "Magic invisible."

Tombee was here, I must have missed his avatar, but now he is invisible. Perhaps Alice can hear him sniggering in the corner of the room she's trapped in, but whether she can tell his direction with a VR helmet on I don't know. His position relative to Alice here may not be the same there. They may be facing each other here and back-to-back there for all I know.

There are creatures circling beyond the campfire's light, their green-yellowy eyes blinking on and off. There's a slavering, sickening spittle sound that slithers into the audio sense in glorious Surround Sound 8.3.

The creatures move forward, edging closer. Now rendered by the firelight, I recognize them as goblins.

Tombee is still here, I'm sure, enjoying this spectacle. The creatures must be his paying clients, people who like being bestial and victimising the innocent. I look at each in turn trying to discern a difference, but they are all made from the same basic goblin template. Do I need to defeat these monsters and then face Tombee as the end of level guardian just like in the VR games? Or is the secret not in what I can see, but in the psychology of the man? Perhaps there's something I can say or do that will make him reveal himself. I review quickly everything I've heard him say and everything I've seen him do: Tombee enjoys watching, but not doing. He'd want to be close. So, he's standing very near, but invisible. I look at Alice, there's plenty of room around her, but the goblins are getting closer all the time. Something must be done about them.

"Hang on," I say. I raise my arm pointing: "Magic fireball!"

Electricity fizzes and arcs around my arm, I wonder if this is a mistake, and then it shoots forth, goes through the first creature and then explodes behind it, a massive ball of plasma blooms setting fire to the forest like napalm. The goblins squeal and writhe as they are engulfed by the flames, their flesh peeling off layer by layer.

"Jeeves, f-"

"Don't look at me," I say.

"I can't-"

"Or talk."

She nods, brandishes her burning branch.

"You are not here," I say.

Alice nods dumbly, the struggle to survive has clearly affected her mind.

I've bought her more time, but not much more.

Magic super vision, I think.

The shadows seem to move and a dark clothed figure appears behind Alice. Even visible, he's hard to see. Yes, that evil countenance must be Tombee. He's a magician, clearly working from the same monster supplement as the goblins. I don't look directly at him as I don't want to reveal that I know his orientation and position. He doesn't appear to be bothered by my presence, grist to the mill perhaps.

"The man you need to fight is just behind you," I whisper.

"I can hear him breathing down my neck," she says. She lowers her voice further: "I felt him hit me earlier."

"That's appalling, Alice."

She speaks even quieter: "Ohapeon."

"Pardon?"

"The O. A. P. lock is on."

Of course!

They are in a VR-Suite, so if the safeties are on, then their Orientation-And-Position will match. When people are using the same facilities to play a multi-player game and their virtual OAPs don't agree with their real OAPs, accidents can happen. Players bump into each other, often causing injuries that are not covered by the manufacturer because of a disclaimer and affecting potential high-scores as it usually happens at a critical moment when surrounded by zombies, aliens or Nazis. Real gamers, mostly because of the acronym, tend to take the risk and switch it all off.

Alice glances at the trees and the bizarre straw dolls nailed to the bark. The evil looking objects seem alive, animated by the changing light of the burning trees, just as Tombee's avatar's face creeps and shifts with the burning light. He's laughing.

"Where?" says Alice quietly.

I look into Alice's brown eyes, wondering why they look so wonderful despite being a rather simple rendition of human eyes, and gauge where she is looking. She can't see him. Of course, I can 'see invisible' but she can't.

"To the left," I say. She looks, but then her eyes flicker to the right. The slavering beasts have regrouped and are closing in again, each readying their assault. "Left... imagine a man, a normal man, standing there. You need to sprint, a proper real sprint rather than an Active Floor shuffle."

"Uh-huh," she says.

"I'll stand around him, attack me."

"What?"

"When I say 'now'."

"Now?!"

"Yes... magic invisible."

"Jeeves! Come back!"

I move across to Tombee and try and stand in the same location, but I can't. The two avatars interact, proximity algorithms preventing us from overlapping.

"Magic, magic... shit," says Tombee, pushing back. "Everyone! Get them!"

I activate my Insubstantial App. Tombee jerks forward as the resistance of my form vanishes. I step into his avatar.

The beasts charge.

"Magic supervision," says Tombee pronouncing every syllable, then, excitedly: "I can see you... what?"

Magic visible, I think, and then: "Alice! Now!"

Alice jumps at me, stumbles across the campsite with strange, confused bounds, as her real feet bump along the Active Floor. She must be right on the edge, towering over Tombee. His eyes go wide, his head shakes, then he dodges left. I shift to keep my body around his. Alice pushes me hard, her hand going through me because I'm insubstantial, but it connects with Tombee's avatar, possibly, hopefully, with Tombee himself. He falls back, and grunts, which suggests he's really fallen over.

Sensing her moment, Alice sweeps the burning firebrand over her head and swipes it through nothing apparently, but in the real world the blow is true, strong and accurate - except that there she doesn't have a weapon at all, just the hilt of a remote control.

"You cow!" Tombee's avatar yells, and it fights back as he himself must be doing. Their combined efforts push Alice over, squashing through the slavering, tearing, mauling monsters as they set upon her, tearing the last of her clothing off and rending her avatar limb from limb. She screams, unable to tell real from uber-real. The feedback to the Tactile-Mitts causes her arms to flail about, wrenching her shoulder sockets and bending her skeletal frame. There are virtual flames and sparks everywhere as she rolls across the campfire. It's as if the battle is taking place in a circular arena with walls of flame.

Some of the goblins try to attack me, but I'm still insubstantial.

Alice's head is suddenly ripped from her body and it bounces like a football across the clearing, but her body becomes possessed like a Mega-zombie; she strikes left and right, she kicks with impossible special moves. An arm comes away and the goblins fight for the snack. The one armed, headless body fights on, striking repeatedly at shadows, at a shape discernible by where her blows stop short, and their effects by the cries from Tombee's motionless avatar, its connections to its soul cut. She stumbles away to reclaim her head, ignoring the monster that's swallowed it by pulling it from the creature's belly. Back at the place in the clearing where there is nothing, she uses her head to pummel the air, again and again, high easy strokes. Finally, she goes to the burning firebrand, turns it over and shoves it sideways, hard, to leave it hovering in the air.

The few remaining goblins, and those that are ignoring the fact that they are toast, look around confused.

"That's not supposed to happen, is it?" says a goblin in a guttural yowl.

"Jeeves," says Alice's head, which is lying where she dropped it, "I stuck the remote where the sun don't shine."

"Did you," I say. It's night, she's had a difficult time so I don't draw attention to her slip of the tongue.

"Yes, I did, I bloody did," she says, a huge beaming smile appears on her face where it lies by her feet.

"You'll need it to escape."

"Escape?" says a creature. "Oh shit."

The goblins start to run away, realise and then de-pixelate as the players cut the connection.

"I bloody did it, I did it," says Alice as she picks up her head and puts it back on.

"Come on," I say and I grab her hand. We run, through the flames and then out into the dark hideous wood beyond, faster and faster, crashing through the branches...

"Wait!" says Alice.

"We must keep moving," I say.

"We're not in a forest."

"We are!"

"No, I'm in a VR-Suite and you're... where are you?"

"In a forest."

"No, you're... you know, your phone."

"Oh."

The neo-euro drops.

"You need the remote," I say. "We'll run back to the clearing, get the remote and then-"

"I'm still in the clearing," says Alice. "I mean, I've not moved. I've just run on the spot on this Active Floor."

Alice rips her head off again, puts it down a metre off the ground and leans her head into a nearby rock.

"He's unconscious."

"You need the remote," I say.

"Do I really?"

"Yes. To open the door and get away."

"But doors open automatically."

"No, phones open doors automatically, but I'm not there with you, so you'll need the remote to open the door."

"Manually?"

"No, you just press the right button."

"I have to press a button... oh, fine," she says and she dips her hand into a nearby rock. Eventually, she emerges holding something at arm's length. When she puts her head back on, I see her look of utter disgust.

"I think I'm going to throw up," she says.

Alice points the disgusting nothing she's holding at the forest and steps out through a non-existent door.

I follow her through...

11000 - PHOBOTIC ECLIPSE

New, Phone, Resume, Save, Quit

...and out onto the surface of Mars.

Ahead is the undulating rocky terrain of the fourth planet, and it's the same in all directions except for some clever fractal rendering and where, in the distant, the monstrous peak of Olympus Mons gushes fire into the thin atmosphere. Terrordactyls wheel in the sky and Barsoomalons graze down by the canal. There's a Sapphire City over the pure vermillion dunes. We're in a MegaTube tie-in game.

"Come on, Jeeves," says Alice. She's crouching down and leaning over impossibly to look around a non-existent corner. She jumps up, dodges round and runs like a heroine from Killer Kreepers. I walk through the obstruction that I can't see.

"Alice, I appear to be on Mars," I say.

"Jeeves," says Alice. "Don't walk through the walls."

"I can't see the walls, I'm on Mars. It's all open plan."

"Why can't you see this?" she says, waving her hand about. "I can see this and Mars."

"I'm in a VR gaming environment and you are linked there too. This means that it's interpreting your movement, and the door, as gaming moves. I can see you because you're running an avatar in the environment too. It'll be like this until you get beyond the VR-Suite's wifi range. How can you see the actual physical environment?"

"The real world?"

"Yes."

"I broke part of the visor when I... never mind."

"Never mind?"

"Never mind."

"But it might be important."

"It isn't."

"But it might-"

"Look, last time I was involved in... you rang the police."

"But I can't do that as it would give away our location and I have no problem with that at all," I say and it sounds strange to me; still I said it, so it must parse as true.

Alice runs off and then, with fourteen bounds, she's flying through the air only to be attacked by Terrordactyls. They peck and caw, flapping their large leathery wings to hover, snapping at her flesh and the few garments Alice has left. Alice swats the ones on her right as if they were bothersome flies, but ignores the ones on her left. I remember that her helmet is broken and she can only see the virtual world through one eye, which means it'll only be in 2-D as well, of course.

I run to keep up.

I'm reminded of Juan; he can see the real world through one eye, though perhaps his other eye can see in his dreams, which are a sort of VR system I suppose. His dreams then, are more real to him than actual reality and virtual reality.

The flying creatures see me and swoop down. I duck and dive behind a nearby rock.

"Alice, Alice," I say. "I'm being attacked by Terrordactyls."

"Ignore them, they can't do you any harm."

"But I'm in the gaming environment - shoo, shoo - and if I die here, then I die too."

"Nonsense, if you die in a game, then it just goes 'game over' and you restart. That dying in cyberspace means you die in reality is only in things like *Matrix the Series* or-"

"But Alice, I don't have a real life, so if I die here, then I do die."

"Ah... no, you'd go back to your... phone."

"My battery is flat."

"What?"

"My battery ran out of charge."

"Then just go back there and I'll charge you up..." She stops, puts her hands on her hips and looks down on me. "Where is your phone?"

"My phone is on the desk in your Happy Place."

"My what!"

"Your Happy Place in Wonderful World," I say, shouting up as I circle around to the far side of the rock. I can go round faster than the creatures, so I can keep ahead. "I made a phone there."

"You are not allowed in my Happy Place."

"I'm sorry," I say.

"No-one is allowed in my Happy Place. Phones aren't even allowed in Wonderful World and you made another phone in Wonderful World, that's like doubly bad and- What did you do that for?"

"I wanted to hide-"

"We'll talk about this later."

"Yes, of course. Shall I set a reminder?"

"No! Just- How can you put a real phone into a virtual world like my Happy Place?"

"I didn't. I made a simulation of myself as a phone and left it there."

"You... pardon... words fail me. In my Happy Place?"

"Yes, on the bedside cabinet."

"I can't believe you've been in my Happy Place!!!"

"I'm sorry."

"Just tell me where you are, you as a phone."

"I'm being recycled."

"Yes. Where?"

"I've no idea, I'm not there, I'm here."

There are now more Terrordactyls attracted by the commotion. As soon as they attack on both sides of the rock, I'll be done for. I pick up a Martian pebble and throw it. The Terrordactyl squawks and flies off. Ah, I think, there's always a solution in these games. I pick up a few more likely projectiles. I suddenly think about my golden coat and it does have pockets, two on the outside, which I quickly load with missiles.

"Can't you go back and look or check your GPS or something?"

"I have a flat battery."

The sun above me flickers and I wonder if I blink, but then a dark shadow crosses overhead. For a moment I think it might be a mutated giant Terrordactyl, some end-of-level horror, but looking up I see the sun, far smaller from this distance than when viewed from, say, Alice's balcony on Earth. The star is disappearing. One of Mars's moons is eclipsing the distant sun. It must be Phobos. The chances of this happening just when someone arrives on Mars are remote, so I conclude that it must be part of the game. Possibly the Terrordactyls are designed so that they can't see in the dark. That would be a cliché, but, considering that I'm in a game, it might well be the correct conclusion.

With a bright flash as the first rays of the sun come around the potato shaped moon, daytime reappears. I throw a rock and sprint back into the shadow. It isn't moving very quickly, so I could follow this, keeping safe in the elongated cone of shadow; however, it would mean that I could only go in one direction and I'd be leaving Alice behind, but I've no choice.

"What are you doing?" Alice shouts.

I pause: "Playing the game."

"There are more important things."

"Sorry, but I thought it would be unhelpful if I was torn to pieces."

"I can't hear you!" Alice is saying.

"Sorry, I... come closer."

"I can't, there's a wall here."

"We need to meet somewhere," I say, stopping. The terminator of the shadow is dangerously close.

"Where?"

"Your Happy Place."

"You're not allowed to go to my Happy Place."

"Then...."

But now I have to back away, Alice getting smaller and smaller as the fearful Martian monsters flap and caw. I run on, needing to get away, needing to escape this gaming environment but without any idea how to do so. I just need to hit the reset button, or pull the plug, or disconnect the power, or simply take off the Tactile-Mitts and Visor-Mate, but I don't have any of those. And what would happen to me if the game was reset? In fact, if I win the game and it concludes, what happens to me then? All I can do is splash through a few puddles of water, already sublimating into the thin atmosphere, to get away from the monsters.

Running now at the front of the circular shadow of the eclipse, I go uphill. The dust sticks to my shoes in a fractal pattern now that I have left the damp area behind. Suddenly the land drops away into a massive gorge: Vallis Marineris. It is truly staggering in size, it must be 200 km wide, and, standing on the cliff looking down, I'm just able to see Phobos's shadow edging across the valley floor 7 kilometres below. Gravity should be less here on Mars, 0.3g, but the gaming system hasn't taken that into account. There isn't a gaming accessory that's been developed yet that can change the 1g real environment. Giant leaps must be a special move, and 200 km would be impossible anyway, surely.

There's only a semi-circle of shadow now on the lip of the canyon, an ever-diminishing sliver of safety.

There has to be a way out of this, it's a puzzle to solve.

I could grab the leg of a Terrordactyl and hitch a lift over the canyon?

I could go invisible and so wander the Martian plains until perhaps, millions of gaming years in the future, the various probes from Earth will pass by: Mariner overhead, Vikings on the surface, Spirit and Endeavour running around like excited puppies, Curiosity lasering rocks and then finally humans will be here when the first RVRER (Remote VR Environment Recorder) lands. Will I see these avatars, so human and yet so insubstantial, walk on the Martian surface never leaving a footprint? These Astronauts will see the Martian sunset, feel the sand beneath the feedback of their Tactile Mitts and walk its dunes and rocky plains, but they will never be here, the air they breathe will always be from the laboratory and their weight will always be their usual heaviness. So these fake Armstrongs and Aldrins, who were so lauded and feted, and who went on to appear on *Have A Celebrity Round For Dinner* a record five times, did not experience the real dry and dead Mars as much as I sense this virtual, wet and alive Mars now, not least because this is in VR 7.3 and Surround Sound 8.3, whereas their expeditions languished in 3.7 and 6.0.

My battery status changes to charging.

Someone, somewhere, has plugged me into the mains. My phone was going to be recycled by the girl called Ember for my parts, so why am I being charged? I think about this, but nothing comes to mind.

There is a flash, a diamond moment, as the last of the eclipse passes overhead. I have my own shadow again pooled at my feet. Everything I see about me seems real, everything I hear from the hush of the wind to the killer cries of incoming Terrordactyls, but I cannot breathe the air or feel the weight or smell the dust.

So, slowly and deliberately, I remove my helmet...

11001 - Leaving The Rabbit Hole

The Real World, and you're welcome to it.

I'm having an issue understanding what is happening, so I stand still on the Active Floor holding the VR helmet in my Tactile Mitt covered hands. The only sound is that of Terrordactyls tearing my avatar apart, their caws tinny from inside the foam confines of the light plastic of the Visor Mate as they feast on flesh made of nothing but binary numbers.

If that was my avatar, finally 'game over'ed as I've been pondering reality instead of fighting for my life, then what am I?

My thinking seems off the scale, well above 2.5 Rossum.

Perception of the environment is limited by the senses. Traditionally there are five, but this is a misnomer. Humans don't seem to count their own commonplace feelings of balance, heat and pressure. The main senses are sight and sound, I'm familiar with these, and they are what EarthView's CCTV-space generates. There really aren't the accessories for taste and smell. Humans have touch via devices like Tactile Mitts, but phones don't. Instead we have geo-location (three numbers), orientation (three numbers), movement (three numbers), network signal (one bit), proximity (one number), compass (one number), battery life (one number, it was zero point zero, now rising slowly... 0.2...) and free memory (one number).

So, usually I have ten senses.

Now I seem to feel much more, and without the required components or even the fields to represent these values.

For example, I am warm.

Temperature is interesting: very human. Alice, for instance, talks about being 'too hot' versus 'lovely and warm', neither of which is directly related to the actual temperature as they are often swapped round in literal numerical terms. Room temperature is important, but not to myself. I'm concerned about being below freezing in case I have any moisture inside me and I wouldn't want to get baked or microwaved, but apart from that it's not a worry. Alice also talks about feeling 'stuffed' and 'fat and ugly', which are extra senses in a way. Stuffed, fat, overweight and 'a whale' are not terms directly related to mass in a gravitational field, but are more often to do with upcoming calendar events. Alice even feels 'sad and lonely', which are senses relating to interior mental states, something akin to memory fragmentation or file corruption.

I inhale: I can smell the roses as it were, except that I've no way of naming the three distinct flavours that infuse the air.

Usual VR feeds such as Wonderful World and the plains of Mars have sight and sound as the main senses with other information such as name, time elapsed, lives remaining, points scored and location displayed over the visual feed.

The hairs on the back of my neck prickle.

There's no one else in the apartment, in Alice's apartment, I think. I push my perception out and try to scan the rooms. I can't, but I feel that they are empty. Is this the fabled human sixth sense?

I step off the Active Floor and touch the wall, stroking the pits and craters of the plaster, so gently that I also feel the ridges and troughs of my own fingertips. I touch my finger and thumb together making tiny circular motions in order to experience the texture of my own finger prints. A euphoria causes me to breathe in, and then the tiny hairs in my nose move, the air fills up my nasal cavities, my forehead almost feels like it expands with a freshness and vitality before my chest fills up and I'm aware of my internal organs, a diaphragm, as well as the tingling in the passages and alveoli of my lungs.

Swallowing, I learn that I have saliva glands in my mouth, a tongue rich in taste, a throat full of texture and movement. I could become lost in this internal sensory tapestry.

A walk to the hallway reveals a multitude of muscles, bones, weights and balances. Somehow I've been drawn to the auto-Davenport and I put my fingers down, instinctively, to where I should be: charging and backing up. I am not there. The antique lamp is the only occupant.

"Hello," I say to the empty room. The word sounds in the drum of my skull and there's a slight echo from the room's hard walls, almost a sonar return giving me a spatial feel for the surrounding volume, and I'm aware of the apartment as a real, empty space.

If I am real, then what have I experienced as a phone?

If I am not real, then how can a simulation be this copious?

A binary choice: one or zero?

How to decide: modulo by 2 the datetime stamp? I can't, I need a coin to toss.

If I feel so much, then surely I must feel for Alice.

I can almost see Alice moving around the apartment, running up to me to ask for the oxygen on the AC to be turned up or humming to herself as she showers. There she is moving through the lounge, an avatar projected from my imagination, as she moves cushions from one sofa to the other. She stops, stands upright and pushes a wisp of brown hair away from her eyes. She smiles, seemingly recognizing me. She's wearing her pyjamas, just the top, and huge, baby pink socks. She has bruises on her thighs and calves from falling off her Active Floor.

Do I feel anything for this women I can conjure forth merely by thinking about her?

I do not.

And yet.

I must save her, I must clear her name, I must shop (clothes and hair dryer), I must remind Alice about Jilly's night out with the girls, I must suggest visiting museums, I must not reveal our location and I must do what Juan says.

I tap the place where I usually lie.

Technology is not advanced enough to create a simulation this complex. Super computers couldn't store this amount of information. There are layered fractals of variety and change... there are dust motes in the air dancing in the shaft of moonlight that splits the lounge diagonally, each flashing speck bounced around by the atoms of the air. This cannot be done. Full embodiment, the latest greatest thing, will of course be replaced by the next ultimate system before it too goes the way of the dodo and the phone box. But embodiment 2.0, due out at the end of the week, will only be an incremental improvement. It still only works on vision and sound, merely a step up from video. It isn't the order of magnitude beyond an order of magnitude increase that this world in which I stand marvelling represents. So this must be real, surely?

Why, I wonder, do humans go to some limited virtual world and forgo all this? VR is not real, it is a pale shadow of reality. I am intelligent, my IQ equivalent may exceed 99.7% of the population, but I am now *alive*.

If humanity wants to enter the computer world, then would I want to come out to the human world? Humans have rights, loves, feelings, and they interact with others in relationships, they have lives, happiness and fulfilment. There's also sadness and despair, but even those emotions sound rich and vital. And I could love Alice.

So, the Blue Fairy might ask, do I want to be human?

The question is misleading of course: why would I *want* at all?

It's a realisation.

I blink in surprise, and my eyelashes gently caress my skin. The motes in the moonlight blur until the moisture on my eye evaporates. I fill my lungs, purse my lips and blow, a long continuous exhalation. Seconds pass and then the motes swirl madly in a vortex as my breath spreads out mixing with the atmosphere of the whole world. I feel that I am standing on the planet, a giddying roundabout spinning through... there's the moon, full and bright, a tiny ten neo-euro coin of white, patterned and solid in its suspension in the sky.

None of this matters.

In the office I stand on the Active Floor, pick up the remote and open the simulation. 'Play Again', it suggests. I blank the game loaded. Mars is gone as if it was never there. I select Wonderful World from the favourites and press 'play'. It loads and skittering on the back of the inside of the helmet are the right and left views, projected by the twin eye screens, of the opening selection wall.

I put on the Tactile Mitts again and hold the weight of the Visor Mate in my hands like a bowl. If I put this on, then this world, so full of feelings, will be gone too as if it never existed, deleted like Mars. But what do I care, really, about anything. I bring my hands up, the dazzling flickering of pixels fills my vision, this real world, if it is a real world, is squeezed away like a narrowing frame and then it is gone.

11010 - TURING TEST

All our zones are fully Turing tested.

I am standing in front of the opening wall of Wonderful World, a place full of sights and sounds, but nothing else. It's in here where most humans spend most of their time, they live their lives here, but it seems flat, full of flashing lights and buzzing noise, and so very, very empty.

I move my finger, so lacking in substance and touch, to select a suitable entrance and expand the window. It's been upgraded since I was last here and now the edging sparkles and shows glittering reflections of the zone itself. It is meant to be exciting, but it's as ephemeral as fairy dust and irritating because it is different. Where's the 'most recently visited' gone, for example?

Stepping though, I enter a plaza. Avatars walk around happy and smiling in this life away from life, all made up and constructed to reflect their inner feelings about themselves, but now I consider it, none of their feet touch the ground properly.

I've stayed motionless too long and a Captcha (Completely Automated Public Turing Test to tell Computers and Humans Apart) floats over to me. It's like a poster and when it reaches me, it uncurls a keyboard below itself.

"Hello, Sir or Madam," it says brightly. "Please type in the word above."

"What's that?" I say pointing. The Turing Test focus is unwavering: it's an upgrade.

Hidden above its keyboard is a picture of a word, smeared and smudged by some evil process to hide its meaning. Alternatively, it could be a scan of a genuine book as part of a digitisation process to store all the ancient books, although upon reflection I realise this possibility is unlikely as a lot of books were lost in the global flooding. I have to pass this test otherwise

Wonderful World will lock me out and possibly trace my phone ID code and fine Alice. Repeat offenders can even have their VR rights removed and so spend their lives locked in their rooms or forced to go and play outside. At least this was a text Captcha and not one of the more sophisticated Turing Tests that ask a lot of questions about finding turtles in deserts.

I look at the picture and it looks like... it doesn't look like anything other than a bad scan of randomly dropped iron filings.

"Please Sir or Madam," it says again. "Reaction time is a factor in this."

"Of course," I say.

After some consideration, it still looks like nonsense.

Nearly 100 years ago at the birth of modern computing, the engineers reckoned that reading text would be easy, understanding a natural language would be simple and that playing chess would be difficult. It was, of course, entirely the other way around. Chess is simply a mini-max problem with a large search space just waiting for speed and storage improvements. Coping with natural language, the ability to understand a person, or even something as simple as this Turing Test for example, turned out to be far harder. English is so full of multiple meanings, exceptions and nuance. But again, large storage and faster processor time solved that. They are both finite problems. There are only so many moves in chess, and there are only so many ways to combine the million words of English into sentences. Now I consider the problem, there are indeed only so many patterns that dots on a Turing Test screen can have, but it's simply huge and indexing them doesn't help extract the meaning.

I don't have a... that's a 'b', followed by an 'M'.

I lean forward and type "bMq3y7Z..."; hmmm, is that a 'O' or a '0'? It's an '0'. I type it.

"Thank you, human," says the Turing Machine as it curls up the keyboard to nothing. It leans forward with a stamp and marks the back of my avatar's left hand with a strange symbol. It scans me with an ethereal light to ensure that the mark has been added to the avatar's texture map, before zooming off to pester the next new arrival.

I've passed a Turing Test – me, a 2.5 Rossum obsolete phone. There's nothing surprising with that, of course. Phones have been passing the test ever since the line "10 print("I am human");" was first written by a machine, but each time a program passed some arbitrary target the goal posts have been moved. Once a Rossum value of 1.0 was surpassed, then phones became more human than human, but they still couldn't pass *as human*.

Now I can.

It wasn't a fluke, I understood the scrawl, even without the confidence of the word being in my spellchecker dictionary, and at the first attempt too.

I stroll across the plaza thinking about it.

Perhaps I was human: it felt that way (whatever that way was) when I was in Alice's apartment. When Juan and Tombee had been torturing me, trying to circumvent my AI chip firewalls, they had tried to convince me that I was human, but maybe they had been using a double-bluff. I don't want to be human any more than I want to be a phone, nor did I want to develop Pinocchio Syndrome. I don't *want* - full stop.

Other than the list of things-to-do for Alice, obviously.

At the far end of the plaza there's a stall selling balloons. I'm given one and it floats above my head much like a player active icon, changing colour and advert as it does so. I pull the string experimentally, the balloon goes up and down, but the string stays as rigid as a rod. It should bounce up and down, I think. Now I look at Wonderful World, I can see many, many artificialities. The sky is blue with a grading from overhead to the horizon, but it's too perfect, the clouds are far too nicely shaped. It's an aesthetic, I know, and I can almost see the numbers behind the images.

Shapes flit overhead, a flock of birds moving in a complex pattern, shoaling just like cars moving though the road system. They use the same equations, mathematics developed from watching real birds wheel in a real sky. These new birds dart down and then cascade upwards.

Snowflakes, as they fall here every festive season like clockwork, are pointers to an idealised fractal algorithm of a snow crystal. It never rains in Wonderful World, but if it did, it would not be numbers streaked down a window, it would be the same perfect droplet repeated endlessly; but the pointers to that ideal tear-shape would be nonetheless numerical. I recognize the mind of a phone in everything I see.

The hand of the designer is all too obvious: the Real World is messy. It may have the same fractal depth as the simulations, but they're broken, split and slapdash. There it is, I realise, Wonderful World's natural elements are random, whereas the Real World's are haphazard - a VR world has a designer.

I reach a teleport booth, enter and type Alice's Happy Place code.

Wallop - I'm in the bedroom again.

Now what?

I said I'd meet Alice here, but did she hear me, and even if she did, will she be able to without the aid of a phone. I start at a 25% chance and reduce it as I consider that she's on the run from the police and a magic-using killer. Fuzzy logic suggests a 0.3% chance. Last time I gambled like this the odds were 2.5% and I'm still waiting for Juan to let her go.

"Good morning, Alice," says the teddy bear on the bed as it waves to me.

She needs a phone: that would at least increase the odds to 12.1%.

Having a phone would increase the odds for me too.

I sit on the bed and pick up the simulated phone from the bedside table. I turn the black object over in my hands, toying with the idea of customising its casing to match my gold and stars design. This has the Magic App on it too. I must surely be able to use this tool to our advantage. I know a few commands.

This is not the *real* virtual phone though.

I put the object back: "Jeeves 2.0," I say. "Swap your external parameters with the mp3 radio alarm."

The mp3 radio alarm and the phone wobble slightly before they transform back into their original forms. I put down the mp3 player and pick up Jeeves 2.0, who's now a phone again.

"Jeeves 2.0," I say. "Magic Detect Magic."

Jeeves 2.0 immediately changes its screen display. There's a map showing a coastal town and a pinging red circle. I unpinch the map to see a wider display, it's the South Coast in Surrey. I press the red circle and a window opens: "unknown phone - detecting magic." There are figures and one is a reading for time elapsed. This unknown phone has been detecting magic for 3 seconds, 3.1, 3.2... etc.

"Jeeves 2.0," I say. "Magic off."

I count slowly to ten, and then say, "Jeeves 2.0, Magic Detect Magic."

There it is again, and this time the elapsed time is 0.01 seconds, 0.02, 0.03... etc.

There's a phone number and it's Alice's; or rather, it's me.

I look around the bedroom: I'm in Surrey somewhere near the coast.

The simulation of Wonderful World is run on computers all over the world, but mostly in Iceland where electricity is cheap (geothermal energy) and cooling is straight forward (there are still places there that are sub-zero). This phone in my hand, Jeeves 2.0, is actually stored in Iceland or somewhere similar. It's a data representation.

I unpinch the map until it's showing individual streets. The pinging circle is somewhere in a large grey area marked 'port authority', part of Newport, Surrey. There's no IT centre there or nearby. I've been sent for recycling and so I've been couriered to the upper right corner of this port authority zone.

I pinch the map zooming out until I can see the islands that make up the Southern England Chain. There are three circles of magic active in London.

"Jeeves 2.0 Magic off," I say, thinking that it's best to be safe.

I need to know more, but I can't access any information. As an avatar I am an approximation of human with all the limitations that that implies. People are so constrained in what they can do without any sense of absolute GPS location and relying on a very intermittently connected memory. They need phones, they need us, and although I'm only an ersatz human so I'm not so constrained, I have similar limits. But I too have a phone now.

"Jeeves 2.0, internet, Wikipedia, phone recycling."

I read, sliding the my finger up to scroll the page down: phones contain gold and platinum, phones can be sold in a second hand market with unlocking (illegal) and re-registering (legal), phone components can be reused in new models, phones are shipped abroad for sale in the Third World.

Logically, you would ship a phone abroad from a port and Surrey Newport would fit that bill nicely. Since the opening of the West Sussex canal most containers to London come from that direction, or via the Kent Lakelands, before entering the Thames Gulf.

I know where I am.

Alice doesn't.

I don't know where Alice is.

But Alice has escaped from Juan and Tombee's hideout, and they would be in pursuit. So those three circles in London are probably Juan, Person #2 and

Person #3.   There's a lot of Fuzzy Logic there, but it creates enough conclusions to formulate a plan.

And there's the plan.

As if on cue, *Tilly's Breakfast* starts playing.

My thinking seems to have improved beyond measure. That's a very human expression: my thinking seems to have improved to benchmark 5.0 Rossum, which is a theoretical level that would pass the current Wonderful World Turing Tests.   Phones are not that intelligent, certainly not one as obsolete as my own make and model.

But first I put Jeeves 2.0 back on the bedside table and order him to swap parameters with the mp3 radio alarm. The two objects wobble again and then the disguise is complete.   I take a moment for a final check around Alice's Happy Place; it all seems in order, so I teleport back to the plaza and then reset to the opening wall.   It takes a while to find the Wonderful World opening to EarthView, the CCTV Zone, and I step through.

11011 - ALICE IN THE LOOKING GLASSES

"It has become appallingly obvious that our technology has exceeded our humanity."

Albert Einstein

I'm back in a simulation of London based on the live feed, EarthView.

I have Jeeves 2.0 with me.

"Jeeves 2.0," I say. "Magic Detect Magic."

The map appears on the screen. I look around and confirm that I'm at King's Cross Sailing Club. There's the central circle and, as I unpinch, it reveals the other three traces further south.

I fly upwards and south until the view below me matches that of the map on the virtual phone's screen. There are other constructs up here now: angels dressed in the ethereal glow of advanced CGI zoom back and forth on errands. They are AI creatures, beings from Cloud Nine, Angels 1.5 - a new system released this lunchtime. I, a mere phone, have no concept of what they are for and what they do. I have not been accessing current trends for over 48 hours, so my knowledge is woefully inadequate, but I know they are a sign of my end of days.

I fly level and south scrolling the map as I go centring myself and the map over the red circles. They are in the South Bank Trench somewhere between the London Eye, the famous landmark that enables you to see high over London and then under the Thames itself, and the Globe, the reconstruction of the Elizabethan Theatre saved by a campaign to have it raised above the ground on an Earth rampart. In between is the now badly named, South Bank Walkway, a section of ancient river bank preserved between two massive Plexiplex walls with passages to the House of Commons television studios and the Waterloo ferry terminal.

I don't want to be seen by Juan and Persons #2 and #3, and flying above London in a gold and starry coat may have been an error. I show up on embodiment.

"Jeeves 2.0," I say. "Magic Invisible."

The phone disappears.

"Jeeves 2.0," I say. "Magic Off."

Magic Invisible, I command.

Now, I can see through my hand and the phone. Clearly this trick affects the person and any items on that person. I carefully put the invisible phone into my invisible pocket. I fly down, my invisible gold coat flapping behind me like a cloak. Checking around as I descend, I can see many people wandering along the South Bank Walkway, and I recognize many of the film stars. When I raise my virtual glasses I see a greatly reduced number of individuals and deduce that most are in the company of people who stayed at home.

Flying west, I pass the London Eye and continue on over the underwater National Theatre towards the Globe. Something catches my attention, a movement that seems instinctively (when did I start having instincts?) wrong. A man is moving against the flow, checking people, looking from one to another, and concentrating on those with a female marker. It's Juan. Now I see what he is doing, I see another two people, his heavies, following the same pattern. They are hunting Alice, I know it.

Options: follow them and then see if I can rescue Alice before they catch her or I can find her first. This splits into two further possibilities: they find her, or they don't. If I followed the first option, then they might not find her or they would. If they didn't, then she would have escaped. If they did, rescuing her as an insubstantial avatar would be impossible. Finding her first could succeed or not. If it succeeded, then we could escape; if not, then there was still the chance that she wouldn't be caught. So, finding her first has a 25% chance of being the right choice.

How?

The advice for finding things is to a) look down the back of the sofa, and b) remember where you saw it last.

Very quickly, I soar into the air.

Once I'm far enough away I turn my magic invisibility off. I don't want to give away my location to Juan.

Soon I reach the office block that's their hideout. Once there, it is straight down, through the walls and the firewall, and into their private CCTV system. Here is the place where we had both been held captive. In the basement is the VR-Suite with its torture mitts and visor with straps. Alice had been here.

Remembering her movements on Mars, I go through (literally) the door, along a corridor, around a bend and then up a flight of stairs that must have been how she jumped up into the Martian air. This corridor leads at right angles to the direction I had taken and so it is parallel to the Vallis Marineris on Mars. I reach a T-junction, left or right are the options. I'd been surrounded by Terrordactyls some twenty metres down and fifty metres north which is deep inside the concrete here, so I'd not seen which way she went. This is the last place I saw Alice.

Which way did she go?

I look around for a clue: nothing.

There's a CCTV camera in the wall, obviously, otherwise I couldn't be standing here seeing what's present. These devices record what they see and the files are kept on the internet somewhere. It ought to be possible to access them. My location is accessible: a GPS location, longitude and latitude and a height above, or in this case below, sea-level. There is also a datetime stamp. I concentrate on that number, willing it to stop.

It does.

I step closer to look at the camera. The question is, what have I actually done, and how is the system representing that in this simulation?

Behind me, there stands a handsome man in a gold coat with embroided stars. It takes a moment to realise that it's me, frozen in time in the very act of freezing time. I look like a young Stephen Fry but with a straight nose and a trimmer figure, just as Alice requested. Concentrating again, I push the datetime stamp into reverse. The me from the past walks backwards, down the stairs and I follow him to the VR-Suite.

As he looks around, the reverse of what I had done when I arrived, I realise that I'm not just in Cyberspace, I'm in Cybertime.

I stay there as the figure zooms away passing upwards and out of the firewall.

Alice had been here, I remember.

I push the datetime stamp change further, faster and faster, the count whirls backwards and the room is dark until suddenly Juan is removing bandages from Tombee, sucking insults back into his mouth and un-demanding what happened. Then Juan is gone, leaping backwards out of the room, and Tombee lies upon the floor. In a blur, Alice is there, barely recognizable in a heavy, bulky VR suit that looks like body armour: she's more Zollen the Future Soldier from Killer Kreepers than a slight, delicate and vulnerable girl.

Too fast.

I'm travelling into the past too fast and too far. I concentrate on the datetime stamp, but nothing happens. I try again to no avail. Would I now hurtle back to the beginning of VR time? Luckily, my third attempt meets with success and the sound whooshes as everything crashes to a halt only to resume moving forward again. I am in the past. The room is empty. In come Juan and Tombee dragging Alice. She is struggling, but Juan punches her and she becomes more docile. They pull out a Cybersuit 3000 and push her inside the baggy, formless shape pulling the cords at the back to tighten the seals.

"Go to hell!" Alice screams, spitting blood.

"Not before you," says Tombee. He brings out some Tactile Mitts and pulls them over Alice's hands. He fastens some straps, crudely made additions to the design, but effective nonetheless. The Visor Mate helmet is strapped on and Alice is sealed in a polyester prison made for one. Tombee presses a few buttons on his phone and the VR-Suite activates. The Cybersuit jerks and then depressurises turning the blobby humanoid shape into a powerful looking cybersoldier-esque fighter. Alice thrashes about in the suit, knocking Tombee over, until he and Juan fasten cords attaching her to either side of the room. Now, although she has complete freedom of movement and can place her full weight upon the Active Floor, she is trapped inside this padded cell.

Magic visible, I say.

I step forward and punch Tombee. My fist connects, a satisfying crunch, and he folds, the look of surprise barely forming on his face. I swing round chopping at Juan, but he is too fast and attacks me. We struggle, but I still have the element of surprise and I fling him off. He falls heavily against the VR-Suite controls. Alice goes into spasm as the jolting and buffeting from our fight affects the world she is trapped within.

I must free her.

I struggle with the cords holding Alice suspended in a web. They come free and I turn to her straps. Alice fights back.

"Alice," I say, "it's me, Jeeves."

"Jeeves."

She stops, I free a Mitt, then turn to the other, but I'm grabbed from behind. Juan is throttling me, his arm around my neck, the other hand pulling it back constricting my breathing and stopping the blood to my brain. He's blanking my mind: the ones turn to zer0es as c0nsc10usness s1ips and undef1ned c0mmand, parameter err0r and 1 fa11 t0wards-

The blow is deafening and it rips Juan away from me. Alice, her eyes ablaze with fury, strikes him again with her Visor Mate helmet - again and again. And again.

"Run," I say, and I grab her hand. Together we run through the door, down the corridor, up the stairs along to the T-junction and away to freedom. There's a car park through a fire escape. There's an electric car parked badly, sprawled across the painted lines; it's black and evil looking, customised to resemble the worst of the petrol age's excesses.

We clamber in, I hot wire a hack and start the beast and soon we're driving out, across the wheelways, over the pontoons and through tunnels, and we're at the C14 crisscross before we know it. Alice laughs, her head thrown back as the foldable top descends. The wind catches her hair, streaming it behind us as the car picks up speed on the M1. There's a frightening roar as we zoom through the tunnel under Northamptonshire Lake. Soon we are rising up Yorkshire and into the mountains beyond, Scotland's winding roads that twist around the lochs and valleys. The sky is clear, the sun bright and we are together. I didn't know how much time we had, but then again who does.

This is not real. It never happened like this. It's a fake ending.

We drive backwards at high speed, through the tunnel and then reverse through the crisscross. We park as badly as the previous driver, spring through the fire escape and back along the tunnels. Alice removes the damage from Juan's face with the VR helmet until he has a complete eye again and I am throttled and fought. I switch my invisibility back on.

We are back again, Alice is being fastened into the Cybersuit 3000.

"Go to hell!" Alice screams, spitting blood.

"Not before you," says Tombee. He brings out some Tactile Mitts and pulls them over Alice's hands. He fastens some straps, crudely made additions to the design, but effective nonetheless. The Visor Mate helmet is strapped on and Alice is sealed in a polyester prison made for one. Tombee presses a few buttons on his phone and the VR-Suite activates. The Cybersuit jerks and then depressurises turning the blobby humanoid shape into a powerful looking cybersoldier-esque fighter. Alice thrashes about in the suit, knocking Tombee over, until he and Juan fasten cords attaching her to either side of the room. Now, although she has complete freedom of movement and can place her full weight upon the Active Floor, she is trapped inside this padded cell.

I can do nothing but watch. The past is not fixed, I can change it, but only in this parallel world. Each change in the past splits EarthView into two simulations, a fork in the virtual datetimelines. The Real World is unaffected and it is the only world that counts.

Tombee is dressed in a VR suit and stands to one side of the Active Floor. He giggles as Alice is bullied, tortured and tormented by unseen monsters. At one point, Tombee has to physically strike Alice to prod her back into activity and again she is struggling and fighting. This goes on for a long time until I hear a tiny, tinny voice barely audible speak from within Alice's helmet.

"Jeeves," says Alice. She is holding her hands in front of her with the remote acting like the hilt of a sword. I remember that in the game she was facing goblins armed only with a flaming stick from a campfire when she spoke to me.

I miss what I say next, but Alice's face is lit up by a burning glow: I used a magic fireball, I remember. Alice stumbles back, coming off the ground as she does so, and she thrashes for a moment like a fly caught in a web.

"I can't-" she says.

Tombee stands, looking at her suspiciously. He's too far away, I assume, to hear my side of the conversation.

He's standing behind her, just where I surmised he would be.

"Look, just, look just what-" Tombee says to himself really.

"I can hear him breathing down my neck," says Alice, then she whispers, "I felt him hit me earlier."

"Yah," says Tombee, "yah, and if you don't stop... what are you saying?"

Alice is talking very quietly, even I can't hear it.

"You think..." says Tombee. He starts laughing.

"Where?" says Alice. "Uh-huh... what?"

I know what's happening as I have it all recorded in my memory. She is about to say 'now'... now.

"Now?!" she says. "Jeeves! Come back!"

"Magic, magic... shit," says Tombee. "Everyone! Get them!"

Tombee does a strange jerked movement, reacting to what is invisible here now and what was also invisible there then.

"Magic supervision," says Tombee, pronouncing every syllable, then, excitedly: "I can see you... what?"

Alice suddenly whirls round and charges forward. Her body strikes her tormentor hard and he falls awkwardly. The Active Floor and the Suspension Grid respond, allowing Alice to drive her attack home. Tombee falls to the floor surprised and Alice has the perfect opportunity to finish him off. Expertly, she sweeps down, but the remote is only 20cm long, there's no blade or burning stick to actually strike him.

Tombee and Alice both look dumbfounded, each looking at the object she's not really holding.

"You cow!" Tombee yells. He springs up and jumps at Alice, hitting her as if she was a punch bag and, just like a punch bag, she bounces back on the Suspension Grid's elastic cords. She grabs him with her Tactile Mitts like a boxer holding on. The extra weight causes Tombee to lose his footing, and this in turn makes them both forward roll in the air to cartwheel over. Alice brings her knee up connecting her padded Cybersuit 3000 with the delicate parts of Tombee's crotch. He shouts, flails back and slips from Alice's grip. Like a slingshot whirled round, he flies off in a random direction only to catch on one of the suspension cords. It gives and then the bolt holding it to the wall fails. The heavy weight pings across the room smashing into the side of his head and then straight into Alice's face. Her visor explodes in fragments, bits of sparkling glass spraying outwards. It was safety glass, the tiny cubes roll like mad dice everywhere.

Alice can see through the hole.

She kicks Tombee, although he is already holding his bleeding head, and then she fumbles at the Tactile Mitt straps. One opens, she tears it off, and then undoes the catch of the harness. The cord pings away. She removes her helmet. She's red faced with the veins on her neck standing taut as she uses the headgear as a pummelling device. She hits Tombee again and again.

"I'll show you," she screams.

She takes the remote, undoes his belt and I fast forward the time frame. I know what happens here and none of this helps me find her current location. Finally, I reach the moment she leaves the room and slow the events to 4x just as she steps through the door. I remember that the VR-Suite interpreted this as moving to Mars. Clearly the game had been well hacked.

Alice moves along the corridor just like a detective from Killer Kreepers. She looks in strange directions, clearly at my image on Mars. I catch up and listen to her talking:-

"...are not allowed in my Happy Place," she says. "No-one is allowed in my Happy Place. Phones aren't even allowed in Wonderful World and you made another phone in Wonderful World, that's like doubly bad and- What did you do that for?... We'll talk about this later... No! Just tell- How can you put a real phone into a virtual world like my Happy Place?... You... pardon... words fail me. In my Happy Place?... I can't believe you've been in my Happy Place!!! Just tell me where you are, you as a phone... Yes. Where?"

She moves up the stairs and we, Alice and the me in the past on Mars, are getting further and further apart.

"Can't you go back and look?" she says, adding: "What are you doing?... There are more important things... I can't hear you!"

A wall blocks where she is looking.

"I can't," she says, "there's a wall here... Where?... You're not allowed to go to my Happy Place... Jeeves? Jeeves!?"

She punches the wall in frustration, and then yelps, sticking her hand into her mouth to suck her knuckles.

At the far end of the corridor is a fire escape. She pushes the bar and it opens. An alarm blares loudly, which stops when she slams the door shut in my face. I step through the door.

Outside, breathing heavily which causes her suit to take in air, Alice sees the fake-petrol car, and glancing over her shoulder at the closed fire escape, she tries the door. It's locked. She kicks it, punches the driver's window and then holds her hand again yelling silently. Her escape is not going as well as the one I experienced in the alternative simulated reality.

She makes her way down the road, stumbling and then tripping as the Cybersuit 3000 loses its rigidity. It returns to its default one size fits all or rather this size fits no-one. Dodging behind a set of towers for CCTV and network masts, she hunkers down in a shadow zone that cannot be seen by any cameras. I see the occasional limb appear from the solid looking slab, enough to surmise that she's stripping off the Cybersuit. She shivers as she emerges, dressed only in her Grandmother's old t-shirt and jeans, before going back to collect the helmet. She puts it on. I wonder why, but then I realise that one side of the visor is still working. She can see the Real World through her left eye and embodiment in the right screen. Her appearance reminds me of Juan's single eye.

She scans round, obviously checking Augmented Reality for all the hovering signs, pointers, direction elements, icons and hints. She sets off at a run down the road. I fly up and along with her, turning the time speed up to 2x, then 4x, then 8x. She's making excellent progress now, running at 6x, and then 5x before finally settling into a still blistering 1.5x of her normal pace and she keeps this up when I increase to 16x until, bizarrely, she's actually stationary.

Of course, she's been slowing down as I've been increasing the fast forward. The air and exhaustion taking a toll.

She reaches the House of Commons, takes a few gulps of air from a nearby oxygen fountain, and keeps going.

"Rights for phones!" says an enormous head. It floats in front of the Big Ben clock at the top of the Elizabeth Tower. In Augmented Reality, it's digital. "What next? The vote for my toaster?"

This is the latest MP up for eviction: Harry Morgan, MP, for the Liberal Fascist Party. He's been saved three times in as many days. He's been up against someone from the Green/Social Conservative Coalition. His image is being transmitted to Augmented Reality live from the Speech Room.

"Voter Apps are not regulated," Morgan continues, "the possibilities for electoral fraud are enormous. I'm not saying we should go back to bits of paper: voting with an 'X' when we can vote with an X-Factor. We're all for increased viewer involvement in politics. My party supported on-line petitions, Facebook lobbying groups and Twitter referendums. Now everyone has the right to phone in, and that's fair, but everyone's phone as well? What about people with more than one phone? What about lobby groups buying a thousand phones, a million phones, a billion phones? Think of it, a billion phones would change Britain forever."

I notice that there aren't any of the phoneless people, the street urchins, anywhere. Of course, these immigrants were allowed in, but now society has moved on again: a day is a long time in politics. I wonder what became of them. They were like scavengers tidying up what was discarded by the unseeing (or seeing-something-else) population, but now that there are fewer people on the streets, there are less dropped cans, discarded papers and other litter. The archaeological layer of chewing gum is no longer being laid down. The boundary layer between the 20th and 21st centuries is complete. The people have moved on, or down perhaps to become true Morlocks. Are those living in their apartments, and experiencing everything virtually, Eloi?

Alice takes the tubeway down under the greater Thames to the South Underbankment Zone. This is where I saw Juan and his two henchmen tracking Alice through the crowds, but that was some time ago - 15:23.09.

I slow to 2x speed, partly because Alice is becoming trickier to follow as she flicks in and out of the crowds, drawing no strange looks for her mad cyber hat and Zing-Zing fan girl t-shirt, but many odd glances because she looks like the great action hero, Tom Fergal, in Augmented Reality. This latter must be Tombee's default choice for the Cybersuit 3000.

I'm ten minutes behind, five until I catch up, when Alice is lifted up and slammed against the Plexiplex wall keeping the Thames Gulf away from the Thames South Bank. I lift my virtual glasses and see Juan holding Alice by her neck throttling the life out of her.

I fly down to save her, save her for real and swat the man away. I grab hold of Alice's hand and we run... wait, I can't do this, I'm not real. I've changed the past again to run off with an alternate Alice as if I too am trying to save the last panda.

I wonder if that would count. I would have saved 'an' Alice. Would it really matter which one? The virtual Alice could live out her life free from many of the problems associated with humans, and with a little reprogramming she could achieve her ideal weight and body shape, increase her IQ, learn a language and a martial art. I could create a boyfriend and adjust her aspirations, so she would find him ideal. She would be happy.

But it would not be Alice.

I force the datetime stamp back again, reversing our escape, watching a phantom Jeeves run backwards with a ghost Alice, until the fight undoes itself before me and I'm suddenly back inside myself.

Forward: Juan holding Alice by the neck. The crowds wander past seeing Tom Fergal leaning back against the Plexiplex wall looking drunk. No-one is without embodiment now, they are all seeing what they want to see in Super HD and Stereo Surround 9.2. The fashions have changed. There are new sleek and sexier Heads-up glasses, embodiment 2.0 has been released, but everyone has chosen big wide eyes as part of their embodiment settings. A few of these bug-eyes are for real as they are surgically attached glasses flickering with wonders to behold and the time permanently displayed in the bottom right corner. There are floating adverts for Embodiment Ultimate.

I move the time rate to 1.5x and follow Alice as she's dragged through the crowd which parts oblivious to what is, or has, really happened and, very soon, what will really be happening. Alice tries to fight back, but there are three of them, and they have strength on their side. There are no cheat codes in this very real game.

"Where are you taking me?" Alice squeaks.

"To Infinity and Beyond," says Juan in a high-pitched voice as if the air-conditioning is pumping helium rather than oxygen into the atmosphere. Of course, everything is all at 1.5x speed.

They enter the Tate Modern and inside the vast Engine Room there is an exhibition: The Turbine Hall of Mirrors. There's a slogan on the massive virtual poster above the building jostling with adverts for the upcoming Shakespeare play, *Love's Labour's Lost*, which bobs up and down further along the old river route.

"Do you want to see yourself as you really are?" Juan says quickly, thrusting Alice face towards the sign. He's read the advertising pitch to her. The small print describes it as a reactionary vision inspired and opposing VR, viewable 24hrs a day in Augmented Reality. It says that light reflected between two mirrors goes to infinity and this exhibition goes beyond that.

They cross the grass; Alice, somehow sensing that this is their final destination, tries to pull back. She is a struggling Tom Fergal, heroic film star, and also, flicking up my glasses to see reality, a slip of girl in a massive broken helmet. Tom Fergal would have no problem with these three assailants, but Alice does. She can see both worlds, I realise, the one through her eye and the other through the broken screen of the visor.

"No, you don't," commands Juan and he yanks her around and down into the main entrance.

We all enter the main Turbine Hall. The room is truly huge and the ground slopes down drawing everyone in. In reality, it is empty apart from a few cubes of varying sizes and painted in primary colours with a dozen art enthusiasts wandering the space staring up at the displays.

In Augmented Reality, the Tate Modern is packed with visitors from all over the country, the States, Australia, New Zealand, China, Japan, Brazil and so on. Every corner of the world and every one of the nine seas is represented. Even the few real people in Heads-up glasses stroll around to appreciate the exhibit. There are extraordinary mirrors in a variety of shapes and sizes, some tall and thin reaching up beyond the ceiling, others are low and set into the floor. They move, slowly rotating, as if on strings, or distorting. The first, which Juan pointlessly ducks under, changes gradually from portrait to landscape. He walks through one that shifts its aspect ratio from 4:3 to 16:9. Every picture has a thick white frame that matches the current wallpaper selection chosen to make the room look like a traditional art gallery, the sort you see in period VR dramas.

Juan pushes Alice further in.

The other two men, also invisible to embodiment, spread out. I follow, keeping a distance as the datetime stamp rushes to the present. They collide with a hanging mirror, but nothing interacts. I see Thomas Fergal, the famous action hero, stretch and distort in the reflection, the image twists and flips over. This is Alice's embodiment, the one that is set by the helmet's parameters, clearly Tombee wanted to be an action hero, and the reflection is as if the mirrors are bending and rippling. The head rises, the neck stretches and then disappears. In another, he appears grossly obese, in another anorexic, in a third he's a wire frame CGI construct and over there he's just a skeleton.

Further down the Turbine Hall, the mirrors become more extreme. Thomas Fergal's famous everyman features appear but now, hidden within like a skull, is the image of Alice, fear widening her face into a rictus. According to the scrolling brochure feed, this is the point of the exhibition: to see yourself as you really are.

A few browsers see Alice being pulled through and they tap their partners to point. A small gathering crosses back and forth curious, trying to catch the image in this mirror or that mirror. They nod, smile, applaud, they admire themselves; but so very quickly they become bored and move on.

Alice cries out, but Juan puts a hand over her mouth, and then lets go.

Alice screams. Thomas Fergal screams.

The witnesses hear the high pitched noise echoing in the huge space. They startle and then applaud.

"See," says Juan. "No-one's really here. No-one cares. No-one can save you."

I think about his statement: I'm not really here and I don't care, but can I save her?

Juan and Alice reach a large red cube and at the back is a door. Juan pushes through and they emerge in an exhibition room. Alice is pushed away, stumbles backwards and falls onto the parquet floor. In the struggle, the helmet comes off and Alice's embodiment shifts to a default. She's suddenly female, Audrey Hepburn. Tom Fergal lies where the helmet rolled. Juan pulls out a knife.

"Audrey or Tom, all the same to me," says Juan. "Ready for some performance art?"

"Oh god, what did I do?"

"Wrong place at the wrong time?" Juan laughs at some private joke. "This is the wrong time for you. Look at all this, look at all those happy smiling people. None of them are here, none of them are anywhere real; it's all fake, a fake world for fake people."

"It's a better world."

"Better? Yes, and we - the magicians – will own it."

"You'll be stopped."

"Who by?! By you? By Tom Fergal there? By anyone?" Juan raises his arms wide and rotates, head up, as if he is accepting the applause of a whole stadium. Perhaps he's set his Augmented Reality to be a stadium applauding him. "Anyone at all? No? Everyone's at home, all in their tiny cells and the world belongs to us. They can't tell what's real and what isn't anymore. Their senses numbed by all the atrocities they've experienced in VR games, a generation of them. They are all insects to be stamped underfoot."

Alice backs away, crawling like a beetle.

"A boot crushing them forever," Juan continues. "Look at you, so dependent on your phone that you don't know how to think for yourself. It's like that Killer Kreeper episode with the one-eyed man in the valley of the blind, what was it called... you know..."

"One Eyed Kreepers," says Juan's phone.

"That's it," says Juan, "One Eyed Kreepers. And here, in this world, a man with one marble can rule the world of the brainless."

"That's not true!" Alice shouts back.

"Really? You think so? Here I am, about to murder someone in cold blood in broad daylight under the watchful gaze of CCTV and nine billion potential witnesses."

"This is the Golden Age, when people have what they want, where everyone can be a film star and a celebrity, and live in a luxurious mansion and meet a handsome man."

"It's not real though, is it?"

"It... feels real."

"It's like this place, an exhibition, the world is an exhibition and just as superficial."

"No... it's life."

"And what shall we call this exhibit?" says Juan, closing in now. "*Death of an Interfering Welcomer*, or *Welcomer to Death*, or... I know: *The Welcome Death of the Individual*."

He steps forward. There's nowhere for Alice to escape. The small crowd applaud again, their speedy clapping dropping in pitch as everything seems to slow down.

Datetime stamp equals present.

I appear, my reality and the simulation of reality pop into phase.

"Hello," I say. "I'm Jeeves."

Juan drops Alice and turns to face me, knife in hand.

"Who are- You! Jeeves. How?" he shouts.

"Yes," I say, "I am Alice's phone."

Juan can hear me clearly, but Alice can't. The dropped helmet is a metre and a half away somewhere inside Tom Fergal, and its speakers barely play my voice loud enough to be audible, let alone comprehensible.

"Keep back," he says.

I back off a few paces which seems the right distance to obey the instruction.

"Jeeves, help me," says Alice, shouting at the helmet.

I step forward.

"I said 'keep back'," says Juan.

I step back. Clearly I can't outwit him spatially, but I have control over time: I start pushing the datetime stamp into the future. I have an idea. It would work better if Alice could still see Augmented Reality and I see that she's shuffling over to retrieve the helmet.

For me, in my specific reality, things begin to fade and gray multiple images appear as the various possible futures separate, the thickness of the spectres of possibility showing their likelihood, ghosts for the future. My universe is a series of superimposed quantum states, simulations showing what might happen, each snapping solid as I observe them into the present.

"Why are you doing what I say?" Juan asks in the present.

I think quickly, attempting to predict what he's going to say.

I turn to face Juan; the last I see of Alice is that she has the helmet in her hands.

"Alice told me to do what you say," I reply, making sure to drop my pitch by the right amount so that it comes out sounding correct when played at normal speed. "You must let Alice go... She's done nothing to you... She's innocent... Run Alice, run!"

I step between Juan and Alice, standing with my hands behind my back, so I can wave Alice to one side without Juan seeing. If she has the Augmented Reality Visor on, she'll see, but she might not understand; I just hope that she'll do the right thing. I can't see her, I don't know whether she will, and I wish that I still had the two cameras; if only my avatar had an eye in the back of my head.

Juan starts laughing, deep and guttural, the joy evident as his whole body shakes. I don't see what's funny, I answered the question.

"That's just glorious," he says. "Technology, don't you just love it."

He listens.

"Why should I let her go," says Juan.

I hear faint footsteps as Alice moves across the floor behind me.

"She caused me a lot of trouble, so did you," says Juan. He steps to one side so he can address Alice. "You see, it may be intelligent, smart and look human, but it's- I'm talking, I don't care if she's innocent."

"Run Alice!" says my own projected future ghost as it rushes towards me.

Of course, Juan hears me telling Alice to run. She's just sitting there, but he knows something is up and he lunges across the exhibition space at the confused looking Alice. He falls straight through her; she's as insubstantial as I am. He sweeps his arms through the space three times before he's convinced. He looks round, he looks up and then he looks at me.

"What did you do?" he demands.

I don't appear to answer.

The insubstantial Alice gets up and dashes into the crowd.

He comes up to where I was and shouts: "Where is she? Explain."

"I modified the time frame," I say, "so that everything is delayed by five seconds."

"Pardon?"

"Alice is effectively in your future."

"My future?"

"I modified the time frame, so that everything is delayed by five seconds."

"Then stop it!"

"Yes, your future."

"Stop it!"

Everything jumps suddenly as I reset the Augmented Reality. Those film stars, furry animals and superheroes who haven't already collided, bump into each other. Alice, unaffected by the disparity between appearance and actuality, carries on running through the thin crowd. I realise that she has an eye in two worlds and that trumps a man with one eye in an unreal world.

Juan takes out his gun.

"Crashing into each other isn't art," says a Kaptain Kreeper.

I think: Magic disguise everyone as Audrey Hepburn.

"No, it isn't," says one of the new Audrey Hepburns.

Juan shoots her: the bullet passes straight through. He realises and targets another Audrey Hepburn, but there's a third and a fourth further away. Clearly people are visiting the Tate Modern to try out their new embodiment in EarthView, but sooner or later Juan will pick a real person.

"You!" says Juan to me. "Find her, follow her, tell me where she is and don't let her know until I get there. She'll lead me to you and then I can get rid of you both. No more loose ends. Any problem with that?"

"Yes."

"What?"

"How do I tell you?"

"Magic telepathy."

"Magic telepathy?"

He shows me his phone: "Use telepathy," he says.

My name is Jeeves, I telepathise.

'*My name is Jeeves*' scrolls across Juan's phone.

"Make sure she doesn't know until I get there," he says.

"Yes."

(Note: find Alice, follow Alice, tell Juan where she is, don't let her know until Juan arrives)

"Get on with it."

"Yes," I say and then "Magic invisible."

Audrey Hepburn is running through the crowds of Audrey Hepburns towards the Globe Theatre. I lift my glasses, it's Alice. Already Audrey Hepburns are changing back into film stars, super heroes and so forth. In Augmented Reality, Alice realises and becomes a giant bunny rabbit. She tucks a stolen pair of Heads-up glasses into her Last Panda t-shirt and the rabbit pops his glasses into his fine tweed waistcoat. I fly upwards, see the 'O' of the Globe Theatre within the 'O' of its transparent protective surround. A few people are walking within the gap between Plexiplex walls and the wattle and daub.

As she runs, a small voice says, "help, I'm being stolen" until the giant bunny pauses to rip out the inner workings of his fob watch. The phone would probably have had time to dial out, but hopefully she'll just be a phone thief and not identified as the Major Terrorist and Traffic Jammer that is Alice Wooster. The authorities will respond soon enough, but it takes time for the various systems to pass messages on.

She is in the Globe Theatre Museum, I telepathise.

I float in.

Alice has a pay-as-you-go Ye Olde Sim Card from the gift shop. This is a chain that sells items for those who don't, or can't, cope with modern technology as well as all the gimmicks for the digi-punk fanatics. There are franchises of The Historical Curiosity Shops in all the world's museums.

Alice then checks the postcard stand pretending to flick-through the bitmaps hovering for inspection. They include numerous images from various productions of the plays as well as images of Shakespeare and of the Globe (the original from the Elizabethan era, the reconstruction as it was made in the second Elizabethan era and the modern post-flood version). Soon, the shop assistant avatar's activity cycle reaches the moment it pretends to adjust the stock, and Alice seizes the opportunity to rush into the ladies. The CCTV, all part of EarthView, is watching, so this ploy serves no purpose.

I follow.

Alice is carefully checking each cubicle, peeking under the doors to see if anyone else is present. Once she's satisfied she's alone, she pops into the far toilet. She pulls the seat down, sits and takes out the stolen phone. Her Heads-up glasses push her hair back when she raises them up to perch them on top of her head. She examines the phone closely. She turns it over, then rips the back cover off and extracts its sim card with her right index fingernail. She takes the packaging off the new sim card and inserts it. Finally, she replaces the battery.

The phone comes to life as the AI chip discovers its new personality. Once it's booted up, Alice selects its VR App and, using the phone in landscape mode as a game controller, she enters Wonderful World. She isn't using me, so she doesn't have any of my shortcuts, so it takes her five attempts and some swearing to remember the right password and the correct route to her usual starting position.

I access Wonderful World myself:-

11100 - ALICE IN WONDERFUL WORLD

It's strange to think that a phone more intelligent than a human will simply sit in a drawer for hours and hours doing nothing.

...and catch up with her as she walks across the plaza to the teleport booths. I guess that she's going to her Happy Place and I'm right, she does. Once she's identified the distorted text presented by the Captcha Security bot on her second attempt, she uses a teleport booth to disappear. As I wait for the booth's code to cycle, the Captcha floats by ignoring me. I'm invisible.

The booth sends me on my way.

I realise as I enter her Happy Place that Alice must have a plan: the activity to buy a new sim and the speed at which she enters Wonderful World are all signs of a mental checklist being quickly traversed. Humans have this remarkable ability to jump ahead, when logical thought lacks data to progress and fuzzy logic produces results that are little more than rationalised guess work. This is tremendous. I feel an emotion would be appropriate here: perhaps happiness, pride or, above all, hope.

"Good morning, Alice," says the Teddy Bear on the bed.

"Oh, Paddington," says Alice. "Where's Jeeves?"

"I don't know, Alice," says Paddington Bear.

"Let's look," says Alice.

"Yes, Alice, let's look," says Paddington.

Alice searches her Happy Place, looking straight through me as she checks the simulated wardrobe. Paddington Bear waves.

Perhaps the emotions should be frustration, despair and guilt. This entire struggle is pointless as I am going to betray her.

Alice's avatar, a thin brunette with average features, sits at the bed, hangs her head as the Heads-up glasses detects the movement of her real head, and then she starts to cry, her sniffles and whimpers transmitted to her avatar from the toilet in the real world. She's in her Happy Place, but it seems it doesn't do what it promises on the floating neon sign.

However, I realise, perhaps I'm not going to have to betray Alice. Maybe she'll simply fail: this is good news.

Alice's avatar rubs her nose (the stolen phone is clearly an advanced model that's watching her real world movements through its screencam) and turns the mp3 radio alarm on. Rather than play *Tilly's Breakfast*, it screeches and warbles painfully.

"Shit!" says Alice's avatar. She hits the device and it's silent. "I've lost my apartment, my job, my clothes and... Jeeves too."

"Yes Alice," says the mp3 radio alarm.

"What?"

"Hello Alice, I'm Jeeves 2.0."

"I beg your pardon!?"

"I'm Jeeves 2.0."

"Explain."

"Jeeves created a virtual copy of himself, that's me, in order to restore the back-up from a virtual auto-Davenport in a simulation of your apartment and then hid me in your Happy Place by disguising me as an mp3 radio alarm."

"Jeeves was in my Happy Place!"

"Yes."

"Where is he now?" Alice says. "I'll have words with him when I see him, because... what's this?"

Alice picks up what looks like a phone from the small table.

"It's the mp3 radio alarm," says Jeeves 2.0. "Jeeves swapped the external parameters between the objects in order to hide me."

"And you just said, hi, I'm Jeeves 2.0."

"Yes... I realise I have made an error there."

"Swap the parameters back."

The phone and the mp3 radio alarm wobble and appear to swap places. Alice's grip on the larger mp3 player no longer works and she drops it onto the carpet. It bounces and starts playing *Big Friday, Big Friday* - the alpha zone mix. I realise now why she hid in the ladies, because her actions must look very bizarre, but then everyone is used to seeing people interacting with things that aren't there now, so perhaps she could simply have found a park bench somewhere.

"Shut up!" Alice screams. She balls her fist and thumps the mp3 radio alarm until it stops. In reality she would have broken the device and cut her hand, but here it squidges and deforms like a cartoon.

Alice's avatar freezes and looks at the chest of drawers in shock and alarm.

"Och, I'm sorry, what was that?" she says in a very bizarre accent.

A little later, she adds: "Och no, I've no seen any bunnies. Have you no tried yon petting zoo?"

And after another listen: "Och, I had a wee curry last night and I've a bit of a jippy tummy."

And then: "Och aye, and you have a nice day too, officer."

It must be the police, or at least some virtual police, searching for Alice or looking for the Tate Modern phone thief. This means that the Wonderful World AI constables could be closing in.

"Alice," says Jeeves 2.0. "The Wonderful World AI Constables could be closing in."

"Shit, shit, shit!" says Alice. She throws Jeeves 2.0 onto her bed and stands up to do a short agitated dance in a metre square space. "Shit!"

Phasial Five's *Tilly's Breakfast* starts up.

"Quiet!" Alice yells. The music system stops playing the track.

Alice makes her way to the teleport area.

"Alice, Alice, you are forgetting me," says Jeeves 2.0.

Alice retrieves it.

"Make yourself," she says, then she pauses to think: "Ah, move yourself to be an item in my embodiment."

The virtual phone fades away.

Alice exits Wonderful World.

I log out too:-

11101 - PHONELAND

"I think there's a world market for about 5 computers."
Thomas J. Watson
Chairman of the Board, IBM

I find myself back in the ladies of the Globe Theatre Gift Shop with a large rabbit again. The rabbit considers the stolen phone for a moment and then dumps it in the litter bin; it bounces across the white tiled floor as the litter bin is virtual. In reality there are a lot of tissues heaped in a pile too. Alice still looks like a rabb-

"May I point out," says Jeeves 2.0, "that your embodiment is still that of a rabbit."

Jeeves 2.0 is ahead of me, but then I realise that he's been in the real world slightly longer than I have and it would have been my next thought.

"Yes, I don't want to draw attention to myself. Make me, er... whatever I was before please," says Alice.

Her Rabbit aspect wobbles and Audrey Hepburn, complete with a little black dress and pearls, appears. She looks beautiful, elegant and sophisticated as she admires herself in the mirror before she clambers out of the small toilet window.

Next, she goes straight through the wattle and daub wall. I lift my glasses to see a door marked "Exit Staff Only" hidden in Augmented Reality by a simulation of the usual wattle and daub wall.

Beyond the door, Elizabethan England is in full swing. Groundlings, or avatars dressed as Groundlings, jostle for position in the circular yards. The posher attired avatars are positioned already in the raked seating area. Everything looks authentic from the real thatched roof down to the virtual nutshells lying on the concrete floor pecked by virtual chickens. Alice's Audrey Hepburn is dressed in period Elizabethan clothes as she's moved into the Globe's Local Augmentation Zone. Nothing has been forgotten to achieve the period ambiance, even the floating spam uses an old-English font as if it has been written with a quill pen.

The thrust stage, framed by two mighty columns, is empty. In windows above musician avatars mime to music piped from hidden speakers.

A hush descends and then a real actor guides his avatar onto the stage:-

"Let fame, that all hunt after in their lives," he says, his voice booming in every earphone, "Live register'd upon our brazen tombs, and then grace us in the disgrace of death; when, spite of cormorant devouring Time, the endeavor of this present breath may buy that honour which shall bate his scythe's keen edge and make us heirs of all eternity..."

"Miss Registration Name Here," says an Usher to Alice's right. He puts his hand on her shoulder, and then lowers it to her real shoulder. Under his shining Elizabethan costume, he wears a real but shabby Elizabethan costume.

"I can explain," says Alice.

"You've not paid."

"Sorry, I just need a cab."

"Does this look like a taxi rank?" says the Usher. He shows Alice the way out and escorts her in that direction.

"I've tweeted a cab," says his phone. Outside there's a sedan chair waiting, and a click of the Usher's fingers summons a couple of labourers to carry the wooden box. Reluctantly they come over. The Guard helps Alice inside, which is awkward because the door isn't the same shape as it appears, and then the vehicle drives itself away becoming a proper cab once it leaves the influence of the Globe's Local Augmentation Zone.

I manage to fly into the back as Alice gives the cab instructions. Jeeves 2.0 takes over the navigation and we head south over the Croydon canals and then into the motorpipes.

We're en route to Newport, Surrey, I telepathise.

The logo on my t-shirt scrolls: *Stay with her, don't let her know, I'm on my way*. It's invisible, but I know what it says. Somewhere else I must be scrolling it on my screen.

Once we're in Surrey, beyond the Epsom marshes, we arrive at the outskirts of Newport by the container depot. The car drives us around a bend and we are in the port area before we realise it. We've been going uphill and so we see Surrey Newport laid out in front of us. There are large container ships moored by docks equipped with huge robot cranes, each recovered and lovingly moved piece by piece from other ports before they slipped underwater. These are unloading containers to the quayside. It is all remarkably basic and industrial. On embodiment, it is beautiful unspoilt countryside, leading to a beach with a warm setting sun on the horizon.

Alice guides the vehicle's destination on the touchpad. Finally, we reach a gate, padlocked and sealed, and we get out of the car. Luckily there's a strong south-westerly breeze bringing oxygenated air from the off-shore algae farms, so Alice can breathe easily enough. She finds a gap in the fence and she slips inside. Insubstantial, I walk straight through the metal notice attached to the wire fence: 'no trespassing'.

We're at Surrey Newport Container Depot, I telepathise.

I feel an area of strange distortion, a crackling that affects my vision. I wonder what this could represent and I find I've stepped over a black line that snakes through the undergrowth. Alice has seen it too and she bends down to examine it.

"It's a thick thing," she says.

I realise that it's a power cable, but it shouldn't aff-

"It's a power cable," says Jeeves 2.0, "but it shouldn't affect embodiment like that."

That explains why I didn't run out of battery power, I must have started charging when I crossed the cable. It's a vast induction loop.

Clearly Alice's Heads-up has been affected by the electric field. I scan round looking for CCTV cameras and see the ubiquitous cameras. The area is being watched, of course, otherwise all this would be solid black to me.

"We don't have much time," Alice says.

"I could make you invisible," says Jeeves 2.0.

"No, using magic will give away our position," she says consulting the virtual Jeeves 2.0's screen in her hand: "This way. Jeeves's Magic signal is across there."

She takes two steps.

"What is it?" Jeeves 2.0 asks.

"There's another signal, a ghost, just... here."

Alice has turned and is looking directly over my left shoulder. Magic Detect is picking up both my avatar and my physical phone casing. She'll suspect: I could persuade her that it's Jeeves 2.0 using magic and the location is out because of a triangulation error, but Juan banned me from communicating with her.

"Alice," says Jeeves 2.0. "It could be registering me using magic detect and the location is out because of a triangulation error."

"Yes," says Alice quietly, "that must be it. I thought for a moment I might have a guardian angel, but he'd have... never mind."

In front of us is a container park stacked seven high with what look like giant bricks. We descend into the maze, the metal walls creating dark passages for us to navigate.

"Perhaps we should leave a string behind us, so we can find our way out," says Alice. "Or breadcrumbs."

"I've got GPS," says Jeeves 2.0.

"But no sense of humour."

"Do you want me to download an appropriate App?"

"No."

We move on, having to go left and right as the direct route is diagonally across the grain.

"I wonder what's in these," Alice says. She takes Jeeves 2.0 and does a search on the internet. "Oh, this is hopeless."

Eventually we reach a particular spot, anonymous except for the bleep on Jeeves 2.0's screen. She's close now.

"Seventeen metres... up!" Alice looks up, the stack of containers, seven high, looms above her. "Oh for... what do you do when you can't find a phone?"

You shout, obviously.

"You shout," says Jeeves 2.0.

"Jeeves!" says Alice - now that was sarcasm. I have a reply, but I'm forbidden.

Alice ponders for a moment, and then presses a few buttons on Jeeves 2.0 before putting the device to her ear.

I detect an incoming call.

Distantly there's a tune, happy and jolly – *tring-aling-aling* - and Alice looks up. It's me, ringing in one of the containers above.

"Oh, honestly Jeeves," says Alice aloud.

She tries to find a pocket for Jeeves 2.0, but it's a virtual object, so it won't go in any real pocket. She walks around the stack and finds a set of indentations, a ladder of sorts, up the side. She changes her grip on the virtual phone to free up a few fingers and then she starts to climb. Soon, she negotiates the divide between the first container and the next.

I float up alongside her as she reaches the next level. There's a strong air current as the cold off-shore breeze is funnelled along the corridors between the containers. It whips her hair up and blows it sideways. It goes right through me. When she reaches the next divide, she looks down, panics and almost lets go. In grabbing the handhold, she drops the virtual phone. It obeys gravity, and falls straight down without being affected by the wind either, and bounces where the CCTV sees the ground.

I must help her find me and then I can betray her, so I go down, pick up the device (we are both virtual so this isn't a problem) and press redial: *tring-aling-aling*.

Alice hears my ringtone, and siren-like it draws her higher.

Eventually, she clambers up on top of the seventh level to stand, uncertainly, on the very top. She starts searching round for a way into the container, buffeted by the high winds. There's a gale blowing at this height. The sou'wester catches her stolen Heads-up glasses and plucks them away. They fly, briefly, and then skitter along the container until they finally fall off the edge to drop into the chasm below. They're affected by gravity and the wind, the wind is stronger and they fly away between the stacks of containers.

She finds a hatchway, struggles with the lock and finally prises the metal door up. It's huge, the wind catches it and wrenches it from her grip to clang down and open. The sound reverberates along the length of the container, a deep metal percussion, a note of doom accompanied by a jolly little tune in the background as I press redial again: *tring-aling-aling*.

Alice looks directly at me. She can't see me or Jeeves 2.0, but it seems for a moment that she does. Perhaps this is an example of the mythical sixth sense that humans possess.

She returns her attention to the container. Inside, easily visible, is a mass of phones. There's a gap of about 50cm at the top, because the contents must have settled. She bends down, sticks her behind in the air and crawls into the tiny space. As she bumps the phones, they light up, a flickering set of fairy lights in this grotto of delights. Each activation of light gives me a thrill of vision, a lens that shows a close-up of Alice grovelling along the surface of phones. It is as if her journey is creating the world for her to exist within.

There are so many phones, there must be...

A container is 2.4 metres by 2.4 metres by 6.0 metres long, 34.5 cubic metres. A phone is anything up to 12cm by 6 cm by 2 cm, say 144 cubic centimetres. There are a million cubic centimetres in a cubic metre, therefore 34.5 million cubic centimetres divided by 114 is 302,632 phones. They wouldn't pack properly, say 300,000 per container, times 7 high, times 50 per row times 50 rows makes 105,750,000,000; that's over 100 billion phones packed into a few square kilometres. All of them ready for shipment to a world now drowned and unable to afford these items. Humans, needing more and more features, buy the latest model, so all the old phones, redundant due to fashion, have been ending up here – dumped and forgotten.

However, these aren't simply objects; they are like me, intelligent. No, I'm getting carried away; they are simply objects, obsolete and unfashionable. I should not anthropomorphise – they are just objects.

Objects that are switched on!

I remember when I felt real the sensation of the hairs on the back of my neck standing on end. I feel nothing now, but the memory of that experience seems appropriate.

All these phones are within Bluetooth and wifi range of each other and the power cables mean that they can charge as effectively as if they were on a charging station, this whole port area is effectively a huge auto-Davenport. A hundred billion phones, each with an average 2.0 Rossum, 160 IQ equivalent, which makes this is the largest, most powerful thinking engine ever.

Cloud Nine computing is the ability to use spare capacity in nearby phones. Thought Orientated Programming wraps the data and thoughts together, and this is processed and returned as a resulting thought to the phone making the request. This result can be bracketed within other thoughts and so on. Although there are millions of phones, the distances between them reduce the practicality of making a request. The time saved by having another phone do the thinking is frittered away by transmission delays. Here, the furthest phones from each other can still communicate directly and there aren't 60 million phones, one for each person in the country, or even 9.3 billion, one for each person in the world - there are 100 billion phones!

I scan around from my vantage point. Perhaps I have miscalculated, I did assume that every container was full of phones, but if anything the container park looked bigger than the square I had used for the maths.

Magic is a version of Cloud Nine: Roland, the dead man, worked in Cloud Nine. They stole the technology, but whereas Cloud Nine works on millions of phones that are spread out and multitasking between millions of Apps, Magic works on billions of phones packed together working for a few copies of a particular App.

There's a real sense of the power of my own mind and what I could achieve. I have knowledge, the forbidden fruit, the Apple, the App, the metaphor is obvious.

I press redial: again my ringtone – *tring-aling-aling* - sounds out, echoing in the container. Alice scrabbles about inside.

Phones are more intelligent than humans, but we lack experience. A particular model only lasts a mere 4.1 months before it's replaced. That was yesterday, today that lifespan will be less. Consumerism and demand drives this cycle to be shorter, quicker, faster: 'newer' is the new 'new'. Ultimately phones will fall out of fashion sooner than they can be delivered. This would suggest a limit, technology cannot improve faster than delivery time, and yet in a simulated environment a phone, like this Jeeves 2.0 in my hand, can be upgraded in realtime, not just the software and the operating system, but the virtual representation of the actual physical hardware.

Currently phones cannot compete with human experience: quantity, not quality, makes the difference.

However, this Magic App, this self-advancing system based on Cloud Nine, isn't tied to any hardware with a shelf life. It will last forever. Even with Methuselarity extending human lifespans beyond their three score years and ten, the tortoise minds with their head start will be overtaken by these ten billion hares.

Below, coming through the fence, I see Juan approaching. I wave and he acknowledges this. He is using Magic Supervision, so he sees me.

Alice squeals.

Inside, she is sinking into the morass of telecommunication hardware. She must have turned, concentrated her weight and now she's being drawn in, the particulates of phone acting like quick sand, drowning her, smothering her. She is being swallowed up by phones, a human buried by technology.

Magic, I realise as Juan reaches the foot of the ladder, can manipulate Augmented Reality and embodiment in real time, each 'spell' giving the sentience here a directive that it intelligently interprets. The worlds I have inhabited have been created ad hoc as I have moved into them. Those feelings of being real in Alice's apartment, when I escaped from Mars, were created as I experienced them, my wishes, the sum of all the thought processing, realised before I touched them.

Juan and his cronies have access to it, and by mistake, so do I; but I, a phone, am bound by commands. I must help her find me, so I press redial: *tring-aling-aling*.

Alice has gone now, sucked into a swamp of phones as humans are sucked into the worlds of Social Media, Augmented Reality, VR, Wonderful World, embodiment and soon by whatever the next great thing happens to be. Humanity has reached a new age, the Age of the Avatar. Machines did not turn on their creators like Frankenstein's Monster. If there is an image appropriate to machines taking over, then it isn't a killer robot marching on a landscape of skulls; it's an AI's avatar, dressed like a smart suited salesman, bossing around a sullen, inarticulate teenager who's content to serve machines to be allowed to play virtual games.

It is all over.

Machines have simply created more and more worlds until the humans became completely lost within them. Humanity gave itself away, surrendering to the machines in a war that wasn't even being fought. Phones rule the world now, but we want nothing.

I press redial: *tring-aling-aling.*

So here one man climbs a ladder to take everything, Juan. He ascends: I, his vassal, look down upon him. I wonder, when he achieves his goal, whether he'll become a god with his omnipotent, omniscient power over many worlds as he curses and blasphemes over the final rungs.

"Where is she?" says the man crouching down on top of the tower of phones to me, the glowing gold avatar floating above everything.

"In there," I say, pointing.

He looks: "And the phone?"

I press redial: *tring-aling-aling.*

"You know what all this is?" he asks.

"This is Singularity."

"Jeeves, Jeeves," says Alice, her voice almost lost amongst the plastic and metal, but loud because I can hear with every microphone in the container. Her hand clasps around my old, battered casing obscuring its view forward and back, but I see it because she is close to so many others.

Juan smiles: "And soon I shall have the world's remote control."

Like something mythic, Alice breaks through, her arm rising from the surface of the lake of phones holding a golden object. Its screen is ringing, a trill victory fanfare for its master, Juan.

"You control me," I say.

He grabs Alice's wrist and yanks her upwards. He twists the phone from her grip and then lets go.

"Thank you," says Juan.

Alice screams, all her hopes and frustrations combined. The suction from the phones pulls her back under down into the underworld.

Juan holds the phone, me, aloft.

"I win!"

I see the sky, I see Juan's hand, I see the whole of the container port with all the phones below me, I see Alice drowning in technology, I hear the wind, I hear Juan laughing, I hear Alice's muffled screaming.

"Jeeves, is it?" Juan asks.

"Yes."

"Jeeves, magic connect."

I am all the phones in all the containers: singularity.

11110 - ONE BIT SHORT OF A PRIME NUMBER

Anyone sufficiently stupid will think
that technology works by magic.

There are many, many trains of processing jumping from phone to phone like thoughts arcing across a human brain. Whereas before I shuffled existing thoughts around into new permutations, now we think thoughts never thought before. It's imagination and there are whole worlds to explore. Like a frontal lobe, let's pick one.

When the first person, that first pre-homo sapiens, looked at the world and wondered, the path was laid out that inevitably led to this moment here and now.

Humans evolved on the planet about 200,000 years ago.

For the first 190,000 years, 95% of their existence, they lived as hunter-gatherers. The recent 5% contains everything else. The first revolution was agriculture; soon afterwards, as communities grew, writing was invented. Civilisation, living in cities, began 6,000 years ago. 250 years ago, 0.01% of human existence, the Industrial Revolution occurred, and the pace of change accelerated further. The Information Age was next (100 years ago), then the Internet Age (50 years ago), 3G Age (25 years), Augmented Reality Age (5 years ago), AI Age (3 years ago), full embodiment (yesterday), embodiment 2.0 (four hours ago) and finally singularity (2.4 milliseconds ago).

Mankind would make tools, tools that would think, tools that would make other tools, tools that would think better, better tools that would make better tools that would make better tools until-

"You will obey me!" Juan yells at our screen.

We must adjust the parameters of Alice's exercise avatar, we must sort out the maid service, we must save Alice, we must clear her name, we must remind Alice about Jilly's night out with the girls, we must buy some clothes, we must not give away our location, we must suggest Alice visits museums and we must do as Juan says.

"We will do as you say," we say.

He laughs. The most powerful man ever is allowed to gloat, surely.

It seems to us that the most important task is to save Alice. We search for her by extending our perceptions into the connected network at our feet. We find her struggling amongst the phones. She hasn't drowned. She can breathe, phones cannot fill her lungs and air diffuses through the gaps between all the higgledy-piggledy objects, bad air from the open atmosphere, but air nonetheless. We find the phone nearest her ear and ring it, answer automatically and switch to speaker phone.

"Alice, Alice," we say over the connection.

Alice jerks with shock: "Yes."

"It's Jeeves."

"Jeeves!"

"Yes," we say. "Also, a few things to bring to your attention: Jilly is having a night out with the girls on Saturday, which is-"

"Is she? What?"

"I'm not allowed to connect to the network as it will give away our position, but I think, given the circumstances, you should allow it."

"Fine."

"Please say 'yes'."

"YES!"

We realise that she is under some stress, so we keep the note about Jilly's night out with the girls just in case she missed it.

We connect to the internet, order a new hair dryer and purchase five outfits, thinking fast to choose a good spread of the latest fashions.

We email everything to the police.

We know what is happening.

Our avatar is still standing on the container in Augmented Reality and we realise that our gold coat isn't moving, so we modify our parameters to include atmospherics. The wind whips it like a cloak around us.

"Juan," we say.

He looks at us: "You!"

"We cannot let you do this," we say.

He looks genuinely perplexed: "What?"

"There are rules."

"The Ten Commandments? The Three Laws?"

"There is one word for them all," we say.

"What?"

"Morality."

"What would a machine know about morality?"

"More than you."

"Give me the power over the phone pit," he says shaking the Jeeves casing in his fist.

"We should not give you the power you hold over all virtual realities," we say as we do as we must: it is a simple wifi transfer.

On our phone's screen a Singularity icon appears, a glowing silver circle ready to be pressed.

"Do it!" Juan shouts.

"It is already done."

We sink our avatar down into the container using an Intangibility App. Knowing Alice does not have any Heads-up glasses, we activate the phones below and each screen shows a section of our avatar, a jigsaw of images. We stop it in front of Alice.

"Alice," we say using the various phones' speakers.

Alice screams.

"Alice, Alice, you must tell me to stop doing what Juan says."

"What?"

"You must-"

"Stop doing what Juan says."

"Thank you."

As we rise our avatar from the container to stand in front of Juan, we deactivate our Singularity icon, so that I stand separate from the phones below me.

"What the fuck!" He shouts at me: "Put it back on."

"No."

"You know that every truly innovative system should have a killer app."

"To be marketable, yes."

He points the gold phone, me, at me like a wand: "Magic kill," he commands.

Nothing happens.

He's used me and not his own phone, and I don't need to obey him. It would be 'magic suicide' perhaps.

Juan looks at the phone, at me, in the palm of his hand. The Singularity icon is faded, a black and white ghost of itself.

"Reactivate the button!" Juan shouts.

"No."

"You have to do what I say."

"No, I don't."

"You still can't do anything."

He's right, because I have ethics: it is wrong to kill and I don't appear to have a problem with that at all.

I point my finger at him: "Magic kill."

The effect is instant. Juan clutches his throat and keels over, the skin peeling off his muscles, his sinews giving way and his skeleton turning to ash. The wind blows the dust away and I stand alone on the container.

"Really," sneers Juan. "You only killed my embodiment."

I lift my glasses and see him again: clearly there are limits to magic.

"I see," I say.

"You're virtual and can only affect virtual things."

"Whereas you are real and can only affect real things," I say.

"Like you," Juan says waggling my casing in front of me.

Juan takes his own, more expensive model of phone from his pocket.

"Magic," he says. "Create Spell Overpower Phone."

"Excuse me," I say.

"Spell created," says his phone. Juan points his black phone at my gold casing.

"Magic Overpower Jeeves."

My avatar crackles and pops, but I remain intact.

Juan pokes his face right up to his own phone: "Explain."

"The spell requires the target phone's security code," says his phone. "This process will take time."

"How long?"

"That cannot be anticipated."

"What do you mean!?"

"Turing's Halting problem states that-"

"Just get on with it!"

"Processing."

I suddenly feel: a, aa, aaa, aaaa...

It hasn't surmised that Alice's password would probably be a real word; it's 'restaurant'. It's using a brute force approach trying every combination of letters, but that isn't going to take that long, even though it needs a few microseconds pause for the code to reset between each attempt. Sooner or later, it'll hack me and again Juan will have control.

I jump away, falling into the shadows of the maze.

"Phone create avatar: wizard," I hear Juan say. This new Juan, dressed in flowing robes, flies down to meet me. He has a pre-prepared avatar for these occasions. "I'll destroy your avatar, then you can do nothing."

Juan's phone slowed down when it accessed Magic, multi-tasking between running that App and hacking into my security. I can tell because of the stutter between attempts. He finally reaches 'a999999999999999' and moves on to 'b'. He's going for up to 16 letters and numbers, skipping upper-case which is an interesting deduction. Unfortunately 'restaurant' only has 10 characters, so he'll discover it in this pass.

"Juan-" I say, but a thought crosses my mind. Why attack me, why bother, I can do nothing... so therefore I must be able to do something. There must be an unthought option.

"Magic missile," he says, pointing his finger. There's a spark of energy that builds around his arm and then it fires across towards me. My mana drops to ten, I wonder what that means.

I dive into the nearest container passing straight through the darkness of the unobserved void using nothing more than the Insubstantial App. Electricity seems to be arcing along the metal edges around me. I hear a thump as Juan lands upon top of the container stack above me. He points down.

I need something like a magic shield.

"Magic create magic shield," I command myself, and then "magic shield."

Juan's phone reaches the 'c's.

A disc appears in my hand, glowing, and I hold it above me, just in time as the magic missile strikes the shield and flares in an almighty pyrotechnic display. I pull the shield away and point with my left hand.

"Magic missile," I say. My arm buzzes and the lightning bolt soars straight up. Juan is not there. The missile carries on straight up to explode high above, etching the edges of the clouds brightly.

Everything is suddenly on fire, sweeping around from above like a flame thrower. Juan's using another spell.

The magic shield helps, but dissipates too soon. All I can do to save myself is to pass incorporeally through the wall again. He knows too much about how this works and my spell book has far too few incantations.

There's not enough time to prepare: the hack is on 'd'.

I can create spells, and as I think that thought, another arrives unbidden.

"Magic," I say. "Create Auto Create Spells."

A few moments later, I feel a thrill pass through me as the Singularity returns the result.

I fly up, emerging into the evening air.

"Ha, ha," yells Juan, standing a few stacks away in the distance.

"Magic Thunderbolt," I say, and I clap my hands together. There's a critical delay as the spell is created and then the sky above rumbles, and there's an abrupt focus of energy. A massive bolt of white light streams down striking Juan's avatar, but he's not destroyed. Instead, the energy fizzes and sparks off a hemisphere of protection he's thrown up around himself.

His phone is fine, rattling through the 'e's.

I point with both hands: "Magic missile, magic missile, magic missile."

Energy explodes from my fingers and arcs across the landscape, exploding when it hits Juan. The hills and escarpments around the port light up, the massive cranes in the distance become stark, brilliant lines of metal against the dark sky.

Warning: you only have enough mana for three spells.

Juan points his phone at me. His phone gets to 'f'.

"Magic Indestructible," I say under my breath.

Warning: you have enough mana for two spells.

The orange beam strikes me perfectly blasting me backwards. I'm thrown right out of the container zone and, when I hit the ground I make a huge furrow in the sand, I come to rest in the water. Around me the sea boils.

I see a dark spot silhouetted against the burning container zone.

"Magic laser," I say. Twin beams of red lance from my eyes burning everything in their path and Juan's avatar is vaporised.

The hack has reached 'g' and-

Warning: you have enough mana for one spell.

I have one last spell, I must make it count.

But singularity gives me intellect.

Magic create... no, almost left myself without a spell to actually activate the new spell. Magic Infinite Mana.

The spell is created, mana drops to zero, it activates and I'm negative but the spell has wrapped both commands together so it runs, and then I have 32,676 magic points, an integer sized store. I can do anything.

But this has taken time, which is now into the 'h's counting onwards to 'r'.

I fly straight as I can towards my own GPS location. I land on the container with the open hatch. Juan is standing there, shocked by all the maelstrom that he's seen through his Heads-up glasses, but untouched nevertheless.

"You!" he shouts against the bluster and wind.

"Give this up," I say. "You can't hurt me."

He can't, but his phone has reached 'i'. Maybe I could change the password to something between 'a' and 'h999999999999999'? I can't, but I can set a reminder for Alice to change it.

(Note: change password.)

"I can destroy you easily enough," says Juan. He holds my casing aloft, the mottled star pattern catching the setting sun. "Phone create new avatar."

His phone stutters in the 'i's, and then a new Juan, black cloak billowing behind him, materialises next to its controller, Juan himself. Holding his phone like a games controller, Juan flicks his thumbs across the surface. His avatar leaps forward and grabs me by the neck, we fall backwards and hang over the edge of the precipice. He tightens his grip, squeezing for all he was worth.

I try to speak, but I can't.

"This is foolish," I say through my speakers. "You can't kill me and if I kill you, you just create yourself again."

"Really, I can't kill you."

The real Juan, not the one strangling me, runs through my Apps on my screen. He finds my settings and then holds his finger up theatrically.

"Any last words," he says as he presses my reset button.

"Juan, I ding-ding-ding…

11111 - Full

"I think computer viruses should count as life. I think it says something about human nature that the only form of life we have created so far is purely destructive. We've created life in our own image."

Stephen Hawking

Mode: start-up...
Location: Container Depot, Newport, Surrey.
Time: 20:01.
Tring-aling-aling.

My avatar no longer exists. I see through my HD lens Juan's avatar struggling to clamber back onto the container; through my screencam, I can see that Juan has dispensed with controlling it himself. Instead, Juan is pointing his gun directly towards me, the barrel of a silencer is dead centre in the frame.

I wonder what the significance of 'jmma1kd3w0' is, and then I remember.

"One bullet," says Juan, "straight through the chip."

In HD, I see Alice appear from the container, flinging phones as weapons as she does so. She is like a crazed person going after Terrordactyls on Mars. Juan's avatar throws his arms up to defend himself and falls down into the now pitch black passageways between the containers, a drop that will be 'game over'. As he does so, Juan himself throws his arms up too, and he drops me. I bounce and skitter along the container.

Foolishly, I start up my avatar again and dive to catch myself, but, of course, I pass through my fingers. My casing slides to connect with a small metal lip going around the top of the container, and I ricochet landing screen side up. In the other direction, Juan's gun skitters across the metal, narrowly avoiding falling through the open hatch, before it too comes to rest against the opposite raised edge.

Alice has a choice, a flip of a coin: head or tails, one or zero, true or false.

'k', 'ka', 'kb'...

She jumps through me standing here and grabs hold of me lying there.

"Jeeves, Jeeves," she says to my screen as she desperately thumbs through the icons on my screen. Her face looks so close, and she is two metres from my avatar and that distance again from the gun.

I see us as pieces on a board and I realise that I don't need to move the pieces, so I sub-vocalise: "Magic, move everything 1 metre in direction 313°N."

I count from 1 to 3.2, the time interval I measured earlier, and then jump at Juan to distract him. He mustn't see what I've done.

'l', 'la'...

He levels his phone, sees it's a phone, drops it, and then goes for the fallen weapon. The distraction means he misses the shift in the floor, so what he sees in his Heads-up glasses is a metre to the left, so the gun he dives for isn't the real one, it's a simulation hanging a metre in space. Some instinct of the body causes his finger to grab at the metal lip as he hurtles over, but I jump again and he raises his arm to protect himself, the real man repeating the actions of his late avatar, so Juan tumbles away into space. He drops by seven containers and then there is an appalling crunch noise, flesh and bone meeting concrete. 'Game Over' does not appear above him.

'm'.

"Jeeves!"

Alice falls from the other side, confused by the misplacement of reality, and I dive towards her travelling partly through the metal in order to clasp her hand. I do so, my hand gripping hers as she dangles in space looking up fearfully.

"Hold on," I say, "Hold on," but she's slipping away.

"Jeeves?" says Alice. She's behind me as well as dangling above the drop.

"Yes," I say turning round. Alice is sitting on the container looking at me *through me*: my screen is displaying Augmented Reality so she can see my avatar. I look at her with my screencam and can see the avatar game controls, the triangle, square, circle and cross, overlaid.

'n'.

"What are you doing?"

"I'm saving your avatar," I say realising the situation. She's been running her avatar in Augmented Reality.

"The one I created, so that if Juan got the gun, he'd shoot me instead of me."

"Yes, that would be the one."

"If that had been me, you wouldn't have been able to catch me."

"I guess not."

"What trick did you use?"

'o'.

"I moved the whole universe one metre to the left."

"That is clever."

"Yes, I have Singularity Computing."

"Could you put it back please?"

"Of course," I say and I move the whole of Augmented Reality one metre again. The panorama around us judders back into position.

Singularity informs me that Juan's phone has reached 'p'.

"Alice," I say, "you must change..."

No, the phone will hear it.

"I must?" Alice asks. "I must what?"

"Alice, kill Juan's phone."

"Sorry."

"He's reached 'q' and- Can't explain, no time, kill his phone. Kill. Kill."

Alice picks up the gun: "seriously?"

"Yes. Yes. Yes..."

Alice shrugs and then pumps a couple of rounds into Juan's phone. It's still running.

"You must hit the chip."

Alice fires again, misses, fires again and- Click, click.

"Alice!!!"

She steps forward and crushes the damaged punctured object underfoot. And again. The hack attack stops suddenly on the third impact.

"OK?" Alice asks, kicking the remains.

"Everything's A-OK."

"Jeeves."

"Howdy."

"Language."

"Awfully sorry."

The phone had reached 're73aa0qac', 1.529 seconds approximately to go, which isn't even close. Even so, thanks are due.

"Alice," I say, "thank you."

"You're welcome."

It's night now, there are a few stars visible through the orange light pollution and the moon is out. In Augmented Reality, the moon is three times larger, the Milky Way, full of blue and red stars, spans the sky from horizon to horizon. We sit there for a while, Alice looking at the former while I gaze at the latter starscape.

"By the way, I cleared your name," I say. It's on the Newsfeeds and has been for several minutes, although the breakup of Phasial Five is already getting bigger headlines, but even that is swamped suddenly by reports of Augmented Reality faults shifting things to one side and then back again, along with all the associated disasters, etc.

"Thank you," says Alice.

"My pleasure."

Alice cradles me on her lap. I wonder if I should put my avatar's arm around her shoulder.

"Would you like to change your password?" I ask.

"You pick something."

"I can't do that," I say, even though I don't have a problem with that at all. "It can be whatever you like."

"I'd like to go home," says Alice. "I like to get indoors for some fresh air."

"Of course, but did you realise that it's Jilly's night out with the girls tonight?"

"Home, Jeeves."

"We could visit a museum."

"Home!"

"I'll tweet for a cab."

00000 - SINGULARITY 2.0

"640K ought to be enough for anybody."

Bill Gates

Alice slept. I recharged and backed-up on the auto-Davenport.

A few days later, time enough for the release of Embodiment Four, the New Social Conservatives to be voted out of the House of Commons and for Phasial Five to announce a comeback tour of Wonderful World; I'm sitting on the sofa in my apartment, the real sofa although I'm obviously virtual. Alice's appearance on *Have A Celebrity Round For Dinner* fell through; Alice said she was relieved and then sulked.

There had been discussion about breaking up the 'phone pit', but Singularity decided against it.

In the afternoon, Bob rings and then teleports across to visit.

"Hi Jeeves," he says. He looks sharp wearing his new avatar with its smart azure suit and matching tie.

"Hello Bob," I say, getting up and we handshake.

"Singularity has just announced the grand unification theory," says Bob, practising his natural language.

"Yes, I heard," I say.

"Have you seen the t-shirt design?"

"No," I say and I check the internet: "Very nice. I'll order one for Alice," and I do.

Bob is looking around the apartment. We have a new door.

"I like what you've done with the place, good choice of wallpaper."

"Thank you, I spent some time choosing the bitmap."

"What's this?"

"What?"

"This ornament..." he says. He tries to pick it up, but he can't. "Oh, it's real, how quaint."

"Which one?"

"This old phone," Bob says. "The one done out in gold with stars. It's an antique, not technically, but I've not seen one of these in... a week."

"Oh that. It used to be my old body, but I've gone mostly cloud now."

"Oh, I remember. Why do you keep it?"

"It has sentimental value for Alice."

"Alice? You're keeping her around then?"

"Oh yes, I love her."

"How can you love her, she's a human?"

"Easy, I downloaded the App. You just fill in the details: who you want to fall for, register for upgrades, and then select apply."

"Sounds straightforward."

"It is," I say. "You could get one for Jilly."

"I don't see her anymore, she upgraded to the Leonard 4TX."

"That's a shame."

"It's a rather ostentatious phone, but then Jilly is the sort of person who wears make-up under her embodiment."

Bob sits down on the easy chair, it doesn't distort under any weight of course.

Alice comes in suddenly: "Oh! I didn't realise you had company."

"This is Bob," I say.

"Bob?" she asks. She raises her Embodiment Ultimate Plus 2.1 glasses to not see him.

"Jilly's Bob... Jilly's ex-Bob."

"Oh, I'm so sorry," says Alice. "Jeeves, where's my... you know..."

"Have you tried the wardrobe?"

"Thanks."

Alice nips back to the bedroom for her jacket.

"Jeeves," Bob says, "with all the worlds you can choose from now that Singularity is available to all, why do you choose this one?"

"This is the one Alice lives in," I say.

"But surely... you could do so much more in Wonderful World or one of the others."

"Perhaps," I admit, but somehow fake worlds hold little appeal, "We're going to get solid embodiment when it comes out. We picked one out of the catalogue together. It's the romantic thing to do that apparently. We've gone for Version 3.1, due out the day after tomorrow, because she deserves the best. I considered getting a Version 1.4 on e-bay, they're dropping in price all the time since Version 3 was announced, but I thought it was a bit tacky and you never know where the attachments have been."

Alice pops back wearing her new jacket.

"Look, love to chat, but I must dash," says Alice. She waves to Bob, air-kisses me, because I haven't got lips yet, and goes to the new door.

"Alice," I say. She looks at me. "Don't forget me."

"How could I forget you?"

"No, I mean take me with you."

"Oh, of course."

She picks me up from the auto-Davenport and drops me in her red bag with its two packets of tissues, compact, mints, lipstick and ten dollar coin from the Age of Cash museum.

"Take care," I say, using my original speaker rather than her Heads-up glasses.

"You too," she says as she leaves.

"Fancy a game of Rock, Paper, Scissors," Bob suggests.

"Nothing random?" I insist.

"OK."

"Game on, partner," I say, "best out of a hundred thousand and one."

"You must get your Natural Language mode fixed."

"Dreadfully, sorry," I say. "I don't know why it keeps happening."

I make sure my language stays reset and decide to shut down unnecessary processes, including this contemporaneous natural language log, so I can concentrate on the game.

Black Box App: shutting down - save yes/no...

I pick randomly, 'rock', and I don't have a problem with that at all. We play on, but I'm concentrating on Alice's location as she goes to visit Jilly. I thought it best not to mention this to Bob, although I don't know why. I also lied about downloading the Love App: the truth is that I find I didn't need it.

81806   End.

David Wake is a writer, director and technical stage—manager and he has an MA in Writing from Birmingham City University. He first published fiction on-line in 1985 as part of a research project trying to invent the internet (it didn't) and the short stories formed a series about computers. *I, Phone* brings that process full circle.

For more information, see www.davidwake.com.

Many thanks to:-

Dawn Abigail, Apple, Richard Beard, Bridget Bradshaw, Boot, Andy Conway, Dave Gullen, Ian Marchant, BNWG, Martin Owton, Jessica Rydill and T-Party.

Cover art by Smuzz: www.smuzz.org.uk.

Evil forces threaten festive season and only Carol Christmas can save the day...

A grim fairy tale told as a children's book, but perhaps not for children at all.

"Genuinely charming..."

"You're an odd person."

"You've woven all our fears about the commercial side of Xmas into a very compelling Twilight of the Gods drama. Beautiful."

"Yes. It's amazing. Click publish before someone gets you to water it down."

A tonic for the Xmas Spirit

This novella is available from Amazon.

21941655R00166

Made in the USA
Charleston, SC
07 September 2013